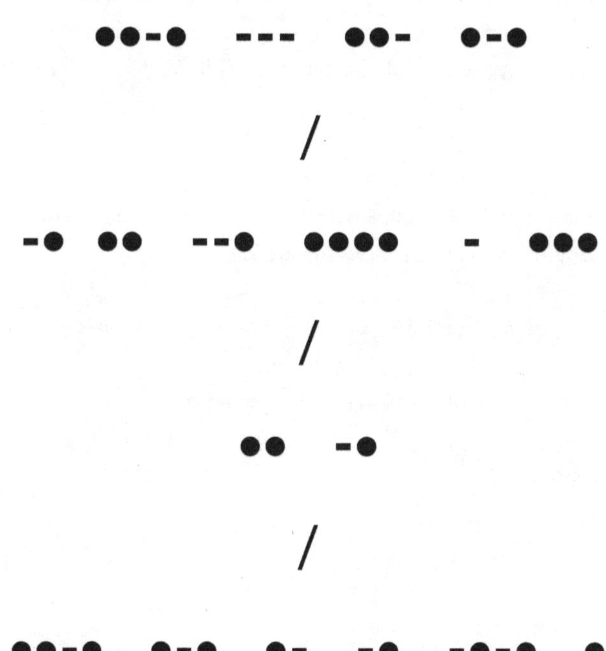

I0836251

CALL the Doctors Publishing
7 St James Drive
Belgian Gardens
Townsville 4810
Queensland, Australia

© 2026 CALL the Doctors Publishing

This publication is copyright. Except as expressly provided in the Copyright Act 1968 and the Copyright Amendment (Digital Agenda) 2000, no part of this publication may be reproduced, stored in any retrieval system or transmitted by any means (including electronic, mechanical, micro copying, photocopying, recording or otherwise) without prior written permission from the publisher.

Every attempt has been made to trace and acknowledge copyright, but in some cases this may have not been possible. The publisher apologizes for any accidental infringement and would welcome any information to redress any deficit.

This work is fictional, and any resemblance to persons real or imagined is entirely unintended.

National Library of Australia Cataloguing-in-Publication Data

Lawton, Luke Douglas.
Four Nights in France
Luke D Lawton,
1st Ed
ISBN: 978-0-9924245-3-4

Publisher: Luke Lawton
Publishing Services Manager: Corinne Ryan
Editor in Chief: Corinne Ryan
Cover Design: Luke Lawton

For Corinne, Sidney and Emmett:

I love you all very much.

FOUR NIGHTS IN FRANCE

Luke Lawton

CONTENTS

PROLOGUE

Alone in the East

Late November 1938.

Gunter Kohl had never really existed, yet still Charles Montgomerie was sad to see him die. He stood alone in the freezing morning air and reflected that espionage was a cruel and bitter game. Above him Bruncvik, the Bohemian warrior hero, struck a lone and silent silhouette against the predawn sky. The safety of Britain, perhaps the world, required Kohl to vanish, and so with professional detachment Montgomerie had carefully tied a rock around Kohl's passport and tossed it into the Vltava River. He'd picked the hour carefully. He knew the minutes before dawn were the safest ones, being generally too early for the law abiding and too late for the lawless. As Kohl's papers slipped beneath the icy water meandering under the Charles Bridge there was a rumble of a backfiring Skoda in the distance. Montgomerie turned quickly at the sound, but a rapid inspection of his surrounds reassured him that he remained alone in the gloom. For the moment, he had lost the Nazis.

He turned and trudged east towards the old town, walking at a speed that had he been observed would imply no particular purpose. Snow crystals broke with a soft dull crunch, crushed against the worn cobblestones by barely less worn boots. Ice clung to the ramshackle shingles of Prague's mediaeval towers, which were starting to gleam fitfully as the sun struggled up. The entire city shimmered white, beneath a slate grey sky. Winter had come early to Europe this year.

Glancing upwards briefly, Montgomerie had to acknowledge the beauty of the scene. Prague, effortlessly chic, was taking the opportunity to shine. Hácha had closed the borders shortly after Munich, and few foreigners would have the opportunity to see the city.

"Silver linings old man," he murmured, breath steaming even with such minimal volume.

He glanced around him again. The bridge was still empty, for which he was thankful. His Czech wasn't up to much, and a casual conversation would mark him as a foreigner.

"Bit too early for Section S I suppose," he muttered derisively.

Montgomerie was running for his life just like the hares chased by the South Gloucestershire Harriers, with whom he had ridden as a younger man. He'd slept at a local tavern near the castle, risen very early, and departed through a first-floor window. He'd paid the landlord handsomely to encourage discretion (money was one of few problems he didn't presently have), but even with that insurance he wouldn't trust the man if the Germans came calling. That was why Kohl had to go. He'd entered Prague on that passport and so needed to leave on another. He wouldn't get far on a train if he carried the papers of a man on a Section S wanted list. Unfortunately, the only passport he had left was his own. As his mind turned over the problem the temperature, the season, and the ephemeral beauty at the heart of the city of Prague were all lost on Charles Montgomerie as he crossed the bridge. He pulled his greatcoat tighter, and walked on, lost in thought. His position was precarious and he had some very serious decisions to make.

Montgomerie was by nature an optimist and believed that any job worth doing should be done properly. He was only now alive because of a lifetime habit of meticulous preparedness combined with impossible risks. Two nights ago he had made a daring leap between moving trains beneath the soft falling snow in southern Poland, a flash of madness in a night chase born of chaos. Alone and unwatched this morning in Prague he considered it likely that his mad acrobatics outside Krakow had for the present won him a reprieve. Hopefully his pursuers from the German foreign intelligence service were languishing on a slow train running south to Budapest while he was safely hidden within the borders of the Third Reich itself.

He was fairly sure that by now his hunters would have realized that he had not joined them winding through the Tatra Mountains on their way to Hungary, but until the train reached Keleti station in Budapest there would be little they could do. He also would have bet two good silver pounds that even when they found him absent in Hungary the Abwehr agents chasing him would struggle to believe his current location. They'd expect him to do many things: double back to Gdansk, try for a ship through the Baltic, run for Riga, seek safe haven in a city without Nazi influence; but he gambled on the hope that no sane man would head west towards Germany itself. What fox hid from the hunting pack in a dog kennel? Montgomerie's move to Prague showed finesse worthy of a master player of contract bridge.

"Ballsy's just another word for stupid, Charles" he reminded himself as he stepped off the bridge.

Budapest would have placed him under the very nose of the Arrow Cross Party, the fascist junta that allowed Nazi Party rule by proxy in Hungary. Entering the occupied Sudetenland however meant placing oneself within the grasp of the Sicherheitsdienst, the malevolent evil that grasped at the heart of Hitler's Germany. 'Section S' were mentioned by the British services with the same breathless fear as the Gestapo, for they were infamous for brutality during the interrogation of their foes. Coming here to Prague and placing oneself knowingly within their reach was borderline suicidal. Capture would mean a slow and anonymous death in an unmarked room beneath a faceless building. Montgomerie understood the risk and the agents pursuing him knew it too, yet he walked on secure in the knowledge that the Germans were oblivious to his presence in Prague's cold morning air.

Montgomerie also knew that he had a high card left to play in the closing tricks. It wasn't an ace, he thought, shaking his head. Not that spectacular at all really. It was more like he held a queen hidden cunningly to draw a ten, but certainly the Germans' bid was not yet won. His employers in British Intelligence had long known of the fraught relationship between the Abwehr and the Section S. It stemmed from a vicious personal enmity between Wilhelm Canaris and Reinhard Heydrich, each of whom chaired an agency. The relationship between the two intelligence services only really functioned because of a well-defined partition between both bodies. The Abwehr dealt almost exclusively with foreign intelligence matters, while the concerns of the Sicherheitsdienst were predominantly domestic.

The Germans were always logical to a fault and by form then Montgomerie knew it had to have been the Abwehr who'd picked him up in Warsaw and chased him south through Poland. Here inside the new boundaries of the Third Reich he was relatively safe from their shadow, and if Section S noticed Montgomerie's presence in Prague he hoped that they wouldn't necessarily pass it onto their foreign counterintelligence colleagues with any urgency. Hopefully the Abwehr had also 'forgotten' to inform their colleagues of Montgomerie's significance.

He intended to make dissent between the partners his ally and steal the match while they dithered. A quick slip through the Sudetenland, shaking the Abwehr in the process, and he'd leave through a discontinuous border and be in Western Europe with a clear run to the British Isles in front of him. Barring mishap, the slender lead between Montgomerie and his pursuers should be maintained. Getting here had cost him three passports, and now he was forced to use his own authentic British papers, issued by His Majesty in '32 no less. He knew his lead was worth the heavy expense. The exposure of three false identities had given him a chance of seeing England again and so he considered his current situation marginally satisfactory.

Montgomerie also prided himself on being a realist. If he was caught, it wouldn't make a difference whichever agency it was. The Germans had already proven themselves ruthless, and at least two dead men in Warsaw bore testament to this. After the disappearances of Viktor Pilch and Pawel Szokolay the Biuro Szyfrów had panicked. They were mathematicians used to the elegance and immutable truth of code theory and therefore unprepared for the callous reality of modern espionage. Even now the remaining members of the Biuro were preparing to go into hiding whilst simultaneously couriering the most important of their work to their collaborators in London. Contacting the British Embassy had been a move of desperation on their part, but the insidious roots of Nazi intelligence had infiltrated large portions of the Polish State. The espionage community had a saying, "there are no state secrets west of Paris," and in Warsaw only the British were held to be above suspicion.

The combined brains of the Biuro and the British secret service knew that the Germans would unhesitatingly add more disappearances to their current tally of two, so the decision had been to courier Pilch and Szokolay's research in secrecy. As the resident 'passport control officer' in the British Embassy to Poland the task had fallen to Charles Montgomerie.

He'd barely taken possession of his charge when pursuit came swiftly and with determination. Charles Montgomerie had to admit that he hadn't anticipated such zeal on the part of Nazi intelligence. He'd been picked up by a German team as he took delivery of the package meaning he'd had scant time to prepare thorough cover, fake identities, false trails. It was only because he was habitually ready for an immediate departure that he was able to leave

Poland. His departure from Warsaw was too urgent to arrange a rendezvous and request some protection from home. He had to make it all the way to England on his own merits. He was honest enough to admit that he simply hadn't anticipated the heat he'd attract, and so now he was travelling using his real name. He was truly on his own. The real hell of it was that Montgomerie didn't even know what he was carrying. All this risk for an unknown package!

Questions about the reason for his task flitted round the edge of his consciousness as he trod the icy cobblestones of the Charles Bridge, but he quashed them ruthlessly. His parcel was something to consider later. Nine hundred miles separated the cold icy morning of Prague, and the welcoming grey of London. Nazi Germany stood squarely in between. Switzerland was out. Both the Third Reich and the Swiss Army had significantly tightened their border inspections as the flames of imperialism burned ever brighter across Europe. Quite simply Montgomerie had no legitimate reason to be in the Reich, and even less reason to be crossing the border for Basel. Trying to improvise a cover story explaining his unstamped British passport to the Germans at the Swiss border would be foolish, akin to presenting at the local SD office admitting to being a British spy. Cheering for the local ruggers on a rainy afternoon at the Bath County Recreation Fields was about as masochistic as Montgomerie got.

The previous night on the train between Krakow and Budapest he'd even considered doubling back to Poland and trying to secure a berth on a ship bound for Edinburgh. He had abandoned the idea though, reasoning that if the Germans were ready to commit murder in a sovereign country that they would have few qualms about using the Kriegsmarine to interdict him. The Abwehr's casual murder of Polish nationals in their own homes telegraphed blatant contempt for international laws. A simple 'customs inspection', or any other such pretext for boarding a vessel at sea, and he'd be bound for Abwehr headquarters at Tirpitzufer Strasse, Berlin. No, the dangers of the Baltic Sea were too great. Montgomerie had no choice but to continue as he had and try to maintain his slender lead in the race for his life. A dash south to Vienna sprinkled with some luck and he could be out of the Third Reich using its least closely guarded border.

"Italy," he whispered determinedly.

Charles Montgomerie feared the Germans, but he shared the collective opinion within British Military Intelligence's Operations Division that Mussolini and his Italian stooges couldn't catch a cold, let alone an experienced British spy. As he formulated his plans in the cold morning air Montgomerie knew that he was betting his life on that assumption. He was confident that if he got to Venice, he could cross west to Milan and lose himself in the mountains north of Torino. From there it was a short hop across the border to France, and relative safety. Misdirection had always been his preferred method of operation. He used the same methods in the field and at the card table, and right now Montgomerie was in his element. He had time and he had space. He intended to use both to his greatest advantage.

He knew what he carried was important. The cable to Warsaw from London had been uncharacteristically clear on that score. The clouds of war again gathered over Europe and Montgomerie suspected he was conducting the opening skirmish. If he was interdicted he could be certain of heading the British casualty list, albeit unofficially. They'd hoist a jug to his memory in Buckinghamshire but that was all he could expect.

Yesterday he'd cabled London from the station's post office requesting some necessary assistance. He had no way of knowing if military intelligence could make the necessary arrangements, nor could they contact him for confirmation. If help came it would be up to him to meet it. He hoped he'd make his rendezvous. For today, no matter how optimistic his mood and how devious his mind, the fact remained that Charles Montgomerie was cold and utterly alone in the clear Prague winter morning.

• -• •• --• -- •-

The evening weather in Buckinghamshire was as typical for England as biting cold mornings were of Prague. The wipers of the black Bentley were hard pressed to manage the ugly, heavy splatter that showered down while its tyres struggled through the thick, soupy mud churned up by the deluge. Outside the mist was thick and the air was cold. In the rear seat Sinclair's breath steamed beneath his mustache. The car shook as it hit a rut in the unsealed surface and the leather seats creaked as they contracted while the temperature dropped.

It had been a less than pleasant trip up from London, but it was finally coming to an end. The car turned right into a drive and passed a wooden guard box where a young soldier huddled over a kerosene burner. He jerked his head up at the noise of the engine and scrambled to attention as the car passed. Above him sodden fir trees stood silent sentinel in the gloom as Sir Hugh Sinclair's chauffeur slowly coaxed the car towards Bletchley Manor. The famously eclectic facade was masked by the weather tonight, and Sinclair was grateful. He knew his opinions on the subject marked him as old fashioned, but he simply could not understand how any architect could mix the baroque and gothic styles. They were too disparate, too uncomplimentary, high opulence squatting beneath brooding ceilings. He was well aware that some wags in government circles regarded his bald pate and luxuriant mustache in the same vein.

"Bloody ugly building," he remarked testily.

"Yes sir," murmured his chauffeur, eyes fixed on the messy mud road reaching through the firs.

Bletchley Manor stood on the Varsity Line between the old, venerable and beautiful institutions of Oxford and Cambridge. It stood in the middle of 58 acres of forest, and the regulars at the house referred to the entire estate as Bletchley Park. Sinclair had purchased the deceased estate in May with the approval of the inner cabinet. He had used his personal funds and regarded the estate as his fief. Bletchley Park was small and ugly and kept a low profile, but Magdalene's finest mathematicians and the sharpest logicians from King's were now in his employ. It was a constant source of amusement to him that his institution (the word was never capitalized in his mind) was fast becoming the principal destination in the country for the finest graduates of Oxbridge.

Sinclair might have used such prestige to further his career but at his own insistence secrecy was paramount. He maintained quiet pride by necessity and only boasted to two or three of the most discreet cabinet members. The Prime Minister himself was largely ignorant of what went on at Bletchley Manor. Sinclair had no faith in Chamberlain's promise of peace for anyone's time.

As the car drew up the doors swung open to reveal a servant outlined beneath an umbrella against the doorway. Above him a faint glow radiated from the windows of the manor, dampened noticeably by the rain. Sir Hugh knew that in his first-floor office a fire's warmth awaited, a small luxury in an otherwise austere and impersonal job. He was known to most people only by the epigram C after his predecessor, Sir George Manning Smith-Cumming. When the old boy had retired Sinclair had inherited both the letter and the job of Commander of British Military Intelligence, Branch Six. For everyone familiar with the brusqueness of Sir Hugh Sinclair it seemed fitting that the quiet man with the piercing eyes have a strong, singular title. C's day had been particularly long, and he craved the warmth from both fire in his office and the whisky he stored in the oaken sideboard beside the hearth.

Half an hour later in his office C sighed gently. He savored a long slow draw from his crystal glass as he gazed out at the rain through a large Tudor window. It was getting heavier, and his mood was darkening with the downpour. C liked his whisky mixed with just a small drop of water to open up the bouquet of the liquor. He also much preferred the urbanity of London, but he couldn't deny that the peace of Buckinghamshire was conducive to clear thought processes. Peering out into the dark, he could see where Hut One stood, squat and dark across the estate's main drive. He'd had that one newly built, to expand his operation. Hopefully the work to be conducted there would go as smoothly as the small hut's spartan construction works. Distressingly, tonight's impasse threatened to cruel his aspirations.

He placed his drink on the desk when he heard hardened leather soles clapped brusquely on the bare wooden floorboards of the corridor. The stride was a quick beat, purposeful in rhythm. In Bletchley Manor only Alan Denning walked that way. There was a perfunctory knock on the door followed by a high-pitched creak as it eased open. In stepped a tall man, dark haired, gaunt, and wholly unremarkable. He bore an air of deferential authority above a face wholly forgettable. No passing acquaintance would have fingered such a man as a master spy, but Denning was one of the best C had seen. He had spent his formative years in the field, mainly in Spain apprising Britain of the troubles the Germans had been encouraging there. Madrid had been a dangerous place in the early '30s, where intelligence operatives who lived longest were often the most nondescript. Denning was living testament to this maxim.

C had brought him home to help build his own legacy. Denning's mathematical skills were unassuming when compared to some of the academics working on the ground floor of the mansion. His logic, tenacity and gift for planning however were legendary amongst the small fraternity of MI-6. His gifts lay outside the academic sphere, but C knew Denning was sharp, someone the Clapham bus crowd would refer to as a 'regular genius'. The London tabloids would have named him a master spy, had Fleet Street known of his existence.

Denning ran C's nascent 'school'. It was he who had coined the politically correct term with C over a port one night, with the aim of disguising the true nature of their activities from any overly interested parties. C had an eye for picking good people, and he privately considered Denning one of his best. The man kept a parsimonious purse and had a gift for coaxing the best out of brilliant but sometimes fractious minds. Of course, C had never told Denning his opinions. He didn't want the man getting too big for his shoes after all, but really Denning was invaluable to him.

He didn't turn from the window to address Denning or express a greeting. The chief of military intelligence wasn't a man for pleasantries, especially after the day he'd endured. A rough day at Admiralty House followed by bad news via wire meant all Denning got was a gruff statement, a growl rather than a sentence.

"We've a problem."

Denning simply raised an eyebrow in reply. C saw him do so. Reflected in the rough glass window by the hearth's flickering light his expression contorted into a shocked look of theatrical proportions.

"It's the Warsaw data," C continued, turning back towards his desk.

"Sir, we need that information," Denning replied, emphasizing every word. Before C could elaborate, he continued quickly, "the Poles are at least six months ahead of us. Word is they've built a working machine, one that's beginning to show results."

"And how close are we?" asked C.

"I've a bright young lad named Turing, just back from the United States, Princeton University more precisely. We've put him to work on the problem, and he tells me that with the Polish data that he'd be able to knock up something of a working prototype for us. We have the principles, and the theory. We just need a circuit model to begin testing our decryption algorithms," Denning explained.

C grunted again. Even his un-mathematical mind understood well enough the implications of Denning's words. He motioned Denning over to the sideboard where a hand decrypted telegram sat crumpled by the crystal flagon of golden whiskey. C spoke as Denning read.

"We've someone on their way down to make the rendezvous but it sounds like our man is quite under the hammer. If that data is as important as you're telling me we'd better hope for a damn sight more luck than what it sounds like we're having presently."

Denning looked down at the handwritten cipher where C's bold capitals spelled out the hidden message. The short telegram read:

"Pursued. Sea and embassy closed. Running for Chamonix. Two weeks".

• -• •• --• -- •-

In the cold night air outside the rail yard in Budapest, Schmidt watched the stars. Cold blue eyes turned grey by the moonlight scanned the silent trains while the other two Abwehr agents prowled amongst the carriages sleeping in the dark. Their heads were down, demoralized, like hounds desperately seeking a failing scent. Montgomerie was not in Hungary, Schmidt was sure. He must have run East. He must be heading South. Word had been sent back to Berlin. The Reich's intelligence networks would grind into action and steer Schmidt back towards the British spy. How he'd slipped past the Abwehr team Schmidt did not know, but they would find him, and then they would kill him. Schmidt was sure of this.

• -• •• --• -- •-

At midnight in Chamonix the wind howled curses at the stars and the temperature plummeted to levels that even the Alps would protest were they capable of speech. A glacial maelstrom raged outside a log cabin on the slopes of *Les Grands Montets* high above the village. Inside, Richard Melvold was happily oblivious to it all. With the warmth of the fire playing across his feet that pulled up by the hearth grate Melvold was content. He'd had a testing day hiking his lanky frame up through the forests to the snow line. The few fellow walkers out passed a tall smiling man with wavy brown hair and an aquiline nose. He had greeted each with a smile and a brief nod. It felt so satisfying to remove himself from the bustle of Edgware Road! Returning to Europe after two productive but tiring two years in British India had been an exhausting change of pace.

The colonies had been good to him on the whole, but it was nice to be back within the bounds of the truly "civilized" world. The Raj had a way to go, he thought, before it earned that title. The cabin where he was lodging for a fortnight was certainly comfortable enough, all squared off wooden beams, rustic furniture, and white linen. At dinner the housekeeper had proved herself a capable cook, although privately Melvold felt that *duck a l'orange* would be much improved by more potato and less *l'orange*, although he'd never admit it to a French cook. His public-school manners were far too refined for that.

He was especially happy to be in France. There was something of the amateur naturalist in Melvold. He'd hoped for some late season hiking, but he would have quite been content with some early season skiing had the winter snows fallen early. In the event, it looked like he'd have a good couple of weeks of clear skies to enjoy the French Alps. He'd already contracted with the *Compagnie des Guides de Chamonix* to head up on the large glacier near the village tomorrow. *La mer du glac*e, the locals called it, the sea of ice. He'd walked it a decade ago in his mid twenties. While he did not relish the descent down the thin, steep iron ladder from Montenvers to the surface of the ice, the thought of once again walking the frozen waves that slept between the *Montets* and the Mont Blanc massif was enticing.

Melvold had lasted two weeks on his return to London. Straight off the ship from Calcutta and already questions from his mother about why he wasn't married and why he hadn't been advancing himself in society?

Why had he seen fit to fritter almost two years away in (using his mother's words) a heathen land full of "godless barbarians"?

Never mind that he'd more than tripled the small fortune his Dutch grandfather had left him five years ago and returned with personal letters of commendation from both the governor of Cawnpore and the superintendent of the newly nationalized railway service. In his mother's eyes his escape from London would always represent youth misspent.

Richard had hoped to rely on his younger brother Harry for some moral support, but it turned out that Harry wasn't in London either. He was up in Manchester, something to do with amalgamating failed steel mills that had been strangled by the great depression. Richard's mother hadn't known the details, and Richard hadn't pressed her. Even his club seemed to have grown old and empty, victim to an incipient dementia with a predilection for licensed establishments. All his friends had married, moved on or migrated to other areas of the United Kingdom. One had even shipped off to Boston!

At every turn, every day the substance of a memory was undone by the reality of 1938 London. Melvold had never liked Yeats much. He was much too melancholy, even for an Irishman, but after a week back in London Richard was beginning to understand the sad lonely lament of *Sailing to Byzantium*. Depressed by the grand facades, empty bars, and dismal weather and faced with a city that seemed but an echo of the vibrant town he remembered Melvold had himself chosen to escape. And therefore this night he found himself slightly maudlin, dallying over a *digestif* high in the mountains above Chamonix. He loved Southern France and was pleasantly surprised by how little it had changed. He was sure he'd have a lovely two weeks.

THE FIRST NIGHT

Chamonix.

Early December 1938.

Two Weeks Later.

I

Once Upon a Winter's Night

The roofs of Chamonix village were blanketed with snow in the freezing darkness that December night when Richard Melvold's great adventure began. In the streets iron lamp posts cast ruddy light up at the groaning eaves and down over leafless bushes. Frost masked the great clock face on the *Hôtel de Ville's* highest tower and a drift was steadily piling up in the churchyard. Snowflakes drifted slowly down through the air. The dark firs upon the slopes above town were cloaked in icy majesty.

Night had come early this evening, as heavy grey snow clouds rolled over the southern mountains to hang above the valley. So complete was the night that the vast outline of Mont Blanc itself was invisible where it towered above the town. There was just an occasional muffled rumble as the fresh powder settled on its slopes. With the gutters clogged and their boots wet, tonight the residents of Chamonix had moved indoors early. The day of the first winter snows was a momentous occasion, unique in the calendar of the alpine year. Across the street from the station, *Elevation 850*, the front bar of the *Maison Gustav*, was festive.

Every time the doors swung open a pleasing hubbub of mixed languages became a cocktail of excited tones and half heard phrases spilling out into the night air. The thick old glass panes set in the windows framed tourists and ruddy faced Frenchmen mixing freely as they celebrated the snowfall. From inside, the same frost sullied panes and the glimpse of the frozen street outside made the wooden tables of the bar and the thick beams overhead seem warm and homely. The entire scene was bathed in the light of a crackling log fire, which regaled the room with a symphony of snaps and pops. The hotel was doing a roaring trade.

"Bit premature for snow, isn't it?" Richard Melvold asked the barman. "We're only twenty-seven hundred feet above the Mediterranean. It shouldn't snow here until Christmas, but the station roof's already under a foot of the damn stuff."

"*Oui monsieur*," replied the bartender, resplendent in a crisp white shirt and black tie. "Usually, it will be late in December before we see a fall, *mais,* when the snow falls, it is the tradition to celebrate," he nodded firmly.

"Yes, it's perfect," muttered Melvold turning to survey the near riot going on around him.

"*Pardon monsieur?*" asked the barman. "The noise, you *comprend,* it is hard to hear you speak."

"How much are your cigars?" asked Melvold, pointing above the old oak bar to where a wooden box full of fat Julietas rested on one end of the creaky spirit shelf hung precariously close above the bartender's head. "I haven't had one of those for nigh on two years. Horribly expensive out in the Indies, even in the best of clubs. And the local tabac is so thick and tarry that it's impossible to roll. Had to take up this," he said, waving an ivory pipe jovially at the bartender. "Bit old fashioned really, reminds me of my grandfather, mother's side. Right old Victorian gent he was. Still the habit's sticking."

The bartender looked at him bemusedly.

"Never mind old chap," continued Melvold. "I'll have a think about the cigar, but I'll stand for a drink now."

"Ah Monsieur, an *aperitif*? Pernod perhaps? A gin and tonic?" asked the bartender relievedly.

English exposition was clearly not his forte and he seemed happy to be back on familiar ground.

"Don't be silly," Melvold replied absently. "It's cold. I want something to warm the belly and revitalize the spirit. I haven't had a gin since I left the Indies, it's too chilly in Europe. I'll have whisky, neat. Make it a double."

"Of course. Do you have a preference?"

The barman waved his arm at the array of bottles behind him.

"The Cragganmore please," said Melvold, pointing. "All the way from Ballindaloch."

"Of course, *monsieur*."

"Cheers old boy," replied Melvold. "Happy to be here tonight," he continued, raising his glass. "Highlight of the holiday and all that."

The bartender looked at him blankly, and Melvold resolved to speak French next time he ordered a drink.

As he wound his way through the crowd to his table at the edge of the roaring hearth, he reflected that he was glad he'd come down from his room to join in the mirth. The occasion definitely called for whisky. He sat, placed his drink carefully on the table and crisply struck a match. He lit his pipe and waved the match vigorously to put it out.

Around him the room was filled with exuberant locals dressed in dark woolen sweaters, thick high leather boots, and warmly functional trousers. There was a perpetual musical chime as cold glasses of beer were brought together in salute. The Londoner in Melvold said the locals wore their hair too long and their coattails too short, but he couldn't deny that they possessed a particularly alpine *joie de vivre*. Ruefully, he reflected that even wearing his Fleet Street tailored grey English drape suit and wide blue cotton tie he was firmly out of place tonight. Certainly, no one else in the mountain village had a tan burned by unforgiving Indian sun over countless hours inspecting train lines. Inconspicuous! He might as well have just walked in naked. Richard took another sip of whisky and sniggered. If he'd been down in the Spanish

Riviera he might just have tried. That would have taken the party tonight up a notch! He snorted into his glass and slid deeper into his chair.

As the continued frivolity washed over him, he stretched his legs towards the fire and thought over his last fortnight. The last two weeks hiking in the Chamonix valley had been cracking good fun. He'd enjoyed the chance to take the fresh mountain air. Wide packed dirt trails had led him up the sides of the *Aiguilles Rouges* and *Le Brevent*, through the groves of fir trees to the open slopes above. Stunning vistas of the Chamonix Valley opened up at every turn and the air was clear and refreshing. For Melvold, the highlight of each walk was the moment he reached the snow line. Up high the fir trees first thinned, then vanished at the same time the birdsong fell quiet. Then there was only barren, hardy grass that clung tenaciously to the mountainside in silence. The wind whipped across the exposed summits with a cutting chill but somehow Melvold found it satisfying to be wrapped in his brand new oilskin coat.

Up there he was alone and free, high above the concerns of the world and safe and secure from Nature's wiles. The valley below was peopled by beautiful hamlets – *Les Bossons*, *Les Praz*, *Argentiere* – and there Richard Melvold had whiled away several afternoons drinking strong black coffee and honing his Southern French accent talking to the local farmers, who simultaneously pulled off both rustic and *chic*. Even their pigs looked like they'd been groomed, and the farmers were much friendlier than the Parisians. Melvold had had an absolutely fantastic time, and it was with regret that he'd left his comfortable log cabin up in the *Montets* two nights ago. He hadn't wanted to go but he'd felt the evening air cooling, a herald of incipient blizzard. The road up to the overhang where he was staying was precarious and prone to closure in inclement weather, and Richard did not want to be snowed in for a week or more in the mountains. Waiting for the *Col des*

Montets to reopen subsisting on progressively stale croissants was not a prospect he relished, especially when coupled with ever dwindling supplies of firewood and tobacco.

Now, reclining by the blazing fire in *Elevation 850* Richard Melvold smiled. His weather sense was still acute even after two years sweating time away in Cawnpore sun, and he had indeed correctly forecast the snow. Winter was here, and he had enjoyed his vacation. It was now truly the end of the hiking season and so he'd decided to travel slowly home to London. He'd planned to take the train up to Lyon two days ago on his return to the valley floor, but a heavy fall further down the Chamonix valley had seen the rail line closed. That was the day he'd shifted down from the *Montets*. It was not entirely his own idea to still be in Chamonix, enjoying the modest comforts of the *Maison Gustav* but since he was here and it was a special night, Melvold was determined to enjoy the party. Of course, the roads up to valley were still open and it was still possible to cross the Italian border to Torino, but Richard had no desire to travel in that direction.

Not only was it the wrong direction for London, but Richard Melvold harboured a dislike of northern Italy that rivaled his love of southern France. To him the lands across the border were irrevocably scarred by a series of industrial towns where the only food available was a horrid mix of basil and tomatoes. Not a good roast for a hundred miles! No hint of civilization until Tuscany, and even that was long removed from the splendour of Rome. To Melvold it was no coincidence that a depressing land had birthed a dire son. In true Italian style several towns in the region claimed the honour of being the birthplace of *Il Duce*, despite the clear fact that all except one must be mistaken.

Why this was boast-worthy was beyond Richard. If he'd been the local mayor of the town where Mussolini was born, he would happily and quietly disown the man. Mussolini was the sort who made his soldiers ride motorbikes wearing helmets festooned with peacock feathers. He was a buffoon, who had transformed Italy into a nation of dilettantes and ditherers, guarded by an army that spent substantially more time on parade than practicing military drills. The Raj hadn't conquered India by looking pretty and like his forbears Richard Melvold was a man concerned with substance rather than appearance. No, Italy and its denizens were not for him.

So, here he was, happily marooned by fall of snow in Chamonix. As he downed the last of his drink, he signaled the barman for a second. Melvold ruefully reflected that although he could still predict the weather, he'd never be able to control it. Until the snow lifted a little, here he would remain. Luckily, he was enjoying himself.

Besides tonight's unexpected festivity, his enforced layover had another compensation. Richard smiled again at the thought. A young English lady named Anne Hamilton had arrived at the Gustav on the same day as him and as soon as Richard had laid eyes on her he'd been smitten. He'd sounded her out with some subtly worded questions – no, she was not married or otherwise engaged - and then he'd gone to work. Carefully discrete at first, he'd become emboldened and openly flirtatious when Anne appeared to return his interest. The real reason he was in *Elevation 850* rather than out wandering Chamonix looking for a good *fondue* or *raclette*, aside from the snow which really didn't bother him that much, was that Anne had promised to meet him for a drink.

Melvold's relationship with a young Scottish lady had ended just before his departure from London for India. He'd never told anyone, but it was the relationship that had first driven him to seek broader pastures in the colonies. He'd decided fairly early on that he wasn't interested in marriage, and running away was easier than arguing with a Scot. His mother, who like all mothers took vicarious pleasure in examining every aspect of Richard's life through a microscope, had been very upset. Isabelle had been in her words "most suitable" as a match for Richard. Of course, Isabelle's father was in the lower house, and Richard rather suspected that his mother simply wished to boast in the tea rooms of London that she was the mother-in-law of the daughter of the Member for Edinburgh South. Richard shuddered at this thought. What daft things were important to members of his parents' generation!

As the celebrations continued Richard decided he really was quite happy waiting at his old wooden table by the fire. He was back in the clear air of Europe. There was no heat full of such humidity that one could feel its weight upon one's shoulders, no miasma of soured spices tainting the evening air. In the streets of Chamonix there were no vendors shouting harassments as one drank tea in the marketplace, nor was he awakened every morning by the incessant call to prayer of the local imams.

Tonight, Richard's world consisted of the liquid fire of his drink and the symphony of conversation that swelled as the patrons became ever more inebriated. Behind him the bar reverberated with clinking glasses and excited voices clamouring for more beer.

"La neige!" cried a large Frenchman dressed in the wax coat of the company of guides.

"La neige!" roared back the bar.

Everyone was enthusiastically celebrating winter's first fall.

"The snow," echoed Melvold quietly with a smile, as he raised his own glass.

He sat back, well satisfied, and made a small mental reminder to himself not to drink too much before Anne arrived.

• -• •• --• -- •-

As glasses clinked in the background, drowned by the tumult of the toast, Montgomerie cursed silently to himself. He was bone tired.

“Thrice damned snow!” he muttered.

If he reached London alive, he’d never again travel anywhere prone to snowfall. His arms and legs were heavy, his muscles drained by ceaseless flight. He had a dull throb in his forehead. It stopped short of a full headache, but it was irritating enough to intrude on his consciousness and distract clear thought. He couldn’t remember when last he’d slept peacefully for more than sixty minutes. Constant stress made a poor travel companion.

Travelling on his real passport for the last two weeks was straightforward but it left a trail that a blind man could follow. He was very easy to track now should anyone be interested in doing so, and Charles Montgomerie knew he was still a marked and hunted man. Happily, as he came south through Austria and Northern Italy he’d seen no evidence of any coordinated pursuit, and it appeared that he had maintained the lead he’d opened up on the Nazis in Prague.

But the early snowfall as he’d been making his way down to Lyon through the Chamonix valley had halted his progress more efficiently than the German secret services could ever hope to do. No trains running meant no exit from the Alps. The lead he’d gained by gambling his very life was slender to begin with. Tonight, Montgomerie worried that it was altogether gone, frittered away by forty-eight wasted hours in Chamonix. Despite his cable sent to headquarters a fortnight ago advising the hamlet as his entry point back into allied territory, he’d seen no signs of help over the two days he’d been forced to act the tourist at the Maison Gustav. It appeared that MI-6 had no reach here and so still Charles Montgomerie remained alone. Like a tiring fox hunted across Europe, he was being gradually run to ground. Now even the weather conspired against him. He was trapped!

For a man in such a desperate position there weren't many cards left to play. He was reduced to trying to hide in the open and brazen out his disguise. The old proverb about the wood and trees was a well-worn aphorism at Bletchley, and Montgomerie knew that sometimes the best place to be invisible was in the open. It was a good theory, and he'd even spent an inane afternoon wandering round the dimly lit rooms of the *Musee des Guides* to discover that there were only so many brown tinted oil paintings of Mont Blanc that one could look at without developing an invidious headache. He'd gone for a tense walk through town this afternoon pretending to stop to admire the town statue. It was a large bronze of a heroic looking Horace-Benedict de Suassure, ice axe raised willing Mont Blanc into submission. Heroic, striking to be sure, but Charles Montgomerie had struggled to evince the proper show of touristic admiration. He had other things on his mind: survival, misdirection, a search for allies. With two churches and only a few main streets Chamonix was just too small to hide in. He knew his disguise was poor and tonight he'd found out how very thin it was. When he returned from his afternoon walk, he'd noticed that the thin hairs he'd left sitting in the join of his suitcase were gone. His toiletry bag was packed ever so slightly differently to the complex and unusual order in which he'd deliberately left it. The implications were unmistakable. His room had been searched. The Germans had found him.

From his dark corner of *Elevation 850* Montgomerie scanned the bar, a pint of local bitter untouched in front of him. He tossed a silver shilling over and over in the dark recess of his mind. With the Germans this close there was no way he'd make it to Paris, let alone London. The snow must have derailed his MI-6 contact coming into Chamonix, just as it delayed him getting out. Of course the Nazis, following him in from Italy had no such problems. It was a frightful shame. The presence of a fellow agent would have changed the game. They could have brought money and papers, or even used Montgomerie as a stalking horse to flush out and eliminate the Abwehr agents now surely resident in Chamonix. But alone and exposed with only his own passport to travel on the situation was indeed grim. If C hadn't arranged help to meet him when he arrived there was no point in waiting for it now. Running back up the valley to Italy carried an unacceptable risk. Chamonix itself was small and there was precious little chance he could hide himself and shake off his pursuers, but unless he broke for Italy Montgomerie was stuck!

"If I can't run, and I can't hide, then what's left?" he asked no one in particular.

None of the locals seemed to hear him over the raucous merriment of the bar.

Montgomerie took a deep breath to calm himself at the end of such a disturbing chain of thought. It was a riddle with no answer and so the only choice seemed to be to change the rules of the game. Fortunately, he did have an idea, albeit outlandish and unorthodox. Certainly, something he'd never seen written up in the School's protocols or records. He'd never heard any of his colleagues try it before and he knew he'd need to be lucky. There would still be great danger for him and also for the unknowing person he needs must involve in any ruse, but what choice had he? If it worked, he'd be able to dine out on his exploits for the next decade. If it failed, he'd be dead. In either event, he'd have few regrets.

The coin dropped to rest silently on the floor of his mind. His decision made, Charles Montgomerie stood, took a deep breath, and walked through the crush of revelers. Slowly he moved across the room to take what he considered was both his best and also only option.

• -• •• --• -- •-

Agent Schmidt was as close to happy as a dispassionate countenance allowed. The suggestion of a smile danced in the cold blue eyes. Charles Montgomerie was worthy quarry. It had been a long chase from the rail yard in Budapest. Once the Sicherheitsdienst had cabled from Prague, the trail long gone cold, Schmidt's team had moved to intercept. Even with a head start, it had been a close-run thing. The Abwehr had just missed the Briton in Vienna and then he'd opened another lead as he fled south to Italy. As one professional appraising another Schmidt had to acknowledge that Montgomerie was an exceptional spy. Even travelling without a cover identity, he was efficient and hard to track. Without the snow closing the rail line to Lyon he might have slipped the Abwehr altogether and carried the day. Here though in Chamonix, he was trapped, and the Abwehr had caught him. Schmidt's colleagues, two brothers, had searched the British spy's room this afternoon while Schmidt had diligently trailed Montgomerie around the village. He was truly alone, Schmidt was sure. His masters from MI-6 had not deigned to rescue him, or maybe the snow had foiled them too. Schmidt did not care. From a corner of *Elevation 850* agent the German watched Montgomerie cross the room. The chase was almost over.

• -• •• --• -- •-

At the same time that Montgomerie moved dreamlike through the press in *Elevation 850*, Wilhelm Canaris answered a knock on the door of his office.

In Berlin, far north of Chamonix the air had been cold and the streets icy for several weeks. Canaris sat alone in the grim grey stone building at 78 Tirpitzufer Strasse. He was a tall man, slim and intense. The golden light emanating from the strong bulb hanging naked above him transformed him into a demonic caricature of a naval officer. Shadows cast across his jacket by his epaulettes gave him bulk larger than a normal man, his bushy eyebrows frowned, and the dark recesses of his face bore a Mephistophelian ire. Tonight, he too was a man under stress. The director of the Abwehr always ran a busy agency. They had many operations, gathering intelligence from the four corners of Europe and beyond, but in the last two weeks one operation had assumed paramount importance in his office. The Abwehr had a spy to catch and a secret to save.

The knock sounded again, more urgently.

“Enter,” he said curtly, with a veneer of irritation.

“Admiral,” said his aide tonelessly, coming to attention in the doorway. “An urgent telegram.”

“Bring it here,” a sharp motion to the desk.

Much rode on the import of what Schmidt had encoded in this latest message. Canaris hoped the scratching of his pencil would detail the conclusion of a chase begun on the backstreet cobblestones of old Warsaw. He worked quickly to unmask Schmidt’s missive and when he’d finished he laid the pencil gently on the old oak worktop of his desk. Just this winter he’d felt the first touches of rheumatism in his hands and he shook his fingers briskly to alleviate the cramps he’d generated with his haste. He looked up briefly at his aide.

“Schnapps,” he waved his hands irritably while the aide walked to the side cupboard where he pulled down a bottle of apple liqueur.

With the blaze of sweet, strong Schnapps warming his core, Canaris smiled. Schmidt had found the British courier. One up on that prancing fool Reinhard Heydrich who’d carelessly let the Nazi party’s biggest intelligence coup for a decade slip through the Third Reich all the way from Prague to Vienna. In the cut and thrust of Reich politics Canaris’ personal ascendancy would grow as the Abwehr prospered. Now, it was time to end this operation and bask in the glory of reflected triumph.

"Do you know what this is?" he asked the staff captain locked ramrod straight at attention in front of his desk. "Of course you don't," he continued blithely, never extending the adjutant the courtesy of formulating a response.

Canaris looked him up and down with silent contempt. His aides were assigned by High Command and he suspected that most of them reported his business back there regularly. The clandestine struggle for primacy in the Reich was never ending, and so he never shared anything important with the junior officers assigned to his staff. Information was initiative, a way to control one's position in the hierarchy. Canaris always personally delivered his good news to the Führer to maximize his credit. He was also adept at ensuring blame for less good news was assigned as far as possible from his own desk. Endemic distrust notwithstanding, he was still yet to find an aide bright enough to bother with on his own merits. This current version was proving no exception.

"This is victory," Canaris gloated. Let Goering stew on that for a while! "Now get out!"

He waved his hand in a summary gesture of dismissal.

In contrast to the oaf who had just left after the straightest of arm salutes, Canaris acknowledged that the British man had been particularly good. They usually were. He had personal experience of that. British Military Intelligence had barely missed killing him on a posting to Spain during the Great War almost twenty years ago. He frowned at the the memory. He had survived but several trusted colleagues, good friends rare in his profession, had died. Unconsciously he rubbed his right shoulder where the scars left by the fire of a Sten submachinegun bore testament to British audacity. That day the victory had been theirs. Tonight, it would be his. Schmidt lived up to an already formidable reputation. The courier was trapped. The last copy of the research of those bastard Polish academics was almost within his grasp.

II

The Chamonix Affair

Large logs snapped and popped behind the old fire grill. The air inside the bar was alive. Neither local, nor planning a stay for the ski season Melvold was still swept up in evening's elan. The celebratory atmosphere of *Elevation 850* was seductive, and he had almost forgotten his original purpose. He'd drunk his second whisky quickly and he was moving towards finishing a third. The alcohol had infiltrated Melvold's consciousness, slipping under his defenses and threatening to carry him off in a pleasant tide of warmth. He blinked and shifted his weight to rise. It was time for a cigar. He'd only gotten halfway up when he felt a hand grasp his right shoulder from behind. A deep voice spoke.

"Excuse me, do you happen to speak English?"

Melvold nodded. Caught in the act of standing and with whisky spinning in his ears he was a little surprised. After two weeks in the valley speaking only French it was strange to hear his native tongue. Obviously his manner of dress had marked him as from the Isles and a compatriot had singled him out.

"Excellent," the voice continued. "I thought I might join you for a drink".

Richard shrugged nonchalantly and gestured in a friendly manner to a vacant chair at his table. Anne hadn't arrived yet, and a little company would be welcome. There was a scraping as one of the other chairs at Richard's table was pulled out, and then he was looking into the face of a middle-aged man, who smiled hesitantly and hoisted a full glass of beer. In the flickering firelight his face was ruddy, and there were dark bags under his eyes. To Richard, he looked terribly stressed.

"Charles Montgomerie," he said. "Most recently of Milan, but more permanently of Islington. I'm on my way home now, but I've been stuck in this benighted town while we wait for the damned snow to clear."

He spoke in a baritone with the hint of a Scottish accent that must have mellowed with time, much as rocks by the sea become smooth and weathered after a life of exposure. It was a voice that inspired trust in Richard Melvold.

Montgomerie continued "It's all very convivial here tonight but it's a bit lost on me. I don't speak French you see."

Richard laughed. "Melvold," he said. "Richard Melvold."

He reached across the table to shake hands.

"I'm in exactly the same position with the travel, got down from some time in the mountains just in time to see the last train out of town for two days pull out of the station. Thought I should at least be a bit social, pop into the hotel bar for a couple and take up a little atmosphere while I'm here. My French is quite passable, but I must admit it's nice to speak the King's after a few weeks away. Where did you get in here from?"

"I've just popped across the border from Turin. I've been off on a bank trip to Milan and now I'm off to Paris, sort of a courier in chief for my organization, before I head back to London for the Christmas holidays."

Montgomerie gestured towards Melvold's empty tumbler.

"Let me get you a fresh one. My round. Might ask the barman if he'd sort us out a plate of nibbles too. What's the French word for that lovely cured ham they do down this way?"

"*Jambon Serrano*."

"Jam-bon," repeated Montgomerie, mangling the French word horribly with overemphasis.

On his way to the bar the British spy grinned to himself. He'd been in the bar for an hour looking for a likely collaborator and had selected Melvold as almost certainly being from the Isles. No one but a Brit would be dressed that way and drinking whisky in a French country pub. Bad luck for him that he'd been fingered, but Montgomerie needed help. Being British there was a good chance the stranger would buck up for King and Country when needed to. When he reached the bar he leaned against the wood and waited, still thinking hard. His idea was looking promising, but he still had a bit of sounding out to do. Working things out on the run was always tricky and he wasn't planning on telling his unwitting co-conspirator his entire backstory.

At the table waiting for Montgomerie and his drink Richard reflected on the ubiquitous nature of the British. There was that old maxim about the sun and the Empire of course, but the presence of his countrymen everywhere he travelled always amazed him. There was no sign of Anne yet. Women these days were taking the concept of fashionable lateness to extremes, he thought. He quite fancied a bit of properly civilized conversation while he waited. He hadn't been paying any attention to the outside world and it would be nice to be updated on the news. Even though he'd spent the last two years in India, Richard had always tried to keep abreast of the affairs of the Empire and he was fully cognizant that the ambitions of nations moved apace in Europe.

The crowd was becoming rowdier by the minute and the noise level in the bar was rising. He saw Montgomerie coming back, a tumbler with what looked like a double grasped firmly in his hand.

"Good man," said Melvold as Montgomerie handed him the glass.

In return Montgomerie said something that Richard didn't quite catch over cacophony in the bar.

"I beg your pardon?" he asked.

"I was asking," said Montgomerie, "what you do to earn your keep." He continued, "You've heard my story, big on the money front but not on the interesting side of things. What about you? Finances, medicine?"

"Actually, I've been in India for the last two years," replied Richard Melvold.

"India?"

"India. I worked up near Cawnpore."

Another cheer rocked the bar. Two older men faced off on the oak top, engaged in an alpine drinking ritual. They toasted each other and seemed to drain their glasses in a single gulp.

"Would you look at that?" asked Melvold. "Those two have been at it for the last hour and a half. It's like they're drinking water! I'd be on the floor by now. Must be last man standing wins."

"It's bloody hard to keep a conversation together with all these continentals carrying on," agreed Montgomerie. "They do seem to be picking up the ball and running with it, so to speak. I always wanted to visit the Colonies myself," he continued, "but never had the time to make the voyage out. Always thought there was something vaguely magical about the thought of a sea passage and then some time in the tropics."

"India's a bloody good wicket Charles!" said Melvold with enthusiasm. "A little hot, the sun as well as the lamb vindaloo! And of course they'll never be able to play any quality cricket, but on balance it's a land of opportunity. It was certainly good to me. Made one or two good friends out there. The local regiment doctor was a real larrikin. The natives can be hard to understand sometimes, but the educated ones are quite interesting. Of course, if you're not talking to a pandy from the Service it's not worth taking the time to say hullo."

"The service?" asked Montgomerie, quite taken aback.

He wondered if for a moment he had misjudged Melvold. He'd never heard that Military Intelligence was active in India, but Melvold's next sentence quashed any misunderstanding.

"The Indian Civil Service," nodded Richard. "We started letting the odd local in back in the twenties. Best thing we ever did for India, tightened up the local governments. They've more money to spend on improving the country, much more efficient you see. There's no more ten men taking five days to do an afternoon's work for one."

"The place is all a bit up in the air at the moment with this business of nationalizing the railways, but I think Ackworth knows what he's doing. I was up at Cawnpore, involved in a bit of it, and for all the chaos Indian Railways is bringing, there's an awful lot of opportunity for people who want to do well."

He winked.

Montgomerie raised an eyebrow over his still largely untouched pint. Melvold, enthusiasm kindled by talk of India, had already downed half his whisky and the spy was happy to let him do most of the talking. His was a dangerous game and drinking heavily was not part of his strategy. On the other hand, he needed Melvold compliant and plying him with drink seemed the easiest way to assure that. Besides he knew that anyone who did a lot of talking revealed much about themselves to anyone who cared to listen. Montgomerie was about to bet the pot on the last trick of the game and so needless to say he was very interested in learning all about Richard Melvold.

"Sorry, drifted off for a moment," he said, taking his first sip of beer for the evening. "Do go on."

"I don't mean illegal things," Melvold elaborated. "There were lots of opportunities to advance oneself while on the business of the company. Buy low, sell high, that sort of thing. Lots of cargo going at cheap prices, all perfectly legitimately. There were some people who played a little harder than me, but Ackworth, he's the head man see, and his men are beginning to frown quite heavily on anything that's not strictly above board. I thought it best to leave anything illegal well alone."

"If you were doing so well out there, why come back?" asked Montgomerie.

Melvold snorted, an amalgam of laugher and chagrin.

"It's more a case of why I left in the first place," he explained. "I was involved with a young Scottish lady in London, but things didn't turn out so well. I don't know if you've ever met any Scots, but if you have, you'll know to stay well out of their way when they're angry. In fact, how two Scots ever manage to stop fighting for long enough to breed is quite beyond me!"

Melvold seemed to have forgotten that Montgomerie's name was among one of Scotland's oldest and most respected. Luckily the Scotsman had other priorities on this particular night than defending his national honour.

"A lucky escape," he murmured.

"A friend of my father's had just returned with fantastic stories of the colonies, and between his tales and my social circumstances, I found myself inspired to explore the Empire. I'd read a little philosophy, a little literature, and more usefully, quite a chunk of economics at the Imperial College, so I managed to wrangle myself a position with Indian Railways and off I went."

Montgomerie nodded encouragingly.

"Anyway," continued Melvold blithely "last I heard in India, Isabelle, my erstwhile Celtic lover, was happily married and had returned to Glasgow so I decided to chance a very low profile," another wink, "return to London. I'd made my money and seen the colonies. The one thing I hadn't done was see Surrey play cricket for a good three years, so I decided to make the voyage home. It was lovely to get back to my townhouse in Hammersmith. I haven't had a good plate of ham and eggs for breakfast since nineteen thirty-six!

"And then," this said with an outright laugh, "it took me about three days of my mother nagging me about still being unmarried to make me wish I'd never stepped back onto the quay at the P&O dock. So, I escaped here to fortify myself enough to deal with the old dear over Christmas. I'm heading down to Lyon tomorrow, or whenever the blasted tracks are clear, and then spending a couple of nights on the left bank in Paris. It's the hotel *Fleur D'Or*. Do you know it?"

"No," said Montgomerie, shaking his head

"Pity," replied Melvold. "Fancy name and all, means golden flower in French, but it's worth the price. One of the only places I've ever stayed in Paris where you don't have to have the obligatory croissant for breakfast, and they don't serve raw meat at dinner either."

There was a stir in the air of the bar and both Melvold and Montgomerie turned towards the door. Any further exposition from Melvold was interrupted as a vision of loveliness strolled her way through the portal connecting bar and hotel lobby. She was five feet nine inches tall with powder blue eyes framed by golden curls falling over bare shoulders.

"Her name's Anne," Melvold whispered to Montgomerie. "Anne Hamilton. I'm meeting her for a drink tonight."

She was dressed in an elegant white silk evening gown that shimmered in the bar's dim light. A black pashmina was thrown casually over her left shoulder.

"She looks even more out of place than you Melvold," replied Montgomerie appreciatively. "Elegance personified. She should be hanging off the craps table in Monaco with a glass of *Verve Cliquot* in her hand, not strolling through the pig farmers in a county pub."

"Yes, she's rather striking, isn't she?" replied Richard.

She nodded a gracious *"bonsoir"* to the bartender and spoke briefly to him. As she sashayed through the crowd he took a few moments to close his bottom jaw and resume pouring drinks. Carefully she made her way slowly through the crowded bar to the table by the fire where Melvold and Montgomerie both rose to meet her. Melvold directed his most winning smile at Anne.

"Miss Anne Hamilton," he gestured, "please meet mister Charles Montgomerie."

He gallantly pulled her chair out as she made to sit.

The bartender had followed her over to the table.

"*Pardon Madame, Messieurs*," he began. "*Un* gin *et* tonic," he pronounced the English words badly with his southern French accent, "*pour madame*".

"Thank you," replied Anne, smiling.

"I'll have another please," said Melvold to the barman, waggling his glass.

"*Oui monsieur*."

"Gin? When it's snowing?" asked Richard, turning to Anne. "Why not have something warmer? Schnapps perhaps? Or mulled wine?"

"Schnapps has never really been my drink," she replied with a smile. "I know this is usually a cool drink for warm weather," she raised her glass, "but sometimes I think one simply has to embrace the prevailing theme of a season. If it's cold outside why not embrace it inside?"

"You know, I think I approve of that," remarked Melvold. "In any event," he held out his hand open palm towards Charles, "I should introduce mister Montgomerie properly. We've joined forces you see, as the only two here who speak a civil tongue, although I must admit he's left the lion's share of the talking to me. Jolly good form because I'm terribly interesting even if I do say so myself!"

He waved an arm depreciatingly

Richard turned to Montgomerie. "Charles, this is Miss Anne Hamilton. I was fortunate enough to join her for coffee in the lobby yesterday. I believe she has also spent the last several weeks in Milan, studying if I recall, although the exact subject escapes me at this point." He clicked his fingers and rubbed his temples. "It's here somewhere."

"Some architecture," supplied Anne, "some literature, anything really for a chance to escape London. I'd even have considered chemistry!"

This last was said with a somewhat theatrical roll of her eyes. "The city is so gloomy in the weeks before Christmas. I had to get away."

"Milan?" asked Montgomerie. "I would have thought Rome or Florence would be more suitable for any serious student of architecture". After a moment, he added, "Or literature."

"I'd be lying if I said there weren't other, um, personal reasons for my trip," said Anne, levelly. "But I'd prefer not to discuss them here. It's a girl's prerogative to keep a few secrets".

This last was said with a slightly cheeky wink at Richard.

"Charles was in Milan!" exclaimed Melvold, his enthusiasm for Anne's approval sharpened by three whiskies too many.

At this Montgomerie's expression froze, just for a moment. Anne was looking directly at him when it happened. She raised an eyebrow.

"Banking my dear," he qualified urbanely. "Glorified errand running really, for some jumped up suits back in Piccadilly."

"You must have been there only briefly," she suggested.

"Yes," Charles replied. "Would have liked to have a better look around, but time and tide you know.... I needed to be in France, and then to get back to business in London."

"It's certainly not the most exciting city in the world, architecturally speaking, although the Duomo di Milano is something to behold," Anne rallied. "It took five hundred years to build. In fact, academically speaking they've still not finished but it's a wonderful display of how gothic architecture has developed since the fifteenth century. I'm thinking of a dissertation on the subject, or at least that's my official reason for travelling to Milan. Of course, I could have chosen Seville. The cathedral there is particularly impressive, but Milan suited me better for other reasons."

"I'm surprised you two didn't meet while you were in Milan," observed Melvold. "There can't be too many of us from the Isles running around the centre of the city".

"Well, I would have simply loved to meet Mr Montgomerie in Milan," said Anne politely.

She looked across the table directly into Charles's eyes.

"I'm sure we would have found simply piles of things to discuss there".

There was a slight catch in her voice at the end of her sentence as if Anne Hamilton had not appreciably warmed to Charles Montgomerie. Taking the cue Mongtomerie looked at his watch and stood.

"It rather seems the evening has gotten away from me a little, so I do apologize for being such a middle-aged bore and leaving. I'd love to stay and explore your experience of Milanese church decor further Ms Hamilton, but you see, my bank cabled me this afternoon. They want me to run up to Geneva." He grimaced. "Apparently there's a spot of bother with one of our accounts up there and they need someone who speaks proper English with a little seniority to go and have a glance at things. I suspect that another drink or two with Mister Melvold, and my institution might be rather in the red tomorrow."

"But we're all snowed in, we can't go anywhere!" protested Melvold. "Probably a blessing for you too! I've been to Geneva, and it's even more boring than Milan. It's just full of cuckoo clocks and large women who eat too much chocolate." He thought about this for a second, and then added as an aside to Anne, "Although I'm sure the cathedral's beautiful".

As Charles Montgomerie pulled his coat off the back of the old wooden chair he'd been sitting on, and turned to walk away, he said, "I'm afraid the road up the valley to Annecy is still open old boy, and that means I've no valid excuse not to be up in Switzerland tomorrow night. I'd love to stay and have another beer with you-"

"But you've barely touched your first one! My local vicar is more companionable at the pub!"

"I'd love to stay and have another drink," repeated Montgomerie, "and it's really nothing to do with religion but I really must be off. I'll certainly see you in London for a drink. My club does a wonderful clam soup and broiled beef the first Monday of the month. I'll show you some top-notch London nosh. No oranges within sight of a good roast duck."

He grinned and knuckled his forehead, public school style.

"Ms Hamilton, charmed, do take care."

Then he held out his hand to Richard. "It was good making your acquaintance Richard; a real pleasure to meet you son. Make sure you look me up in London."

With that final salutation, Charles Montgomerie left the room and made his way upstairs to the warmth of his bed. He'd learned what he needed to about Richard Melvold. He would do.

Melvold watched Montgomerie's back recede amongst the crowd of oiled pullovers and warm knitwear.

"What an absolute wet blanket!" he said incredulously to Anne. "Not that I'm upset to have you all to myself."

She looked him directly in the eye and reached a hand across the table. Her fingers were long and elegant, hidden in elbow length white silk gloves. "It's fine with me," she said breathily. "I prefer our evening that way."

Richard took her hand and there was a slight pause as he gazed back at her.

“Capital!” he declaimed. “That is also my preference to be devastatingly honest. Charles seems like quite a nice man, but three is a crowd.”

“And two is so much more intimate.”

“I agree,” he smiled. “Now! To move away from Milan and to a more interesting banking story, did I tell you yesterday the tale about our company train being held up for ransom by bandits? We were just south of a town called Lucknow. It’s a frightfully good yarn of wit and bravery. Largely my own I must confess.”

He paused expectantly.

“I don’t believe you did sir,” answered Anne encouragingly.

She squeezed his hand and then signaled with her chin to the bartender for more drinks. It was only a subtle movement, but he must have been watching for he came running to take her order.

“The same again please, for both of us.”

“*Oui madame!*”

He left at pace.

“It is absolutely amazing to me how well you have that man wrapped around your little finger,” remarked Richard.

“Isn’t it?” she replied saucily, raising an eyebrow. “Now, tell me more about this tale of heroism...”

Melvold sat back and lit his pipe as he resumed his charm offensive. As he and Anne bent their heads closer in conversation neither noticed the tall blonde-haired man with the ice-blue eyes leaning quietly against the wall in the far corner of *Elevation 850*. He’d spent the last two hours listening to every word at the trio’s table and with the departure of Montgomerie he finished his drink quickly and silently left the room.

III

Midnight in Berlin

Far north of the merriment in Chamonix Admiral Wilhelm Canaris sat alone and silent in his office. The featureless facade of 78 Tirpitzufer Strasse was darkened and his staff had retired several hours previously. A solitary man, he did much of his thinking alone at night when the distractions of a busy day would not interrupt his train of reason. On a sideboard in the corner of the large office was a half-eaten chicken. He often took dinner in his office and the cooks at the barracks mess next door had become accustomed to his hours.

He sat with a cup of coffee he'd brewed himself and gazed vexed at the telegram he'd rejoiced over earlier in the afternoon. His elation had faded with the setting sun, and his mood had darkened as he debated exactly what instructions to give Schmidt. It was a wrestling match between the two equally compelling needs of secrecy and efficiency.

Although Schmidt had finally run the quarry to ground the crux of the matter was that Montgomerie's presence in Chamonix was a problem. Canaris generally favoured expediency over subtlety but France was not a client state of the Reich such as Austria or Poland. France required discretion. He could of course have Montgomerie murdered, but interdicting a foreign national on the soil of a nominally hostile country was risky business. If the Abwehr were exposed there would be an international incident and diplomats hated having to explain such things. The Reich was already regarded with suspicion by the French and under no circumstances did Canaris wish to create a casus belli. Until the Führer was ready to unleash the flames of war across the continent, provocation of France and her allies was to be strictly avoided.

On the other hand, if Montgomerie made it across France to the British Isles, or even should he cross the Swiss border via the less heavily regulated French boundary, the information he carried could be considered lost to Germany. Reinhard Heydrich would delight in the Abwehr's failure and would surely bring the matter to the attention of the Führer. He would use it to justify his own service's many lapses, ruining Wilhelm Canaris in the process. No matter that Heydrich himself had let the quarry slip unchecked across the Reich, a failure of such magnitude would end the independence of the Abwehr and remove Canaris from the inner circle of the Furher. He had no wish to be called to explain himself in such a manner and thus came his dilemma. How to neutralize the British spy and avoid any unwanted attention?

He allowed himself the luxury of finishing his cup of coffee as he ruminated. It was Lavazza, the product of one of the oldest coffee houses in Tuscany. Smooth and dark it ran down his gullet like warm velvet. He concentrated, allowing the progression of the problem to unfold in his mind's eye.

It all came back to Poland, an unfortunate beginning in the cold mists of Warsaw. The Abwehr had many well-placed informants in the Polish government. Copious volumes of information poured into Tirpitzufer Strasse, troop movements, sailing schedules, ordinance orders, new fortifications. The inside joke in the Abwehr was that Wilhelm Canaris knew more about the Polish army than their own defense minister. All the information he collected went of course straight to high command, and in the eventuality of war he was sure the German army would roll over the Polish like a thunderstorm across a wheat field.

A year ago, his agency had caught word of a new Polish government branch called the Biuro Szyfrów. Canaris owned whole branches of the bureaucracy, but this particular twig was shrouded in secrecy. Unlike the armed services it was a mystery that refused to reveal its secrets to the German spy master. Even a translation of the name, “Cypher Bureau” gave little away. Very few of the Poles even knew the name and such a closely guarded secret could not be readily compromised. The bureau was a challenge to the Abwehr’s professionalism, one which Canaris could not ignore.

He had summoned up the resources of his vast network and begun to push. It was a masterpiece of espionage. Extortion, blackmail, intimidation and murder were all liberally employed. He’d spent lives merely to confirm the existence of the mysterious body! The horror he’d felt when he’d finally divined the meaning behind the cryptic name still returned when he dwelt on the subject. The Poles, nothing but a subhuman race of mongrels in Canaris’ eyes, were on the verge of achieving something impossible. He had gone straight to the office of the Fuhrer with stomach tied in knots once he had confirmed his discoveries.

He remembered the day well. He strode past a row of minor party functionaries sitting outside the Führer’s office whose faces portrayed outrage at his queue jumping. Canaris cared little. He was a lord above the petty party peasantry who existed only to serve such as he. Steeling himself he had placed the typewritten report on the Führer’s desk and saluted smartly. He remembered proudly that he had kept his hands from shaking. The Führer read his report in silence, frowning halfway through and then asked a single question in a quietly poisonous voice.

“You are sure of this?”

Canaris nodded his assent.

“We confirmed everything this morning. We have gotten a man inside their offices. The photographs he sent back confirm that they are working on a machine even now.”

The Führer crunched the brown paper bearing Canaris’ report in his hand and looked up with naked anger etched on his face.

"Eliminate them. Immediately."

And so Canaris had. Somewhat paradoxically, "disappearing" people was often easier than the simple business of information gathering. Once the shield of secrecy surrounding the members of the bureau had been breached it had been a matter of routine. Poland presented none of the issues that presently stymied his French operation and Schmidt et al were experts at the devilry of knives in the dark. The members of the Biuro Syzfrow had died quietly, sequentially. The elaborate chase now played out by Schmidt and Montgomerie was merely the endgame of a yearlong struggle fought amidst the deathly cold mists of Eastern Europe.

Canaris placed his coffee cup carefully on his desk as his thoughts returned to the problem of Montgomerie safe and free in France. Canaris knew that too much effort had been spent to cede the game. What was left now, Canaris asked himself? A huddle of scared men shivering in a dim, bare cellar beneath Krakow Castle? They were no longer a threat to the Reich's waxing might. But if their research made it to the British what then might occur? Despite Chamberlain's cowardice High Command knew that Britain and her Empire would be a formidable foe should Germany's expansionist foreign policy come truly to a test of arms. There would be no repeat of the Sudentenland fiasco, no further free tickets under the pretense of lasting peace.

Like most naval officers Canaris had studied the problem of Britain and her empire throughout his career. It was a favourite pastime of German naval officers, theorizing over how to exact revenge on those who had broken the Kaiser's regiments and humbled Imperial Germany. It was a subject of endless words, spoken at formal planning sessions, with sunrise coffee on the bridge at the end of the dawn watch, and over Schnapps at the officers' club by the naval pier in Hamburg.

The single biggest weakness of the British was their existence as an island nation. Their tenacity and the cohesion of the Empire on which the sun never set was dependent on very vulnerable lines of supply. It was down to the Kriegsmarine then: cut off the lifeblood of the island and watch the famed British fighting spirit wither and die. Secretly, as part of the rearmament program, Canaris knew Germany's admiralty was building a new generation of unterseaboots solely for this exact purpose. In tandem the navy had designed an unbreakable communications system to co-ordinate their strikes. Invisible, untraceable, silent and deadly, the fleet would stalk the Royal Navy, hunt them down and erase the humiliation of two decades past

But while the U-boats were fast and stealthy they relied on surprise to achieve their victories. Thus, the sanctity of naval communications was critical.

Canaris had been but a deck officer aboard the *Dresden* during the Great War. He remembered with great clarity the dreadful might and power of the British fleet. With his own eyes he'd seen the battlecruisers *Inflexible* and *Invincible* sail forth from the morning fog lying over the Falkland Islands. Together in the space of a morning, outnumbered and alone, they had dismantled Vice Admiral Von Spee's expeditionary fleet. The thunder of the British guns and the rattle of his ship's wooden deck were printed indelibly on his conscious, and the crash of exploding rounds and the stink of brimstone hovered at the edge of his mind as he cogitated in the gloom.

Later in the war he'd made his own name in the first U-boat fleet, testing his courage against the best of the Allied mariners. He'd sunk eighteen ships, condemned more than a thousand men to deathly rest beneath the icy water of the Atlantic Ocean. On many, many occasions he'd nearly joined them, but his luck had held and by the end of the war the name of Captain Wilhelm Canaris had become famous amongst the dashing sailors of the Imperial

German Navy. That was the nature of naval warfare, the balance of risk and reward.

Thus, for Canaris the present dilemma was more than just a slight to his espionage credentials. He knew firsthand exactly how dangerous the Royal Navy was. However, he also knew that the hearts of sailors were less a determinant of victory than tactics and logistics. Impregnable communications were a decisive factor in modern naval warfare, one upon which they depended. No U-boat could stand toe to toe with a British battlecruiser, and now a handful of Polish mathematicians had deconstructed the elaborate advantage upon which so many hours of German ingenuity had been spent. With the Enigma encoder compromised, the battle order of the German Navy would be laid bare for all to know. Were that so, Canaris asked himself how might the fragile U-boats fare against the likes of His Majesty's Ships *Inflexible* and *Invincible*? The sea wolves, silent hunters, would themselves become prey, each raid potentially a suicidal charge beneath the expectant guns of the British fleet.

"So Ein Misthaufen!"

Canaris swore in frustration at this train of thought.

What that damnable man Montgomerie carried could decide the future of Europe for the next 50 years! The last gasp whispered testament of the dying Cypher Bureau had been carried all the way through the Reich to France! The Führer would be livid when that came out! But if Canaris could catch the courier he would save Germany and her ambitions. Once he had successfully resolved the current impasse he would delight in bringing Heydrich's own failure to the Führer's attention. Success in this matter was paramount for Canaris, the Abwehr and the Fatherland.

Too much rode on preserving the sanctity of German cryptography. Enigma was the key that would unlock the seas of Europe to the Kriegsmarine and its fields to the Panzergruppen.

He might be the chief of the German Foreign Intelligence service, but Canaris possessed the soul of a sailor. Speed, stealth and a decisive strike were the hallmarks of both the master submariner and the master spy. Hesitation, fear, reticence, these were the qualities in a commander that cost lives. One did not run back to port at the first sign of stormy weather. Alone with his thoughts Canaris put pen to paper and cabled Schmidt some very blunt instructions, care of the *Maison Gustav* in Chamonix.

● -● ●● --● -- ●-

Melvold listed ever so slightly as he walked down the hallway adjoining the bar and guest accommodation proper. He wallowed like a poorly rigged ship weathering heavy sea. Slowly he staggered up the stairs of the Hotel Gustav. His watch told him it was almost midnight.

"That can't be right," he mumbled.

In any event he couldn't wait to find his bed. Doubts as to the accuracy of his watch aside Richard was honest enough with himself to admit that he was moderately drunk. At least it was the result of a good cause. Downstairs the subtle winks of the early evening had progressed. Anne had lain her hand on his, and he could swear he'd felt the touch of her leg on his under the table on more than one occasion. But at the last-minute Anne had demurred with a kiss on the cheek and a promise to meet for dinner in London.

"Women!" Melvold snorted.

Worse, Anne wasn't even on the same train as him tomorrow so that was the end of his chances for the moment. It was a shame. Even his mother, the old dragon, would like Anne. Briefly he fantasized at the thought of arriving for morning tea at the family home with Anne on his arm. Even now he could see the look of shock that would be so prominent upon her face at the audacity of Richard's private life. Deep down, he knew she'd never really approved of Isabelle, treating her with the mild snobbery that was the singular domain of a pure blood Englishwoman. She was ever the English lady deigning to speak with the Celtic peasant. Anne, thought Melvold, was formidable enough to hold her own against the old dragon.

Melvold, really quite drunk, had a small giggle to himself. He wasn't quite sure that seducing Anne while drunk to shock and impress his mother was quite morally up to scratch. Mind you, morals hadn't stopped him before. There had been the lonely young wife of the Cawnpore banker last year after all. It wasn't a life experience he was willing to share with his local vicar, but Melvold was sure that Lord Nelson with mistress in tow would have approved. Besides, he had checked. Anne was fair game.

As he reeled up the corridor Melvold's disequilibrium worsened. The imaginary waves he was riding seemed to be increasing in ferocity, even as steep stairs gave way to flat grey carpet. He'd only just mastered the staircase and in the dimly lit corridor it seemed the walls were moving with malicious intent. It took him a moment or two to get to grips with walking on the flat so it took Melvold a moment longer than it should have to notice Charles Montgomerie standing uncomfortably outside the door to Melvold's room. Richard raised an eyebrow and a hand as he staggered to a halt.

"Good evening again," he mumbled rather disheveledly.

Montgomerie greeted him with an apologetic smile.

"Sorry Melvold old son. I was just about to knock, when I saw you come up the corridor."

He seemed faintly amused at Melvold's state of disrepute.

"I wasn't sure if you'd have company or not."

Melvold raised an eyebrow in response. "Unfortunately," he said, spreading his arms, twirling in the hallway and nearly putting his left shoulder through the plasterboard wall, "Here I am, alone. And drunk," he added a moment later. "Damned French bartenders! No measures at all, just a free pour. Those doubles were more like quintuples! How's a man to keep track?"

"Anyhow," continued Montgomerie, ignoring Melvold's rambling in favour of keeping the conversation moving, "I think I mentioned earlier that I'd been cabled up to Geneva tomorrow. Bit of a bother really, because it's my godson's birthday in a week. I wonder, since you were heading back to London, that's where he lives obviously, if you'd drop in with a present from me? I meant to ask you earlier but forgot until I got back to my room and saw it on my dresser."

Feeling unexpectedly magnanimous, Richard nodded.

"Of course. Always happy to help a countryman."

"Capital!" ejaculated Montgomerie.

He raised his left arm and Melvold saw he was holding a large package wrapped in brown butcher paper. Melvold, whose family traditionally irritated each other at Christmas by trying to guess what a present was before it was opened, thought it looked and felt like quite a large book. It was big enough perhaps to be a text, or something formal. This combination of thinking and standing was too much for Melvold to handle simultaneously and it must have shown.

"I say Melvold, old son, are you alright?" asked Montgomerie.

"Of course, fine, never better!" said Melvold seriously. "Why?"

"It's just that you're swaying quite a lot, bit like a willow in the breeze."

Melvold straightened up and steadied himself against the wall.

"Excuse me," he said politely. "I think it's bedtime for me."

"Jolly good," replied Montgomerie. "I'll just leave this with you, and oh, there's a card too."

He handed Melvold a large white gift card, opened. The card was good quality board and had a small gilded French salutation on the front. Written inside in very small handwriting considering the size of the card, was a simple message.

Dear C,

Hope you find this interesting!

Happy Birthday!

Monty

"Look, he works in my office. Here's my business card. Just pop in here, and ask for C. His name's Charles too, but everyone just calls him that. They'll all know who he is."

Montgomerie handed Melvold a business card that read:

CHARLES MONTGOMERIE

MANNING SMITH CUMMING INVESTMENT BANK

54 BROADWAY

VICTORIA ST

LONDON SW1.

"Sounds like a pretty swanky sort of outfit," remarked Melvold, regarding the card with sudden interest. "Probably quite high powered I imagine."

"Not really," replied Montgomerie. "Just an office with a few telephone lines and a couple of clericals to push the paper. Not hard to find though."

Melvold shrugged.

"I'm sure I'll manage."

"Thanks awfully old chap," Montgomerie concluded. "That really gets me out of a bit of a bind. I won't keep you up any longer. Good night, and safe travels."

He patted Melvold on the right shoulder.

"Welcome," said Melvold looking distractedly at the package. "You too."

Melvold opened the door to his room. It took him a full minute of fumbling to successfully insert the key into the lock. He always had trouble with locks when he was drunk. Then he was in and moving straight towards the large white double bed positioned in the dead centre of the room. He poured himself in and fell asleep almost instantaneously, alone.

• -• •• --• -- •-

As usual it was raining in London. There was a light drizzle in the street and the wet cobbles shone wore a dull sheen in the yellow gas light. The large wooden door swung shut and as he left 54 Broadway for the night Alan Denning sighed. There still had been no word from Mongomerie, either at Bletchley Manor or at the MSC Investment Bank office.

It had been Hugh Sinclair's idea to rent the office in Broadway several years ago. It was an unofficial stopping point for any of his agents who needed to covertly contact the agency without the attention that a formal call to Admiralty House often conferred. The business of London's private banks was by convention discreet and therefore Sinclair's faux offices mimicked a place where furtive comings and goings were the norm. Denning thought it was brilliant – the most secret of spies hiding in plain sight. He also was a believer in the old woods and trees argument.

As he opened his umbrella Denning reflected that intelligence operations in Europe were becoming progressively more complex with each passing year. The current operation had been laid on hastily and was therefore doubly so. At stake was the culmination of years of combined effort on behalf of Great Britain, France and Poland. For C, Denning, and the rest of the School success was imperative. Mongtomerie's flight across Europe represented a problem of myriad antecedents but singular purpose.

In the mid 1920s whispers had begun to reach Britain's intelligence community of German re-emergence; arms building and secret projects that might one day be used to further the Reich's latent imperial ambitions. The business of gathering intelligence involved chasing many such leads, often insubstantial and usually hyperbolic, but nevertheless military intelligence had in due course put out their feelers. Slowly, softly, subtly, the snowball of rumour had grown, built up by half intercepted telegrams, papers retrieved from a trashcan outside an office, or a note from a source within the Reich who valued coin over honour. The stories spoke of an untraceable signal created by an uncrackable mechanical encoder. *Enigma*, they called it.

Three years later intelligence had acquired dramatic proof of the phantom machine when a German company had mistakenly shipped a commercial version of the technology through Polish customs in 1928. Seeing the implications immediately, C had re-designated military intelligence priorities and commenced operations to unveil Enigma's secrets. Signals had been pulled from the electronic soup of wireless broadcasts and cables crossing Europe. Slowly the picture had become clearer. The white noise that the German Navy had been emitting since 1926 without reason or meaning took on a new dimension. It was coded transmissions, and the Royal Navy was deaf to the song.

The significance of the problem was immediately apparent to the highest echelons of the intelligence fraternity. Chamberlain might believe that peace would reign for his time but Sir Hugh Sinclair and the other powers in Admiralty House feared differently. The value of being able to read the enemy's communications had recently been demonstrated most clearly in Poland's triumph over Russia at Warsaw in 1920. Now, suddenly Germans ships and soldiers were talking to each other without the possibility of being overheard. So, the finest minds had gone to work at the Government Code and Cypher School in Bletchley and together with the Cypher Bureau in Warsaw slowly they'd made progress.

The real break came in 1932 when a young experimental mathematician named Marian Rejewski had rather outlandishly applied group theory to the Enigma conundrum. In one stroke of revolutionary mathematics, he turned an impossible problem into a workable theory. The pendulum had reached its apogee and was turning back in the favour of the Reich's foes until earlier in the year when one by one the Polish mathematicians had disappeared mysteriously. Everything had again been turned on its head.

"Pilch has resurfaced," C had told Denning grimly one night in May.

"Where?"

"Face down in the Vistula River. Looked like he'd been beneath the water quite some time."

Denning thought back to the gallows humour with a thin grimace. Two days later Sokolay had been found in a back alley behind the main square of Warsaw's old town. His throat had been cut.

The British cryptographers at Bletchley Park were highly dependent on their Polish colleagues for much of their basic data. As the Poles had died efforts at Bletchley had wilted with them. They were so very close to being able to build a working model of the Enigma machine but without the data from

Poland the British could progress no further. Taken by surprise MI-6 had seen no alternative but to try to courier the last of the Polish data to London.

At short notice Sinclair had arranged for it to be carried personally by one of his most trusted agents, Charles Montgomerie. And thence had the real trouble begun. Pursued, hunted, dogged by the Germans, Montgomerie had spent a month in mortal danger and all the while the British had remained blind to the mysteries of Enigma.

“Where is he?” C had asked Denning five days ago.

“I don’t know,” he had responded testily.

“Is he still alive?”

“I don’t know that either,” Denning replied with a great deal of controlled frustration. “He could be dead in a ditch somewhere in the back mountains of Italy, and we’d never know.”

The last communication from Montgomerie had been two weeks ago, read by both men at Bletchley Park.

“Chamonix then?” C surmised.

“Yes. Montgomerie’s a professional. If he’s not dead, he’ll be there. We need to get someone in position to find out.”

The office in Broadway was being manned day and night, discretely of course, on the off chance that Montgomerie would break cover and make contact. To date those hopes had gone unrewarded.

Alone in the chill London air Denning walked slowly down Victoria Street. In the drizzle he cut a dejected figure under the wan lamplight. His right hand was clenched deep in his overcoat pocket, and he opened and closed it absently as he furiously contemplated the current state of affairs. There really was nothing more he could usefully do. They’d sent some help to Chamonix as quickly as they could mobilize an agent but without more information from Montgomerie a rendezvous was very difficult.

At the “office” tonight, the telegram lines remained silent as they had been for two weeks. Wherever Charles Montgomerie was tonight Denning knew that he was still alone.

THE SECOND NIGHT

By the Lyon Station

IV

A Curious Italian

Cold winter sunlight streamed straight in through the window of Richard's room onto his face, disturbing him but not warming him. He rolled over, enjoying the luxury of the clean cotton sheets in the spacious double bed. Around him dust motes sparkled as they drifted aimlessly above the carpet. As a scene it was quite surreal. Winter sunshine was rare in Chamonix but the morning must had seen a break in the heavy snow clouds that roofed the valley. Outside Melvold could hear burbling as melt water from the previous night's snow trickled down the hotel roof gutters. He sat up and looked out the window. The clay tiled roof of the hotel's barn sparkled as the sun danced off the foot of snow it still supported, and beyond in the village every roof shone as the previous evening's fall dissolved in the sunlight.

Stars exploded behind Melvold's eyes and the beauty of the morning was lost as conscious thought returned in the company of a fierce hangover. The reflected sun on the icy roofs stabbed hot needles through his forehead. He felt as if he'd been run over by a freight train, one of the large ones that served the Cawnpore docks.

He groaned and looked at his wristwatch, a battered old Baum and Mercier which he'd inherited from his grandfather. The dial was pitted and small spots of tarnish speckled the band, but the gold hands still rotated across the ivory face with mechanical precision. Despite the wear it was incredibly valuable and Richard wore it constantly, even while he slept. The timepiece, his unorthodox surname, and a generous inheritance were legacy of his Dutch grandfather. It was this he'd used as base capital in India and now it was worth many times over its starting value. Value and beauty aside, the watch was a physical reminder of Melvold's past.

He looked at it again. Silently the hands informed him it was just after eleven in the morning. No wonder his room was so bright! He'd slept late. Fortunately, the train to Lyon was an afternoon departure. With his hangover this morning he doubted he'd have made an early departure. In fact, at that moment, he'd have given a good portion of his small fortune to make his headache go away.

With a deep breath to quash his nausea Richard Melvold sat up further and looked around the room. His jacket and blue tie were thrown messily on the floor. He didn't even remember taking them off! His trousers by contrast were folded neatly over the back of a chair and his shoes were nowhere to be seen. Goodness he'd had a lot to drink! Montgomerie's package and card sat quietly on the bedside table as if trying not to attract attention to themselves. Above them the antique iron French lantern was still on, presumably the state in which Melvold had left it last night.

As he steadily regarded Montgomerie's consignment another wave of nausea hit him. In the cold light of sobriety Melvold did not feel entirely happy about his countryman's request. It was an extra nuisance, something he could do without. Habitually Melvold was a disorganized traveler. He was sure there were innumerable legions of single socks and the occasional diary that haunted the various hotels of Northeast India, hastily abandoned and easily forgotten as he travelled about his business. The responsibility of being a courier did not thrill, especially with this morning's hangover to exacerbate his forgetful tendencies.

"For goodness' sake" he muttered, more than a little piqued.

He shook his head slowly in frustration as he bit his lower lip.

"England expects every man to do his duty, Melvold old son," he reminded himself.

His mind wandered for a moment as he wondered what his grandfather's perspective on Nelson's aphorism would have been. Despite his rather cavalier approach to the fairer sex Melvold regarded himself as one of few men who still believed in moral absolutes. It was the basis of his business success and on balance was a philosophy by which he had been well served.

"Too late to renege now, anyhow," he decided. "Montgomerie's probably halfway to Annecy."

He rubbed his forehead. A shower was called for. He rose slowly out of bed and moved towards the bathroom. Halfway there he turned back, caught irresistibly by one of those random compunctions that usually emerged and demanded immediate attention when he suffered the effects of overindulgence. He would pack the gift later, but the card was sure to be lost as he put his belongings away. Paperwork was easier to misplace even than socks! Quickly Melvold picked up the card, tucked safely its envelope, and placed it with his travel folio where it would rest with his passport and other travel documents. It would be secure there and well removed from the terrible morning coffee spillages Melvold was prone to when he was especially wrung out.

As he turned on the taps to purge the line of cold, Melvold picked up the brass phone handle by his bed.

"*Bonjour, concierge!*" he heard down the rather tinny line.

"Yes, it's Richard Melvold in room ten," he said.

The hangover was too fierce to bother speaking French, and he knew from checking in that the concierge staff spoke English.

"*Oui monsieur?*"

"I'm taking the train up to Lyon this afternoon, for an overnight connection to Paris. Would you please arrange my effects to be transferred to the station and packed aboard the first-class carriage?"

"Of course, *monsieur*."

The concierge hesitated a moment, perhaps anticipating the reaction his next sentence would elicit.

"*Monsieur*, I am unsure if you are aware that there was a large fall of snow overnight?"

"Don't tell me the bloody train's cancelled again!" exclaimed Melvold irritably. "The sun's out, I just looked!"

"*Non monsieur*, the train will run, but not on time. The stationmaster has asked us to inform the guests that the train will be late this evening, because of the time it will take to clear the tracks. He thinks maybe they will depart at six this evening."

Melvold did some quick calculations in his head.

"But that means I'll miss my connection to Paris," he complained. "It leaves Lyon at eight, and there's no way the train will make the journey in that time."

"*Désolé monsieur*," replied the concierge, "but what would you like me to do?"

Melvold took a deep breath. There was no point in shooting the messenger.

"You're right," he said. "Please accept my apologies. I'm not angry with you, just eager to be home."

"I understand *monsieur*. There is a Wagon-Lit service to Paris that leaves Lyon just before lunch tomorrow. Would you like me to arrange you a ticket?"

"Yes please, first class, single sleeper. Have the conductor reserve me a table in the dining carriage please. I suppose that arranging a hotel in Lyon tonight will be difficult?"

"There is always the station hotel *monsieur*. I can try somewhere else, but at such short notice..."

The concierge trailed off, and Melvold could almost hear the Gallic shrug of his shoulders over the phone line. He growled in frustration.

"Very well. I'm not really one for such places, but if there's no choice, book me the best room you can. You should have my bank details in your file there, just cable the money and I'll pick up the invoice when I check out."

"Very good *monsieur*. Is there anything else I can help you with?"

"No, thank you," said Melvold as he rang off.

By this time there was steam flowing out of the bathroom, and the lure of a shower was very strong. Melvold shambled into the bathroom slapping shaving lotion on his cheeks. He resolved that after his ablutions he would find breakfast incorporating some form of ham and eggs rather sickly-sweet bread.

"*Jambon et oeufs*," he murmured as he patted shaving lotion on his chin.

He simply couldn't face a croissant this morning. In his less than reputable college days Richard thought of the triad of a shower, coffee and breakfast as the basis of 'putting oneself back together'. From experience he knew that in his present condition, it was likely to take some time. He'd need some seriously strong coffee to go with the ham.

• -• •• --• -- •-

High in the Alps the afternoon sun was fading fast above the village of Annecy. Charles Montgomerie was beginning to relax. It seemed his luck was holding. He'd taken a terrible risk running from Chamonix and he knew the Abwehr must have followed him. He'd stepped from the coach in the main plaza of Annecy into a pleasingly chaotic throng of people and promptly employed the best of his street craft to lose any pursuers. Montgomerie knew he was good, he was still alive after all, and again it seemed his skill had triumphed. Alone and hidden among the winding narrow streets, themselves in turn bisected by a multitude of tortuous canals, he'd be hard to find, and so now he hoped he was safe once more. The Swiss border was at hand, and he'd steal a car if he had to. In fact, he was prowling the backstreets of Annecy now trying to do just that because once he crossed into Switzerland the Abwehr must needs abandon their chase. He'd been completely out of options in Chamonix, alone and cornered, and so he'd taken another daring risk. He knew full well that in running he'd draw the Abwehr out, the quarry flushing the hunting pack. The Germans would be in Annecy too.

He gambled his life again, but if he was successful, he'd make the safety of Geneva where he'd have an easy ride back to the haven of the Isles via the embassy. He was desperate, and it was worth the risk.

Meanwhile, Melvold would have left Chamonix for Paris while the Abwehr were fruitlessly combing Annecy for Charles Montgomerie. Innocent, unaware, and free of pursuit he'd sail through to Paris where MI-6, alerted by Montgomerie from Station Geneva could meet him in force and escort the package from Warsaw to C in London. Montgomerie's appraisal of Melvold was that he could be trusted and besides what choice had he, besides surrender to the Germans and eating a bullet in the backstreets of Chamonix?

It was fast approaching four and the sun was no longer visible above the old shingle roofs. Below the village the *Lac D'Annecy* was grey below the mountains. Despite two hours spent searching Montgomerie still had no means of transport to Geneva. No one in the town seemed to own a blasted motorcar! He looked around him furtively, a habitual action, seeking signs of pursuit. He was certainly alone in the cold dark evening air of Annecy and he stopped, struck by the scene. It truly was dark now. A bare fifteen minutes ago the sun had provided enough light to illuminate the street, but now night had truly fallen. Even the old electric lights bracketed in stone walls by rough iron casts only splashed a dim glow across the cobblestones. That was good. If Montgomerie walked canal side of the pavement his face would not be easily seen in the shadows.

As the day waned and the sun vanished the temperature dropped quickly, and while he knew the dark and the cold worked for him Charles Montgomerie found the evening growing still ever more oppressive. Something yet bothered him, but he couldn't quite put a finger on exactly what it was. Perhaps it was the ease with which he'd shaken the Abwehr. That was unusual. They'd been truly tenacious pursuers across the entirety of middle Europe. He shivered in the cold. Chill fingers seemed to grasp at his neck as he drifted deeper into the heart of the old French mountain city.

Fog started to drift in from the lake. Roof tiles threw shadows which quickened and danced over the roughened stone walls of the alley. The slate and stone themselves deepened to dark grey, and the shadows grew ever blacker by the minute. The pleasant medieval French streetscape was visually decaying like the peeling strokes of an old oil painting left in the sun. At the bottom of the street the air was cold against his cheeks. Montgomerie could feel his breath steaming through his lips and merging with the fog as an invisible eddy in the darkness. Drifting down the alley he heard a trace of music from a distant tavern, something classical with hints of gypsy. He would have sought the tavern out, but the alleys of Annecy were a cryptic puzzle that reflected sound and bent light to confuse the uninitiated in their paths. Charles Montgomerie shivered, but with premonition rather than true cold. He quickened his pace and turned down a dark alley, moving further into the maze of alleys behind the old town hall. Still no cars! Damn!

Briefly he contemplated finding somewhere to lay low for the night, but he was loathe to risk whatever lead he had gained on the Abwehr. For the moment he was alone, with only the music, definitely a gypsy air he decided, for company. Maybe it would lead him to a backstreet tavern after all, somewhere he could rent a nondescript room or a corner of a barn. At the very least there might be an automobile outside that he could "borrow". His mood was grim and lips a tight line as he turned left down a side street, pursuing the ghostly lilt of the music. The next alley was darker again, the black gloom unbroken by not even a small cafe or a lively pub. It was as though he passed through the great underworld gate unseen, and the famed words he'd read once while a schoolboy at Eton, *'Abandon hope all ye who enter here,'* settled on his mind. Body wrapped in his cashmere greatcoat, mind drowning in thoughts of doom, Montgomerie was lost and cut off from the world.

He was alone in his isolation, and death was only a moment away.

The bullet hit him square in the chest, just to left of his sternum. A small crack in the dark, no louder than the bark of a dog, and a tiny flash of golden flame were the only heralds to announce Montgomerie's demise. The projectile ripped through his heavy coat, broke two ribs, and sliced a large hole through the wall of his right ventricle. It was deadly, a mortal wound, and it happened so quickly that it was only when he felt a warm burning spread through his chest that he realized he'd been shot.

He fell down, shocked mind grasping at reality, and as he toppled, he saw the black swathed Reaper stepping out of the dark shadows veiling walls built before there was electric light to shine upon them. Beneath the heavy hood worn by the cloaked figure cold blue eyes gazed down with stony indifference to the dying man. In that moment he knew that he had in fact lost the deadly game he had been playing and as his blood ran across the cobbles Charles Montgomerie was clutched by a cold fear. He tried to talk, tried to whisper a prayer, but the only sound to leave his lips was the ragged stream of cold air moving ever more slowly back and forwards. As Charles Montgomerie breathed his last his body shuddered, and with a final breath of the cold French mountain air he was dead.

Schmidt threw back the heavy hood of the cloak worn against the cold grasping tendrils of Annecy's fog. The small Luger pistol was deadly at short range. Even with the restrictions placed on German arms manufacture after Versailles the factories in Cologne still turned out quality arms. It was a shame and quite a large risk to kill Montgomerie here in a small French village, but the orders from Admiral Canaris had been most specific. Schmidt did not like sudden changes to operational plans, but nor did one often see Abwehr telegrams bearing orders to be obeyed at any cost.

They'd waited all afternoon for a chance to catch Montgomerie alone, trailing him diligently around the city, hoping for a chance. Schmidt and the other two had formed a loose box, picking up Montgomerie no matter which way he turned. Finally, opportunity had presented itself. Here, in the deserted back alleys of the old city, in the fog and the dark with everyone indoors, the small pop of Schmidt's revolver and the soft crash of Montgomerie's fall were unlikely to draw any unwanted attention. Schmidt only needed a few moments to search Montgomerie's body after it was dragged behind a pile of rubbish down another smaller blind alley

A quick ruffle through the pockets of Montgomerie's overcoat revealed a British passport, Montgomerie's own, which Schmidt pocketed along with a collection of Francs, both French and Swiss in mostly small denominations. Besides some worn and travel stained clothes Montgomerie's duffle bag was empty. Schmidt swore, heard only by the fog, the cobblestones, and the ancient light brackets. Where was the information Montgomerie had spent his life trying to carry out of Warsaw? Where was the Enigma Dossier? All that risk for nothing! Schmidt knew Wilhelm Canaris would not be pleased at this latest complication, especially given the risks they had incurred.

There had to be something the Abwehr team tracking Montgomerie had missed. The British spy had pulled a wonderful switch in Krakow to shake his pursuers but even so they'd beaten the Englishman to France. It really hadn't been too difficult. They were a well organized and financed team of professionals playing against a single courier running against the clock fettered by the risks of exposure.

The Abwehr had been safely ensconced in Chamonix waiting for Montgomerie while he skulked across the Italian border. Schmidt had suspected that Chamonix might form the point for a rendezvous with another MI6 agent but until last night when he'd had dinner with the Englishman, Melvold, Charles Montgomerie had kept completely to himself. In that time, he'd always had an Abwehr eye trained on him. They'd even searched his room while he was posing as a tourist, wandering through the *musée* of the mountain guides. Momentarily Schmidt considered it might have been this last act which spooked Montgomerie and made him decide to run for the Swiss border, but procedures were procedures. Now Montgomerie was dead, but there was a secret still to be saved.

Certainly, Schmidt was certain that there had been no drop, no exchange of anything with anyone in Chamonix. Nor had there been anything of the sort in Milan, behind the border dividing the Reich and its allies from decadent France. There hadn't been a single sniff of British intelligence on the winter wind in southern Europe. To be sure Schmidt had even radioed Berlin for a background check on Richard Melvold but there was nothing there. He was a dilettante, an adventurer, the sort of man the British Empire had been built by in the 1800s, the sort of well bred fool whom the British still considered the cornerstone of the arch of an empire spanning the globe, the type of man the

Third Reich would soon be correcting about any notions of "proper standing" in the world. Berlin was certain Melvold was not an MI-6 operative, and so Schmidt and the Abwehr had maintained the pressure and surveillance on Charles Montgomerie.

Nevertheless, the fact remained: Montgomerie was clean, and the Enigma Dossier sent by the Biuro Syzfrow to Britain in his care was somewhere else. The only person Charles Montgomerie had contacted was Richard Melvold, and therefore willing and knowledgeable or not, Melvold remained the most likely carrier of the information Schmidt pursued.

That blasted British fop must have the package. The only other alternative Schmidt could think of was that there was no secret, no dossier, that the entire chase was a ruse; and this Agent Schmidt of the German Foreign Intelligence Service simply refused to believe. It would be hard work to get close enough to Richard Melvold to find what the Abwehr sought, but it must be done. Richard Melvold had to be found and compromised. The Enigma files would be retrieved.

With a deep sigh, Schmidt signaled to the other Abwehr agents watching silently in the gloom.

"Throw him in the canal," Schmidt instructed, pointing at Montgomerie's corpse. "I need to return to Chamonix. When you're done cleaning up here, meet me in Lyon. We have business with another British. Our best chance will be while he travels to Paris."

As the brothers stepped forward to tip Montgomerie's corpse into the cold dark water of the canal he'd died besides, Schmidt cursed again and vanished into the gloom. It would have to be a rapid return to the Chamonix Valley if Melvold were to be caught before he left on the evening train. There were cables to send. Berlin would want an update. Melvold could not be allowed to leave Chamonix before the Abwehr re-established contact. They would have to be subtle Schmidt knew, provoke and fool the English into revealing his secrets. Arrangements would have to be made to ensure that Richard Melvold was brought to heel.

• -• •• --• -- •-

Chamonix Mont Blanc station was an impressive site in the cold winter evening. Its pale grey gables sat baroquely beneath two feet of snow. At the base of the drift Melvold could see where the downwards pressure was beginning to turn it to ice, a glacier in miniature above the platforms. The peaks of Mont Blanc towered over the station like a rocky crown worn as a symbol of the station's sovereignty over the valley railway line. Puddles of meltwater glinted in the light cast by the old lamps illuminating the platform. In the front garden where the ground was fully frozen every step elicited a soft fresh crunch.

Melvold thought the old *Corpet-Louvert* locomotive resting quietly at the platform was like something from a previous century. Dimly visible on the rime-caked works plate was the engine number: 1410. The engine was a blocky design with all the driving wheels packed under a square boiler painted bright blue, and Melvold guessed that it probably predated the Great War. It was certainly nothing like the five new Baldwin Diesels that he'd introduced to Cawnpore before his departure. Yet despite its age it was a striking machine and Melvold was charmed. Its wheels were clean and a faint wisp of smoke curled from the stack. The uncovered coal car was full of dark black blocks that absorbed the yellow lamplight illuminating the engine cab. Five carriages rested behind the engine, round grey roofs dusted with snow. Richard acknowledged the old train was well cared for. It bore the air of a machine hand crafted rather than made *en masse*.

Melvold stumped up the platform. The vestiges of his hangover were vanishing in the chill night air.

"The first-class carriage?" he asked the black suited attendant.

"The third car monsieur. May I take your hand luggage?"

"No, it's fine thank you."

He took seat 4A in the first-class cab. Opposite him, 4B was vacant. The only other occupants of the car were a woman and her young son.

"Good evening," he ventured politely.

The woman hesitated slightly. "Good evening signore," she rushed out, bobbing her head.

"Ah, Italian, yes?"

"*Si*," she nodded volubly. "My, ah, English is not so good, but my nama is Francesa, and this my son Pirro. We travel to Lyon, to meet my 'usband. 'E is with the bank there."

"Very good," replied Melvold, realizing that Francesca had probably just exhausted her entire English vocabulary. She would probably understand French, but Melvold didn't really feel a need to indulge in idle chat. He was still feeling irritable from the events of earlier that day and the previous night. Richard Melvold, reduced to a bloody bank courier!

There was a knock at the carriage door.

"*Pardon, madame,*" the conductor said, nodding to Francesca. "*Monsieur*, the train will be delayed for a short period of time."

"Don't tell me the bloody line's still not clear?" asked Melvold crossly. "They've been at it all blasted afternoon!"

"No, *monsieur,* not at all." The conductor shook his head vigorously. "One of the first-class passengers has telegraphed. He is running late and has asked us to hold the train. He is on important business, and there will be temporary delay until he arrives. Please accept the apologies of the line."

He nodded again, smiled at Pirro, and then closed the door quietly.

“I say,” Melvold vented to Francesca. “The train’s already three hours late. If you can’t be on board by departure time, I’m not sure you deserve a ride to Lyon. Probably bribed the damn station manager.”

She looked at him blankly.

“Never mind,” he waved his hand at her. “It’s just been a long day.”

Since he had time to wait, Melvold stood, opened his portable case and took out his novel. It was the latest Christie: *Murder on the Orient Express.* Melvold was a devoted fan. He glanced at his watch after about ten minutes and then looked up as he heard a slight commotion in the corridor outside.

“*Si, si! Grazie, si!*”

The door to the cabin he shared with Francesca and her son opened and a tall man with ice blue eyes and blond hair burst inside. He threw his suitcase on seat 4B and pressed a small package into the hands of the conductor.

“*Buona sera!*” he pronounced loudly.

“*Ah, signore,*” exclaimed Francesca happily.

“*Si, signora, scusi!*” He waved her away dismissively.

He looked like one who’d not spare those beneath him the rough edge of his tongue. With a final grimace at the woman, the man rounded on Richard. Melvold braced himself.

“English, yes?”

Richard, quite taken aback at this, nodded dumbly.

“Yes, I can tell from many things, your way of dressing; your stance; your carriage; you must be from the British Islands.”

Melvold eyed him up and down. He was tall, with cold blue eyes and hair so pale it might have been bleached. He wore a dark suit cut in the latest single-breasted fashion, and above a high lapel he sported a blue sash of colour at the throat.

"And you must have come straight from the Criterion," he parried.

"Scusi?"

"It's a theatre in the West End. Dracula is playing there at the moment. You look like a bloody caricature of Vlad the Impaler, man."

Privately, Melvold thought he was being charitable. A schizophrenic peacock might have been a more appropriate summation of the visitor's dress.

There was a moment's silence in the carriage. Then the visitor laughed, long and hard.

"Dracula?" he asked. "Yes, that is very good. How do you say, I have been called a bloodsucker before, no?"

Even his accent when speaking English was very full. The man with blue eyes held out his right hand towards Richard.

"Marcus Bellini lately of Rome."

He pronounced the 'u' of Marcus like the 'oo' of look. Melvold noticed that he referred to the Italian capital as 'Rome', in the English or German fashion, rather than the Italian *Roma*.

"Richard Melvold."

"I am very pleased to meet an Englishman," declaimed Bellini. "Yours is a powerful country, with many interests abroad, and I think most British have many interesting things to talk about."

Richard was slightly taken aback at this unexpected salvo of conversation.

Bellini continued, "You are travelling to Paris, yes? You have the look of a man who travels on business, and I think that there is no business for someone like you in Lyon. Who do you work for?"

Melvold sighed, eared the page he was halfway down and folded his book closed in his lap.

"Currently I'm not employed. Just back from the colonies actually."

The old locomotive clunked into life and the lights of the local station could be seen gently falling behind the train through the icy window near which Richard and Bellini sat. Darkness closed in over the carriages creating the sense that Richard's entire universe consisted solely of the small carriage room and Signor Bellini. The other two passengers were peripheral, the woman reading gently from a storybook to her son who sat on her lap. It didn't look like it would take long for them both to fall asleep.

Bellini leaned close.

"I have a confession to make. I knew you were English before I spoke to you."

The woman and child had indeed drifted off to sleep, her head resting sideways, his backwards on her breast.

"I asked the conductor if there was anyone English on this train, whom I might converse with," continued the Italian. "The French are all fools, and peasants such as these," a gesture at Francesca and Pirro, "would not be sullying our reputation abroad if *Il Duce* had his way".

"You do realize that you held up this entire train full of people, don't you?" said Richard coldly. "Personally, I'd say that rather puts one beyond the pale, reputation wise."

Bellini waved a hand dismissively.

"It was nothing. I had some business to attend to that simply could not wait, and I paid the stationmaster quite a little bit of money to hold things up for me."

Richard had guessed correctly about both the bribe, and the source of the hold up.

"I see," he murmured.

"I saw you with another man in the bar last night. Where is he today?"

Bellini seemed very well informed about Richard's movements.

"Where is Charles Montgomerie?"

He smiled evilly.

Richard stared at Marcus Bellini, shocked.

"How the devil did you know who he was?"

"I met him once or twice around Chamonix. There are few tourists in the town at this time of year, and so it is very easy to come into contact with all the foreigners who are staying in a particular hotel. He was a friend of yours, no?"

"Not really. We'd just met, one countryman to another, and were sharing a drink, as I'm sure you saw."

"Yes, and then the German woman joined you."

"German? I think you have your countries confused, old boy. Anne Hamilton is as English as strawberries and cream in summer at Wimbledon."

Bellini laughed silently. "Of course, of course! It was her blonde hair that confused me. And is she still with you now, or has she gone back to Berlin?"

"Ms Hamilton, I believe, is travelling tomorrow to Paris. I intend to meet her for a drink in London in a week or so."

"So, you too are travelling to Paris I assume, on your way back to London. Where are you staying?"

"I hadn't really made any arrangements," Melvold lied coolly. "Besides, I am not sure that is any concern of yours. In fact, this whole conversation has felt nothing short of an interrogation since you burst through that door. If I weren't so well bred, I'd tell you that my travel plans, my friends and my job are absolutely none of your bloody business."

"I see. Please excuse my intrusiveness. I was simply hoping for a recommendation of a good hotel, but it is of no matter. And I am trying to practice my English. Often the second language one speaks lends itself more to direct questioning than conversation I think."

"Excuse me," replied Richard. "I did have a rather late night last night. I'm sure my lack of sleep is not assisting my temper."

"And so, will you be also meeting Mister Montgomerie?"

This was said with a cynical laugh.

"No, I don't think so. Charles had to run up to Switzerland on some business. I might try to meet him later in London, but it's a big city, and people's paths don't cross very often."

"So, he is not as you would say, a work colleague?"

Melvold shook his head. He rubbed his temples. In the stuffy air of the cab his hangover was returning, and he was set on putting his head back, reading his book and waiting patiently to arrive at Lyon station. He silently cursed his British public-school upbringing and the ingrained manners that were keeping him talking. Some carefully placed rudeness might have discouraged Marcus Bellini and brought Richard some peace.

Bellini himself seemed very interested in Richard, which made Melvold instantly distrust him. Richard's experience was that most Italians were much more interested in talking about themselves, or Italy. In fact, their sheer arrogance concerning *Il Belpaese* as they called it was one of his main sticking points when it came to dealing with them. For an Italian in Italy, it was as if the rest of the world simply did not exist for all the notice they took of it. Richard had been to Rome, and felt its marvels worthy of praise, but the rest of the country for him was less interesting. Even so, he would have preferred a fat man effusively gushing about the marvels of Bologna to the cold blue eyes and intrusive questions of Marcus Bellini.

Finishing his ruminating on the subject Melvold realized Bellini had continued speaking.

"Excuse me" he said, "I missed your last question. Lost focus for a moment, away with the fairies."

"I said-"

Before Bellini could further question Melvold, there was a knock on the door. The woman started awake although her son continued sleeping. The door opened to reveal the conductor, looking tired and haggard.

"*Excusez moi, messieurs, madame. Votre billets sil vous plaît.*"

"Yes," replied Melvold, "tickets. Of course."

Melvold pulled his ticket out of his travel wallet. He saw Bellini eyeing it with a very proprietary eye. Several large denomination franc notes, and the big white card that Montgomerie had given him were clearly visible. Bellini saw Melvold notice him watching and turned away, rummaging in his own small suitcase.

Suddenly there was a loud double-barreled crack, and the train rocked violently. Bellini started forward and Pirro woke with a start.

"Some ice, left on the tracks *monsieur*," soothed the conductor.

Bellini's suitcase was already unbuttoned in his lap, and it crashed to the floor of the cab. A small book fell from the front pocket onto the train floor. Richard picked it up and made to give it back to Bellini, then stopped, looking at it. The black leather front cover was embossed with a golden eagle grasping the symbol of Europe's new and rising power its claws. The swastika clearly proclaimed that this was a German passport.

Bellini fumbled in his case.

"Here is my ticket *signor.*"

He showed the conductor.

Melvold held out his own ticket for inspection.

"*Merci monsieur.*"

"*De rien.*"

Melvold nodded back at the conductor, who nodded unenthusiastically back in turn and slid the door closed. His shoulders dropped as he continued his round up the train.

Melvold turned his gaze on Bellini and wordlessly held out the passport. Bellini took the passport off Richard and smiled.

"I, ah, occasionally do some diplomatic business for the government of Italy. It involves a lot of travel between Rome and Berlin. *Il Duce* and the Führer have arranged for an exchange of passports between their diplomats, to facilitate travel between our two strong allied powers. I have an Italian passport also" and he pulled a blue Republic of Italy passport from his travel case as he shifted awkwardly in his seat.

"Jolly good," remarked Melvold. "Must make it a bit easier for you then."

It sounded pretty hollow and seeing Bellini looking uncomfortable he seized his opportunity.

"If you don't mind, I'd hoped to knock off a couple of chapters," and he waved his novel at Bellini.

"Of course. I also have some reading to catch up on," said Bellini pulling a black leather folder from his suitcase.

As he raised the book to read Richard turned over the event in his mind. How did one explain an overly caricatured Italian peacock with a German passport? Richard was sure the passport was counterfeit and suspected that Bellini obviously was a man who travelled on the more dubious side of the law and therefore had no desire to ask. Melvold was just grateful for silence in the cabin, although he did briefly check that his wallet was firmly held in his coat pocket in case he went to sleep while reading. Didn't want the Italian criminal indulging in a spot of petty larceny after all.

Marcus Bellini must have been grateful for the reprieve and the lack of questions, because he did not speak again. Occasionally Richard looked up from his novel to find himself being appraised from above folder almost like one would appraise a horse before an auction in the yearling sales. Bellini remained silent as the train rattled through the night.

V

Memories of the Imperial Raj

Melvold's wristwatch showed five past midnight when the train reached Lyon. He had been lulled into a gentle daze by the rocking of the carriage but awoke sharply as the old locomotive juddered shakily to a halt. It was an unnecessarily rough end to a pleasant ride. As Melvold stirred, he saw Bellini standing in the carriage making to leave the compartment. Instinctively he checked the inside of his pocket for his wallet. He'd once been robbed while asleep in India and intended never again to be a victim. Bellini saw him fumbling with his jacket and smirked.

"Rough stop what?" Melvold ventured. "These old French locos have never been famous for the quality of their brakes. And look out the window there," he continued testily as he waved his hand at the three wan bulbs lit above the station hotel.

"Any hotel like that one there is unlikely to extol the quality of its service among its virtues. It's the sort of place that thrives on business during the hours that even criminals, spies and reprobates in general would be soundly in their beds.

"In fact," surmised Melvold quite brightly, "I suspect it will be just your cup of tea, Bellini."

Aside from firmly ingraining manners, ten years at public school had taught Melvold never to miss a chance to sink his boot in.

"Indeed," replied Bellini with an ironic tone.

"In any event, it doesn't present the facade of hotel interested in repeat business," said Melvold. "I very much doubt service will be a quality valued by the management. There's always a certain type of establishment to be found by a port terminal at sunrise, or alone on a smoky station platform at midnight, and that dear chap is it!"

"Good night, *Signor* Melvold," said Bellini firmly.

The Italian picked up his suitcase and made a hasty exit from the cab. Richard regarded Bellini's retreating back with a feeling of mild foreboding. Still, there was nothing to be done tonight. He sighed and resolved to keep his weather eye out for the curious Marcus Bellini.

Unfortunately, the silently brooding hotel fully lived up to Melvold's somewhat meagre expectations. The concierge was rude and unhelpful. The room he was in was much smaller than his room at the Gustav and rustic old wooden dressing tables and the cast iron hat stand in the corner had been replaced by the bare minimum of blocky, solid furniture needed to fill the room's small interior. Gone were the soothing pastel mix of winter whites and warm pinks. Here the pea green walls looked designed to be hosed down when the room was cleaned.

The Hotel's owner must have hired an interior decorator both colour blind and ignorant of modern style. Probably one of those Swedish chaps who thought that squares and windowless buildings were what humanity craved, reflected Richard. If he'd woken with this morning's hangover in this room Richard was not sure he would have kept his insides inside. The paintwork was truly that bad.

However, the bed was made with clean sheets and therefore very inviting to a man as tired as Melvold. After a long and relatively unproductive day it was a relief to finally reach the hotel, shower, and sink into its soft embrace. He was warm and the pillows were plump and plentiful. Drifting off to sleep he decided the clean sheets more than compensated for the rudeness of the concierge and the unfortunate colour scheme of the room. Besides, he was only here for the night.

• -• •• --• -- •-

Melvold awoke feeling quite refreshed the next morning. The pleasant morning trinkle of Chamonix's icy roofs was replaced by the occasional thunder of a passing train but certainly he'd slept well. Richard was always amazed how much more rested he felt after a sober night's sleep. Every minute seemed doubly refreshing.

He remembered once broaching the very subject with a friend in India. Doctor John Husser was the director of the Company's Cawnpore field hospital, a mustached red-faced giant of a man. They'd been sitting on the verandah of the medical mess one sweltering afternoon with their thirst building in the oppressive heat. As the date palms swayed overhead Richard had attempted to indulge his curiosity.

"John, I wanted to pick your brains about alcohol," he'd begun.

"Beer please," John had replied quickly before Melvold could continue. "It's too hot for scotch."

"That's never stopped you before," countered Melvold. "In fact, I've seen you down the vindaloo that that chipper chap sells in the temple market. It's hotter out than the back door of a furnace, and you shovel it in and then follow it with a warm pint of pale".

Husser winked and smiled subversively.

"Find me a beer and I'll answer your question."

He'd had downed the first glass like he'd been marooned on a desert island for weeks and sent Richard back for a second.

"Now, Richard old son. What can I help you with?"

"Idle curiosity really," replied Melvold. "But every afternoon I sit here with you in the heat and have a thousand ales I end up needing toothpicks to hold my eyes open. I go to bed, sleep for ten hours and wake up feeling more tired than when I went to sleep."

"Curious, isn't it?" remarked Husser. "Never understood myself why a soporific makes one feel so detached twenty-four hours later. Seems counter intuitive really."

"No answer then?" asked Richard, pleased to have scored a point. His discussions with Husser often degenerated more towards the nature of a debate than an agreeable fireside chat.

"I'll stick with Hippocrates on this one," said Husser. "'Who would have guessed from the structure of the brain that wine,'" he took a swig from his beer with a pleased smile, "'would so derange its function?'"

"Didn't he also remark that one of the greatest miracles of the body was its ability to turn red wine into urine?" asked Melvold.

"Indeed, he did. I think I mentioned that quote last week."

"You did. I verified it myself on Friday."

"Where did you possibly find a good red all the way out here in this benighted land?"

Melvold laughed.

"Funny story really. About a month ago I was up in Lucknow, Selby sent me up to make sure the new station works were on schedule. The local station master's a funny chap, fair bit of Portuguese in him, and he happened to mention he was looking to move a few crates of '28 Bordeaux. Picked it up from a Bengalese chap six months ago, cheaply, under mysterious circumstances. I didn't really go into it, you know what these types are like, all shady business and dodgy deals."

"Quite," agreed Husser. "Remind me to tell you about the orderly we caught thieving laudanum six months ago. He was bloody selling it to the local opium den!"

"I try not to ask now," said Melvold as he finished his beer. He beckoned over the waiter and waved at the empty glasses. "Two more please."

"I must have not looked particularly keen, because he assured me he could show me the stock at his warehouse."

"And?" asked Husser. "Cheers," he said to the waiter.

"We called into his warehouse, only to interrupt a local band of thieves trying to make off with his goods!" exclaimed Melvold. "It was lucky I had my Enfield in my pocket. I pulled it out, waved it at them and made some noises about the police, and they ran off."

"Cheeky buggers!"

"Absolutely. Anyway, after that not only did the chap insist on showing me his wine, he insisted on sharing it with me. We got horribly drunk, decided to guard his warehouse overnight and fell asleep on the floor."

"Tell me you bought the wine?"

"Most definitely! He gave me a dozen crates for 50 guineas."

"A dozen crates!" exclaimed Husser indignantly. "You robbed the man blind!"

"Yes, but I did it in plain sight, and with his consent," assured Melvold. "Made an absolute killing on the product too. The local governor does like a drop after all, and his butler was most appreciative."

"What did you offload it for?"

"Fifty guineas," answered Melvold, deadpan. "Per case."

There was stunned silence on the verandah for a moment while Husser digested the news.

"Reminds me," remarked Melvold. "I saved you a few bottles."

"Nice of you," groused Husser. "You've got a bloody talent for it, haven't you?"

"I have been doing rather well lately," allowed Richard.

"Well?" exploded Husser. "I heard about that shipment of cottonseed oil you just unloaded. "Talk of the barracks, bloody Richard Melvold and his bloody Midas touch! And here's me, on a poor Company doctor's retainer. You can buy the drinks today."

"Nice to know I'm being talked about," said Melvold drily. "Any time you want me to invest some of your savings for you John, I'd be delighted to assist your fiduciary security."

Melvold had waved for the waiter again and he and Husser had wiled away the afternoon, pleasantly intoxicated. He'd been true to his word too, investing Husser's money alongside his own. The doctor was now quite a wealthy man and was carrying on some of their mutual business enterprises over the railways when his infirmary duties allowed. All in all, it had been a very satisfactory friendship. It was a shame John was contracted to serve in India for another three years. Melvold could have used a friend like him in London this Christmas.

Customarily when awaking feeling rested and clear headed, Melvold resolved to not drink so much in the future. Unfortunately, he was honest enough with himself to realise exactly the value of that promise, especially if he found himself on the deck of a bungalow under the cane palms of Cawnpore with the recidivist Doctor J.M. Husser. What was the saying about good intentions and the road to hell? Melvold laughed out loud to himself. If he ever made it down there to the pits of brimstone in the John's company, Lucifer might just take ship out back to the land of clouds, harps and angels.

He stretched in bed, taking another moment of pure indulgence to begin his day. Then, awake and in tune with the world, Melvold turned his thoughts to the events of the previous evening. Richard had spent the trip engrossed in his novel. Even as a certified man of the world he was still a devotee of good murder mysteries. Certainly, he much preferred Poirot's misrepresentation of the Belgians to Bellini's authentic (and horrible) Italian social graces. Every time Richard had glanced over the top of his page, he'd seen Bellini staring moodily through the window into the dark. Perhaps he feared the possibility of Melvold questioning him more closely on his 'diplomatic' German Passport. Somehow Melvold didn't think so. Bellini had seemed a man lost in thought on more pressing issues.

Thinking back on the issue of the passport it occurred to Richard, who had several distant relatives involved in both the Indian Civil Service and Her Majesty's diplomatic corps, that he had never heard of an exchange of passports between neighbouring nations. That aside it was well documented in Britain that *Il Duce* was mad and the Führer often erratic in matters of state. Melvold shrugged. It was a curiosity, nothing more. He resolved to look into it on his return to London, more from interest than any great need. He was sure that he'd find someone in his club to discuss the issue with, preferably over a whisky. It wouldn't quite be the slow breeze in the cool shade under the date palms with the sound of John's hearty laugh, but it seemed maybe as close as he could get in London.

The remainder of the journey had been extremely uninteresting. Richard himself had glanced out the windows twice, but the heavy clouds had cloaked the stars, and apart from the occasional lights of a small mountain village, there was little to see. Rugged up tightly against the slight chill in the air of the carriage, rocking gently as the train wound its way east through the alps he'd been soothed by the gentle patter of sleet on the thick glass window pane. It was almost the perfect environment for reading and falling asleep.

Today would be different, he was sure, less congenial for the committed reader, more interesting for the devoted traveller. There was a great deal of beautiful countryside to see on his overnight to Paris, vineyards; farms, castles sitting exaltedly above peasant like trees in valleys below. Best of all there was the prospect of spending the day without Signor Bellini. Richard smiled once more at the thought and got up to shower and dress.

Padding around his tiny room looking for his wash bag, he reflected that life had become quite strange in the last two days. He'd drunkenly been co-opted as a courier by a reticent British businessman, and then immediately afterwards plagued by a strange Italian who spoke almost perfect English and carried a passport from the Third Reich. There had been some unusual situations in India, (an episode with the overly amorous truant daughter of a passing French academic sprung to mind), but nothing like this.

He shook his head as he turned the faucet marked *chaud.* It was too much to contemplate before breakfast. It was at least a two-coffee problem.

• -• •• --• -- •-

Outside the hotel on the promenade the air was bracing. Even here away from Chamonix and the snow, winter's breath stroked Richard Melvold's cheeks. He looked up and saw a clear pale blue sky. Richard loved sunny days cold enough to wear heavy clothing, without all the rain, sleet and other general unpleasantness that normally came with winter. The promenade was empty and Richard walked quickly, invigorated by the chill. The door to the station cafe was only a few steps down the pavement and Melvold almost bounced as he walked. The hot shower and cold air had enlivened him almost as much as a coffee.

While the station hotel itself left much to be desired the cafe attached to the train station was pleasant in a whimsical way. A small bell chimed gently overhead as Richard swung the door open. The room itself was all old wrought iron trellis chairs and solid wood tables sitting on a scuffed teak floor. From the far corner of the room an old gramophone sang softly, keeping the diners company with a lively orchestral piece.

Melvold spied a waiter and beckoned him over as he pulled out a chair.

"*Une cafe au lait et la carte, sil vous plaît.*"

"*Oui monsieur.*"

"Wait, don't leave yet."

"*Monsieur?*" The waiter turned.

"Do you do an English breakfast? Ham, eggs?"

"*Oui monsieur*." The waiter switched to English. "I will ask the chef to cook it for you."

"*Merci*."

Breakfast arranged and coffee served Melvold reached for the paper he'd found outside his hotel door. He'd barely straightened the broadsheet when he felt a light gloved hand lightly brush his shoulder.

"Richard!"

It was a tone melodious, and full of pleasure.

He turned to see a fountain of blond curls and shining blue eyes.

"Anne, this is a surprise!"

She was fortified against the cold in a travelling dress and fox fur, and wore a broad smile on her face. Her cheeks were red, from the cold rather than rouge. She was the very picture of an English rose, vibrant and resilient against the chill of Southern France. Richard struggled to collect his thoughts.

"May I join you for *petit déjeuner*?" she asked with an impish smile.

"Of course."

Melvold was never one to miss the moment. He stood and kissed her, lips warm against the cold sheen of her cheek. In a fluid motion he rounded the table to take her chair and seat her whilst he beckoned the waiter animatedly.

"Let me order for you," he suggested, moving back around the table to his own chair. "The coffee here is quite good, so I have high hopes for breakfast. I always dread ordering coffee in France. It's a quirk of mine, you see. The results are so variable, even when one asks for just a simple coffee with milk. You seem to spend a great deal of time either drinking black coffee with barely three drops in it or choking down a horrible bowl of cream with few grains and little taste!"

"Richard!" laughed Anne, "I've missed you, even though it's barely been a day. Chamonix was so desolate without your company that I decided I simply had to make my trip back to London with you. So, I took a late coach from Chamonix last night. I hoped I'd find you here this morning. Failing that, I was going to travel to Paris and try to look you up in your hotel. I think you told me it was on the left bank."

She smiled.

"That's an extraordinary memory you have Anne," he replied. "I was so desolate at the thought of staying here last night, rather uninspired and all. But the coffee is good, the cafe is quite bustling and that gramophone lends the place quite a dash of charm. I was revising my opinion upwards to passable, but the company has rendered even that assessment obsolete."

"It is quite charming, isn't it?" she agreed. "The sort of place one might sit to write a travel diary over endless cake."

"I know you think I'm probably a little flighty," she continued, "but I so enjoyed myself two nights ago, and I was hoping we could maybe pick up where we left off in the Hotel Gustav, although we'll need to find a hotel that serves good whisky by a cracking fire," Anne said breathlessly, all in a rush.

"That's rather bold for a lady, isn't it?" teased Melvold, enjoying himself.

"One thing Italy taught me is that sometimes a lady has to take a chance!" Anne explained. "So! Here we are for breakfast! I've booked a first-class berth on the Wagon Lit service today to Paris. You told me you always travelled first, so I'm hopeful that we'll be travelling in the same car."

"My word, you are forward, aren't you?"

"Only for a good cause."

She winked.

Richard nodded, a little bemused but very happy. English women had obviously become much more independent during his leave of absence from the Isles.

"I daresay you'll be better company than the man I travelled with last night on the way down here," he acknowledged, a widening smile on his face. "He was very strange, Italian I think, but unusual even given that."

"Come now Richard, I've just been there. They're not that bad."

"He wanted to know everything about me, my name, where I'd been, where I was going, where I was staying. It was like he was trying to build a file on me. I've read in the Times that Scotland Yard does something similar to try to catch their criminals these days. They call it psychological profiling, apparently it's all the fashion. I thought he might turn out to be some sort of policeman. Either that, or worse I was half worried he might pull out a deck of the tarot and offer to tell my fortune!"

Anne giggled, and Richard shook his head at the memory.

"I had enough of all that rubbish in India," he explained.

"Well, if we see him again, tell me and I'll put on my angry, grumpy face and scare him off for you. It seemed to work for me on the touts of Milan. They didn't quite know how to approach me," and Anne grimaced for effect.

Richard laughed.

"It's good to see you again Anne. I had so hoped to catch you some time in London, but I didn't dream that we'd meet here in Lyon. Where is that damned waiter?" he finished irritably. "I waved for him when you sat."

"Look, go and drink your coffee before it cools," Anne said, lightly placing her hand across the table on Richard's arm. "I'll just go and place an order at the counter, and we can sit down and catch up properly. You can tell me your name, where you've been, your banking details and I'll give you a detailed horoscope!"

She sauntered casually away and Richard turned back towards his paper. As Anne spoke quietly to the waitress at the coffee counter, he turned his attention to the headlines on page three. He'd just skimmed an article about the local mayor proposing a tax rise, when the saw the large bold headline halfway down the page.

"*Une meutre en Annecy!*" it screamed.

Drawn to such lurid news, he began reading, and it was when he saw the grisly photo in the centre of the broadsheet that he completely lost his equilibrium.

"Goodness! Richard, what's wrong?" cried Anne as she sat demurely opposite him. "You looked so happy a moment ago, and I return to find you looking like your father has just died!"

Wordlessly Melvold turned the paper so that she could see the page he was reading. He shook his head, speechless.

"I'm sorry Richard," she apologized. "Reading French has never been a gift of mine. Italian, I'm your girl, but if it's French, then I'm all at sea."

She shrugged helplessly.

"I'll translate for you," offered Richard.

He began, "The headline reads 'A murder in Annecy. 'Late last night, the body of a man was discovered floating in the *Canal Du Thiou*. Police have provisionally identified him as an Englishman named Charles Montgomerie. Early postmortem,' I think that's what they're saying, but they're not words you often read in French so I'm not positive, 'results revealed that the man was shot in the chest.' Rather seems that no one's been reported missing in the Haute-Savoie region. Police are asking anyone who may be able to assist them to contact them in Annecy's main bureau. There's a phone number here, and a photo below."

Anne leaned across the table gracefully to look at the proffered picture. It was a mugshot of a man, lips dark and cheeks ravaged by immersion. Sightless eyes stared back at her. She raised her eyebrows at Richard and shook her head helplessly.

"Sorry Richard. I don't understand why you're so upset. Is this a friend of yours? Any murder is terrible of course, but why are you so shocked at this?"

"I suppose you wouldn't know, actually, given that you'd met him only briefly," replied Richard. "But, do you remember two nights ago in Chamonix we had a drink at the Hotel Gustav with a countryman of ours named Charles Montgomerie?"

Anne nodded.

"Yes, he did look quite stressed, but he seemed quite the gentleman."

"Well, it's not a good reproduction at all. Obviously, the printing presses down this way aren't quite up to the standards of Fleet Street, but I'd swear that this is a photo of Montgomerie. It's the same nose, same eyes and brows. He was headed up that way two nights ago, I think. He mentioned it to us at Gustav's Bar. Rather looks like he's been done in by a thug. It's bloody terrible!"

He stopped.

"Excuse me," he added. "I shouldn't swear in the presence of a lady."

"Richard! That's terrible news," exclaimed Anne. "How do they know it was him?"

"There's a little more below the photo. Seems Montgomerie was found without wallet or passport. Looks like a robbery gone wrong. The only way they even got his name was from a label stitched into the lining of his overcoat."

He shook his head and looked again at the photo.

"I'd swear blind that's him, I really would. Good Lord, that's terrible. He was a most genteel chap."

They sat in silence contemplating the news. The waiter arrived with two plates of piping hot bacon and eggs and a basket of toast. It was as he took his first mouthful that Melvold remembered the package that Montgomerie had passed onto him in Chamonix, one night before he was murdered. Something flitted around the edge of his consciousness, but he couldn't find the idea and examine it fully. Absently, he put his fork down while he turned his train of thought around in his head. It was only a momentary premonition and Melvold only had the sense of it rather than the details, but he couldn't help feeling a sense of foreboding. Montgomerie had asked Richard to take something to London and now Montgomerie was dead. Was there a connection? Or had Charles Montgomerie just been a man in the wrong place at the wrong time?

Anne ate in silence, but Richard's breakfast lay further undisturbed as he contemplated the news of Montgomerie's death. He gazed absently through the foggy pane of the cafe window trying to come to terms with the unexpected news. Across the street a figure emerged from the telegraph office, and Melvold spied a shock of blond hair held down by a black fedora. Bellini was again outrageously dressed, and, in his hand, he clutched what looked suspiciously like a blue and gold wagon-lit ticket wallet.

Jauntily he crossed the road to the station cafe. The bell chimed softly as he opened the door. Bellini scanned the room animatedly and only stilled when he saw Richard. Deliberately he moved through between the old iron tables to where Richard and Anne sat together.

Anne could see Richard tense as he approached.

"Signor Melvold, good morning," he said, ignoring Anne. "I see you have some company, so I will not detain you. I am travelling to Paris today, I think on your train. Perhaps we will see each other, and continue our conversation of yesterday evening, no? I would very much like to make your acquaintance better."

He seemed to have completely recovered from his embarrassed silence of the night before. There was a determined shine in his ice blue eyes.

"Might have to wait, Bellini old chap," ventured Melvold, raising his eyebrows in Anne's direction.

Bellini looked the two of them up and down, nodded and without further conversation sat down in a corner well away from their own table. He opened a copy of the morning paper and began reading.

Melvold gestured with his chin.

"I think that amply demonstrates my point about the rail journey last night," he said quietly to Anne. "I don't know what his interest in me is, but all my instincts tell me it's not healthy."

"He does seem a little unusual," agreed Anne. "Do you think he's the sort attracted to other men?"

"I don't know." Melvold spread his hands helplessly. "I don't look like I bat for the second eleven, do I? Why would he be interested in me?"

Anne laughed at the euphemism. "No Richard, you don't. I'm on the train with you, and if he continues to hound you, we can make out like we're an item." She raised her eyebrows archly.

He winked at her in reply.

• -• •• ---• -- •-

Reading the very same article as Melvold, seeing reproduced in print the details of the previous night's crime, the cold blue eyes narrowed imperceptibly. There was not a movement of the lips or eyes to give any feelings away to the diners in the Lyon station cafe. Schmidt cursed internally for the second time in twenty-four hours. This was an unusual indulgence for an agent so thoroughly professional. A damned pocket lining label! How could one of the most experienced covert teams in the entire service leave an identifier on a subject? Schmidt had hoped for a day's grace before Montgomerie's body was found and identified. A lowly label in an old jacket had betrayed the operation. Damn!

Remaining outwardly calm despite seething inside agent Schmidt took a deep breath. It was done now, and it was another problem to solve. At least it wasn't as catastrophic as if the murder had been witnessed. Explaining to a passerby why three Germans were picking over the body of a dead Englishman in an unlit back alley of Annecy would have been impossible. Speed had been at a premium last night, but still there was no excuse for sloppy work.

In any event the identification of Charles Montgomerie would make the Abwehr operation centered on Richard Melvold much more complicated. No doubt in short time the Gendarmerie would discover exactly who Charles Montgomerie was and for whom he worked. Shortly after that, *Deuxieme Bureau*, French intelligence, would become involved. Even a fool would realize the murder of a British agent implied that a foreign intelligence operation was underway in France. And surely even if the French were so blind as to miss the implications of Charles Montgomerie's death, their British allies in MI6 would make the connection and then the search would begin.

The hunters of the Abwehr would suddenly become themselves prey. Schmidt's mind raced. Suddenly the very hastily laid on operation to find and interdict Richard Melvold had become even more time critical. Maybe the team had forty-eight hours, maybe a week, but in any case, the Abwehr were now facing that most implacable of foes: time. That which they had applied so successfully to bring Montgomerie to heel now shifted against them. Time pressure meant haste, and in turn carelessness, a trail their own opponents might follow.

Last night Schmidt had obtained a copy of the Wagon Lit first class passenger manifest for the overnight journey to Paris. It hadn't taken long to find a company conductor who'd succumb to the lure of easy francs. As a rule, Schmidt hated bribery, especially of such casual nature. Someone easily bought now might be paid again, or more likely "encouraged" in other ways to remember Schmidt's own description and destination. Bought loyalty was always short lived.

Unfortunately, the Abwehr had needed the information. They'd had to know where to find Melvold so they could get close to him and find their mark. Eliminating the conductor after the transaction had been considered but that was a very dubious proposition too.

Murders were much easier to trace than larceny. Montgomerie's murder in Annecy had been risk enough for Schmidt, but Berlin had made the instructions regarding Charles Montgomerie very clear. The Abwehr would have to be careful now. With the enemy on the alert and a trail of murder and other assorted crimes to lead DGSE and MI-6 to their door, Schmidt would have to play a subtle hand indeed.

Examination of the Wagon-Lits manifest had revealed another migraine brewing for the Abwehr trio. Melvold was going to acquire a travelling companion, booked onto the train at late notice. Another British agent, well disguised, who had to be eliminated, or just a harmless co-incidence? How then best for the Abwehr to proceed? This was a definite complication. The thoughts were dispassionate, but 'he' and 'she' were long forgotten terms to Schmidt. Pronouns were replaced by mere adjectives and 'inconvenient' and 'complication' were as personal as Schmidt ever became. The situation would require instructions from Berlin. Murder in the back alley of a mountain town was one thing, but murder in the first-class carriage of a Wagon-Lit train was best left for books.

● -● ●● --● -- ●-

Earlier that same morning Canaris had read Schmidt's telegram with increasing frustration. The folio was still at large. Those bastard Poles could all be stood against a wall and shot as far as Canaris was concerned!

Enigma itself was simple: mechanical encoding wheels with a cold electronic heart. It had been used by the German Navy since 1926, in one form or another, and time and time over it had proven secure. Messages sent by Enigma were twisted. Words were tortured into submission, bent into cruel and unusual shapes. Their letters were manipulated demonically into order and held together only by the invisible precepts of a mathematical equation, as helpless within its grasp as a fly struggling within the gossamer strands of the spider's web.

It worked. It was unbreakable. And then the unthinkable had happened. The Abwehr network of 1930 reached far and wide. There was not another foreign intelligence service on the continent that could rival its scope and depth. Though not a boastful man Canaris was intensely proud of his agency. He thought of his agents as a giant tree. The Abwehr's tendrils infiltrated most of Europe, drip feeding secrets and information back to Tirpitzufer Strasse - they were roots slowly pulling apart the foundations of a mighty building in a relentless search for water.

Routinely most of his intelligence was handled by subalterns, painstakingly correlating disparate rumours, terse communiques and fragmented messages into reports that found their way to his desk in more cohesive form. Only rarely did an agent's report come directly to Canaris. The report from Warsaw that had begun this whole debacle had been such a message.

Canaris remembered the night well when first he'd read the news. He'd been absorbed in thought over one of Heydrich's latest moves in the internal power struggles of the Reich, and outside his office a mighty thunderstorm had raged. He'd picked up the telegram absently, read lazily, and then dropped his coffee cup in shock. Most of the telegrams that did come to him directly were still less than important, but not the piece of paper coded from Warsaw that night.

It was only a rumour, one report from a trusted agent, but its import was enormous. Enigma, the unbreakable code, had been solved in Poland. The incongruent equations had been balanced, the cloak of mystery shrouding enigma had dissolved in Warsaw like a sandcastle left on the beach in the rain.

The ramifications were immediately obvious to Canaris. This was a disaster for the Reich and had to be corrected forthwith. Since he'd read the first sketchy telegram, Wilhelm Canaris had given the matter his personal attention as a matter of urgency. His best agents had been sent, his bloodhounds set upon the scent to discover the truth. He'd used his assets in the Polish government to infiltrate and evaluate the Biuro Szyfrow, and one by one the scientists had been interrogated, and turned or summarily eliminated. It was a masterful operation, planned swiftly and executed almost flawlessly.

As a last gasp measure the remaining mathematicians had sent their research to Britain, by way of one Charles Montgomerie, and Agent Schmidt had been given the task of clearing up this loose end. Now Montgomerie too was dead, but the final copy of the Warsaw dossier was still missing. If Montgomerie been apprehended in the Reich none of these blasted complications would have occurred.

As a professional, Canaris had to admire Montgomerie's boldness. Running into the Third Reich had been a beautiful move on the part of the MI6 man, and consequently Reinhard Heydrich had let the biggest intelligence coup since the Great War slip through his fingers. Canaris smiled at the thought. Confusion for the SD and Heydrich meant opportunity for the Abwehr, opportunity for Canaris.

He had to find that dossier – his own prestige was one thing, but even more importantly the security of the Fatherland was at stake. This operation was a chance for Canaris and his agents to save the Reich and advance themselves to primacy. What irritated him now was that the matter was moving further and further beyond his control.

THE THIRD NIGHT

Across Southern France

VI

Aboard a Slow Train to Paris

The clear air under the bright sunshine was tinged with just a hint of coal smoke, and Richard breathed deeply as he strode up the platform where his train to Paris waited. The smell brought back so many memories, and this morning he was happy. Anne's hand was resting gently on his raised elbow, and he stopped halfway up the gabled platform of Perrache Station to fully assimilate the welcome atmosphere of such a busy depot.

"Train stations always bring back memories," he confided to Anne. "All that time I spent in India, most of it was in places like this."

"Glazed ceramic roof tiles and purple Art Deco arches?" Anne asked, surprised.

"Well, not *like* this," he clarified. "This is very Parisian. You don't even see this in England. We tend to go in for quaint sturdy bricks and immaculate white line signals. Out in Cawnpore the stations are sprawling affairs, built for volume rather than architectural value. We used to put through two and a half thousand passengers a day."

"Two and a half thousand?" replied Anne. "That's impossible."

"Not in India my dear. Life there is a very different prospect from Europe. The passengers weren't even the real money spinner. Most of them barely have two rupees to rub together. The real driver of Indian Rail is goods, cottonseed oil, ores, mutton, spices. We used to move more goods in a month than the Portsmouth docks do in three."

Anne turned to him and raised an eyebrow.

"No jest," he confirmed. "Boarding a train there is closer to an African expedition than buying a ticket here. One trudges across a yard of dusty tracks lying naked in the sun and steps directly up from the dirt onto the carriage step, often while the train is still moving. No sense of propriety, the natives. Don't bother stopping, just have a leisurely drive through the yard and the passengers will sort themselves out."

Melvold looked again around the station, overcome by memories. In India he'd sweated under iron roofs made rusty by monsoon rain while shoeless boys hawked stale bread and warm beer to the passengers. Here time was kept by modern radium clocks, black hands tracking across white fields and accurate to the second when checked against Melvold's Swiss timepiece. Here there was no bustle, no crowd. Rather a stately stream of men in bright cravats under dark suits and women in white dresses carrying lace parasols moved politely towards the carriages. The station hummed and vibrated with a distinct rhythm, a complex and long forgotten dance that formed part of the ritual of train travel.

Melvold looked north up the platform to where the engine that would carry them to Paris waited. It stood attentively at head of the platform clothed lovingly in the dark blue painted livery of the *Compagnie Internationale de Wagon Lits*. The company's two gilded lions shone on a boiler burnished bright by winter's breath.

"You should have seen the old banger I came down on last night from Chamonix," he said to Anne, waving at the impressive engine. "Nothing like that, surprised we made it here at all."

"Sorry I missed it," she murmured.

Melvold paused and inhaled the cold laden air. He was struck by a thought.

"How did you make it down to Lyon Anne? You said something about a bus, but that's deuced odd. When it looked like the train was going to be snowed in overnight again, I spent the afternoon looking for a ride out of town, but there was none to be had."

Anne hesitated slightly, pinching her lower lip between her teeth.

"I had to arrange it at rather short notice," she confessed. "I used my womanly charms to persuade the hotelier to drive me down himself. Of course, when I say womanly charms, I actually refer to a rather large sum of francs."

"All to see me?" asked Melvold skeptically.

"All to see you Richard," she smiled at him, looking him in the eye. "A girl is allowed to be a little flighty sometimes."

He raised his eyebrows and turned away for a moment, embarrassed. It had been a long time since he'd met someone so forward. The silence between them grew ever so slightly awkward for a moment, and not wanting to lose the rhythm of the moment Melvold turned back to Anne.

"I'm sure you'll love travelling Wagon-Lit Anne," he remarked casually. "I always do. They've made their name ferrying the upper reaches of society all over Europe. Attentive service, pleasantly slow trains, sumptuous food and what. I tell you, I bought trains in India that could have made the leg from Perrache to the Gare du Lyon in Paris by late evening rather than overnight, but I'd much rather have the comfort of a first-class sleeper and a whisky in the lounge car than one of those noisy monstrosities."

The had reached the train and he held his hand up to assist Anne into the first-class carriage. Together they walked down the narrow aisle besides the teak doors that guarded the prestigious suites.

"Number two, that's me," Anne said, stopping outside her door. She hesitated for a moment and then smiled gently at Melvold. "I had a book I was eager to spend some time with, so I might see you a little later on if that's alright."

"Perhaps I could make a reservation for a lengthy dinner tonight," suggested Richard.

"That would be lovely, shall we say eight?"

"Eight it is." Richard leant forwards to open Anne's door for her and kiss her on the cheek. "I shall very much look forward to the hour."

He shut the door quietly behind her and checked his ticket.

"Number five," he muttered to himself.

As he came abreast of his room, he saw Marcus Bellini at the far end of the corridor opening a suite door that must have been number eleven or twelve. Bellini looked back up the corridor, saw Richard watching him and waved jauntily before he stepped inside. Richard sighed and turned the door handle of first-class suit number five.

A long slow trip with Anne Hamilton greatly appealed but the idea of a similar period of time with Marcus Bellini did not evoke the same feelings of anticipation. Still, as he stepped in to the rather spacious sleeper to find his luggage stacked neatly in the corner and a fresh change of clothes laid out on the bed, Melvold reflected that first class tickets, particularly with the Wagon Lits, were truly worth every franc. He sat on the edge of the bed and grasped the tiny bell pull that would summon the carriage steward.

Minutes later, there was a discreet knock at his door. He opened the door to find a tall steward, dressed in the dark blue livery of the company.

"Monsieur?"

"Un cafe au lait s'il vous plaît."

"Oui monsieur. C'est tout?"

"Merci."

"De rien."

The coffee was delivered just as the engine chugged into life, coughing steam and soot with a consumptive burst. Richard sat drinking quietly as with increasingly smooth shunts the train pulled away from Lyon. He sipped the coffee hesitantly. It was not quite up to the standard of the coffee that he'd shared with Anne earlier, but he didn't so much mind. It was his second coffee of the day, and caffeine was more important to him now than flavour.

After about ten minutes he sighed and looked out the window as urban grey gave way to green fields. It had been a tumultuous morning, and only now were all the events of the last twenty-four hours starting to settle in his mind. The more he thought about Charles Montgomerie's actions in Chamonix the more they appeared passing strange. He must have been desperate indeed to give an item of value to a complete stranger and now this morning had come the news that Montgomerie was dead, apparently murdered in Annecy. Was it random chance? Melvold shook his head silently. He didn't know what to make of it. Paranoia and suspicion weren't by nature part of Richard's makeup, but he did feel himself to possess a certain degree of intuition. It had helped him make his pile in India. As he drank his coffee, he watched the train run past frost bitten fields bathed by brilliantly wan winter sunlight and wondered why his sixth sense was telling him to be very careful, especially where Marcus Bellini was concerned. After a moment he shook his head, answerless. There was little to be done for the moment, and so Richard Melvold took his loafers off, jumped on the bed, and reached for his novel. It would be time for lunch in another two hours.

• -• •• --• -- •-

Schmidt left the first-class berth quietly and walked quickly down the train towards the third-class carriages. The other two members of the Abwehr team had booked all six couchettes in a third-class cabin, simply using the names of four fictional passengers to ensure the other beds remained unoccupied. Thus, the Abwehr had a secure room on the train, a base from which to co-ordinate their surveillance of Richard Melvold. Schmidt knocked rapidly four times on the door, waited for a count of two, and then knocked again.

"Well?" Schmidt asked crossly once inside.

The older of the two blonde brothers handed over a telegram.

"You know what this says?" Schmidt groused after reading it.

The brothers nodded together.

"British intelligence is here with us, on the train," the younger confirmed. "Their agent is staying in the first-class carriage, near our mark. The British spy is travelling under the name of -"

"Stop!" ejaculated Schmidt, harshly. "No names, even here. The walls have ears, and passing conductors hear strange things. We have an advantage. Our quarry is unaware of our nature, despite some bad luck. We do not need to lose it."

"So, what will we do?" asked the younger brother quietly.

"It has been less than a day since we eliminated Montgomerie," agreed his elder, "and already the British are on our trail."

Schmidt thought hard for a moment, calculating in the gloom of the cabin.

"We act."

It was said decisively, with authority.

"You two watch Melvold, and I will search his cabin this evening while he is in the dining car. I am sure he will have a dinner engagement with his English friend."

This time it might have been irony, or perhaps contempt, that coloured Schmidt's voice.

"If we find our prize we will exit the train when it stops to take on water in the early hours of the morning. We will be gone before Mister Melvold even realizes something is missing."

"And if he catches us?" asked the younger brother. "We would be hard pressed to explain our actions to the gendarmes."

"Ensure he doesn't," replied Schmidt. "If he attempts to leave the dining car before I return, stop him. Start a brawl if you have to."

"And if he discovers you've been in his cabin?" asked the older.

"That fool? I could wave a German passport under his nose and he wouldn't realize the significance. He's too busy trying to get the English girl into bed to play spy!"

The two brothers nodded thoughtfully. The three agents spent the next hour discussing their plans.

Contingencies to neutralize their competition were laid out. The operation was becoming very complicated.

• -• •• --• -- •-

On Broadway Alan Denning read the latest telegram from France silently. Slowly he picked up the receiver of a plain black phone resting on the oak desk in the corner of his office. It was a direct line to C in Bletchley manor. Denning didn't use it very often, but the situation in France was of serious import for MI-6.

"He's on the train to Paris," said Denning. "We picked him up again this morning in Lyon, but it looks like the opposition are on him too".

Denning habitually kept names and identifying details out of conversations on the telephone but there was no doubting the subjects of his bland pronouns.

All Denning received back down the line from C was a malcontent grunt.

"For the moment, I've asked our agent to make contact, and then observe from the background. We don't want to give ourselves away to our opposition just yet, or for that matter our subject. Hopefully when he arrives in Paris, we'll be able to recover our property without a fuss."

"Keep me informed," was the terse reply.

• -• •• --• -- •-

Stars sparkled overhead as the wagon-lit Lyon-Paris service wound its way through the sleeping vineyards of Burgundy. Richard gazed pensively out at the shadow cloaked vines. He was fast approaching the *dénouement* of the crisis aboard the *Orient Express,* but he found himself increasingly unable to concentrate on Christie's complex web of intrigue. Melvold's sense of unease had grown rather than settled over the course of the day, and his mind turned to the murder of Charles Montgomerie rather than the fictional devil, Ratchett. And so, with Poirot assembling the passengers in the dining car to unmask a murderer Melvold had laid his book aside, ordered a third coffee and sat down to think about his situation. Since his worries so interrupted his day, he might as well focus on them.

He was increasingly disturbed by Montgomerie's death. He frowned and tried to tell himself silently that it might have been purely happenstance, but Melvold truly didn't think so. Montgomerie had looked like a hunted man in Chamonix.

Richard started visibly and almost dropped his coffee as the thought finished in his mind. Now, why had he come up with that? He looked out his window again, and saw the question etched in his reflection.

Montgomerie had been reluctant to indulge in a drink with Richard. That was unusual for a banker on an overseas business jaunt in Melvold's experience. Normally all the drinks went on the company expense account and the next morning's business be damned. Certainly, that had been the way in Cawnpore, particularly if John Husser was at the table. Montgomerie had looked tired and stressed, but there was something more. He'd had dark black bags under his eyes and a heavy frown on his brow, and in the bar of the Gustav his eyes had constantly scanned the room, looking like a man searching for the next direction of attack.

Leaving his impressions of Montgomerie to simmer in his brain a moment, Melvold stood and took out his shaving kit. He glanced at his watch. It was six thirty, definitely time to get ready for dinner. He opened his razor. It was a naked blade and Melvold had always prided himself on his steady hands. Carefully he began to scrape the day's stubble from his skin. As the razor crossed his cheek, he again met his reflection in his small shaving mirror, and the questions returned.

Had Charles Montgomerie been a hunted man? And if so, Richard grimaced, what the bloody hell for?

The razor moved to his chin and Melvold thought on. Had he become mixed up in some underworld criminal activity? He stopped for a moment and shook his head as he stared again into the mirror. He had no insights, but he knew something was badly wrong. And then there was Bellini. The Italian was not being honest, about a great many things, Richard feared. How did he fit in?

Melvold's gaze turned to the bedside table where the brown paper package rested. He should open it, he knew. Maybe he'd find some answers inside. Several times today he moved to do just that, but his British manners recoiled from the notion of so comprehensibly violating another's privacy. Yet as he finished shaving Melvold realized that the package really was the cornerstone at the arch of his concerns. If someone had been chasing Montgomerie, they had murdered him to obtain what Melvold now carried.

The conceptual leap was becoming more definitive with each stroke of Melvold's razor. Logically he thought they would come seeking it again. In fact, if they were willing to commit murder for it, they were obviously serious about obtaining the contents of the brown paper. Maybe they'd even come tonight, while Melvold was at dinner. Peripherally a though came to him that he might be in danger, but he dismissed it.

Melvold liked to consider his subconscious reasoning faculty to be among his most valuable assets. Husser, renowned in the mess for his coldly logical analyses, might have quarrelled with Richard's train of thought tonight, but the pull of Melvold's intuition was strong. In fact, the last time it had been this strong he'd listened and made a fortune trading cottonseed oil securities in Cawnpore.

It was nothing major that had led Melvold to this point, but rather a multitude of small instances: the bags under Montgomerie's eyes; the touch of desperation in his voice; the frailty of his handshake; Bellini's facade of urbanity and overly inquisitive nature. All these had summated somewhere in Melvold's subconscious to stimulate his intuition tonight. Richard Melvold knew from experience that he should listen.

As his battered Baum and Mercier struck seven, Richard decided he would act. He decided to line the underside of the door handle to his cabin with a small amount of talc. Anyone entering his cabin would disrupt the lining and thus betray their presence. It was straight from a Christie novel, although Melvold couldn't for the life of him remember which one. Certainly, it was melodramatic, but Richard Melvold would sleep much better tonight if he returned from dinner to find an intact lining of powder.

More practically Melvold resolved to keep a close eye on the package that Montgomerie had given him. If it was truly valuable, he'd best not lose it. He rang the bell for the steward and there was a knock at the door.

"Monsieur?"

"Do you speak English?"

"Yes *monsieur.*"

"I don't know the French word, but I want some butcher paper see."

At the steward's look of confusion Melvold held up Montgomerie's package.

"Comme ça."

The steward didn't raise a brow beneath his dark blue kepi cap.

"Oui monsieur."

Paper delivered, Melvold picked up his travel guide to Southern France. It was roughly the same dimensions and mass as Montgomerie's package and Richard wrapped it carefully. He placed the wrapped book in the bottom of his suitcase, hidden carelessly under a blue woollen pullover, a pseudo-package hidden in plain sight. If someone wanted to go through his things and find Montgomerie's "package", they would.

Melvold smiled to himself, satisfied. If anyone did trespass in his suite he'd know. Forewarned was forearmed for the future. He'd keep the real package by his side the while and continue to resist the temptation to open it. The smile broadened. In a perverse way, he was having fun. John Husser wouldn't behave this way, and he'd disapprove of Melvold's reasoning, but he'd certainly be entertained by the story of 'Melvold the Spy' when next they met.

The thought that those with one murder already heavy on their conscience might commit a second in their desperation recurred. Melvold took it and examined it. Murder on a crowded and secure train was a very different proposition to a back alley robbery after nightfall in a country town. No, he'd be fine.

Preparations made, intuition assuaged, he began to dress for dinner. At the thought of Anne his troubled thoughts lifted. Decisions made and course set, Richard Melvold was never one to dwell on insoluble problems and so readily he turned his mind towards dinner and his conquest. He thought her the most beautiful flower of English womanhood, and the promise of more time spent with her filled him with anticipation.

Was it just his imagination, or had her hand lingered on his just a little longer than decorum allowed as he'd helped her make the step up from the platform to the carriage this morning? Certainly, her smile mirrored in her clear blue eyes had been genuine.

He donned his black jacket and checked his watch. A quarter to eight. Time flew when one was ruminating. He shrugged to himself. There was little to keep him in his room now and when he'd visited the restaurant car at lunch he'd seen a dusty bottle of Glenmorangie perched precariously atop the carriage bar. He liked the idea of a quick fortifier before dinner. So, with that Richard Melvold picked up his travel wallet and Montgomerie's package and left his berth, locking the door securely behind him, layer of talc intact.

• -• •• --• -- •-

The first-class dining car was only half full when Melvold arrived having successfully negotiated the narrow, swaying passage past the rest of the first-class doors. Bellini's suite was closed tightly with not a sound emanating from it and neither Signor Bellini nor Anne Hamilton, or indeed anyone else that Richard might have recognized was in residence in the restaurant.

A quick glance at the room revealed three couples having dinner, and a pair of fair-haired young men dining together. These last glanced up at Richard as he entered. One was dressed in the dark blue woollens, the other wore a stylish grey linen suit. Together they were sharing a glass of beer. Brothers, Richard speculated, no doubt returning to Paris for Christmas. Strangely Richard could feel the eyes of the pair on his back as he walked through the dining car.

He reached his reserved table, booked earlier with the steward. Set for two midway down the length of the car, it was perfect. The crisp white linen and silver cutlery gave it the elegance normally reserved for the finest restaurants in Leicester Square. It was close enough to the bar to easily hail a waiter but removed enough that the diners would not be disturbed by the constant traffic to and from the oak counter.

Also, Melvold grinned to himself, it was only set for two, and so the mysterious and oily Signor Bellini would have to find another group with which to take his supper. He touched a passing waiter lightly on the arm and ordered a single malt. He toyed with his glass while thinking about nothing in particular, waited for Anne to appear.

• -• •• --• -- •-

Schmidt grinned in the darkness of Melvold's berth. After following Melvold at a distance to the dining car the German had watched Melvold as he sat engrossed in his glass of whisky waiting like a puppy for the woman he was pathetically besotted with. At least Charles Montgomerie had been worthy opposition. Richard Melvold gave every indication of being a fool. An intelligence operative would have spent the night on the train locked in their berth, pistol at the ready. Melvold was busy chasing skirts. He was far too unsophisticated to be a spy himself, but was he being used unknowingly by MI6? Schmidt retained some doubts. The British could be very devious.

And so, while Richard Melvold sipped his whisky and waited in the dining car Agent Schmidt moved quickly through his room. The methods of thievery were highly prized skills taught to all members of the Abwehr academy, and it had taken but a second to force the rather pedestrian lock. After a brief struggle with a stiff latch Schmidt was alone inside, and free to search

Melvold's effects. The Abwehr would be halfway to the Reich before Richard Melvold realized anything was missing.

Flicking the light switch Schmidt searched quickly and carefully. Folded clothes were refolded and placed exactly as they were. Luggage lining was examined for any discrepancies or hidden spaces. Before a case was opened the fastenings were checked, but Schmidt found no carefully placed hair, no small piece of tape or gum that when disrupted would betray the presence of a thief. There was no failsafe to be found and this simply reinforced Schmidt's impression that Melvold quite obviously was an amateur. Even the most cavalier of intelligence agents would have taken some basic precautions.

At the bottom of Melvold's largest suitcase Schmidt found the brown butcher paper wrapped package and stopped. Not knowing what to make of it, Schmidt turned it over slowly, hands running over all the surfaces, trying to infer by touch what was hidden by the wrapping. The seconds weighed heavily in the mind of the Abwehr agent. Take the package? Doing so would surely alert Melvold and the object held in Schmidt's hands might not be what the Abwehr sought. It didn't fit the description they'd been given by Berlin, and such thievery carried the risk of exposure.

Schmidt sighed, a slow exhalation of several days combined frustration. Nothing seemed easy on this job. Removing the item would likely put Melvold on his guard. Worse, MI6 were here, and emerging too soon from the shadow to grasp the prize might just play the Abwehr straight into the jaws of the British secret intelligence service. They were good, and given a chance, a professional MI-6 agent could cause the Abwehr significant problems.

Schmidt took the luxury of another deep breath in, another long breath out, calming the heart, allowing the mind to function unfettered. The decision was made. In such a game, what was one more risk?

The brown paper tore easily in Schmidt's hands. Out slid a book, a simple guide to Southern France. It was a standard publication edition. As Schmidt flipped through the pages it was obvious that it was insignificant.

"Hurensohn!"

Schmidt cursed venomously in the darkness. The hands that had been so steady moments earlier twitched violently.

Now what to do? Leaving the opened package in the cabin was not an option. It was an unmissable sign that someone had been here. Even that fool Melvold wouldn't mistake the implications. It was pointless taking the book, worthless and incriminating. Acting quickly Schmidt quickly forced the small cabin window open and threw the book and wrapping out into the cold night air. It was gone in a second. Hopefully Melvold would think he'd simply left it behind. It was poor procedure, but the best Schmidt could envisage at short notice, and as the guidebook flew Schmidt's mind turned back to the task at hand.

There must be something they were missing. Melvold must have the dossier. It could be nowhere else! The Abwehr team had to find a way in under Melvold's guard. Schmidt knew he would eventually lead them to what they sought. Perhaps he could be deceived into cooperating with the Abwehr, an elegant solution to the problem. But nevertheless, in any such scenario MI-6 would have to be removed or negated.

The game was becoming complex, with many subtleties. Even with the temporary setback Schmidt's pulse quickened. Such a game was lifeblood to an agent of such calibre. MI6 would be dealt with and with them gone Melvold could be turned and eliminated at leisure.

All of a sudden there were loud footsteps in the corridor outside, the sound slowly moving towards where Schmidt skulked in Melvold's cabin. Schmidt froze. Already the search had gone on too long, and it was time to leave.

VII

The Enigma File

Alone in the dining car Richard glanced at his silver watch for the third time. He'd grown so used to his own company in India that he'd forgotten how much trouble women went to when they "dressed for dinner". It was a quarter past the hour, and Anne was still nowhere to be seen. Idly Melvold browsed the *carte vins*. The *Château Sancerre* had long been a favourite of his, and he was delighted to see the '36 vintage third from the top of the wine list, hiding underneath an indifferent *Bordeaux*.

There was the sound of someone clearing a throat at his shoulder. It was the waiter, resplendent in black tie and blue cummerbund.

"Would you like to order sir?"

The man's English was faultless.

"Not yet, thank you. I am expecting company," replied Melvold. "My dining companion will arrive presently, so I wonder please if you would bring me another," he pointed at his empty whisky glass, "as well as a bottle of the '36 *Sancerre*, on ice."

"Of course, sir."

Around him the dining car was rapidly filling up. Richard lightly sipped his whisky while in the background the gentle murmur of voices and the rhythmic clacking of the train wheels played a pleasing symphony. At ease in the opulence of the saloon Melvold stretched his legs under the table, closed his eyes for a moment and put his head back. If Anne delayed her arrival too much longer, she might arrive to find a rather somnolent dinner partner. Richard was surprisingly tired, especially considering his day of inactivity.

He was idly watching the entry to the car when the door opened. Richard sat violently back up as the unpleasant sight of Signor Bellini strode through the door. The Italian was dressed in a garish black jacket with purple lapels that could pass for acceptable dinner attire only in Italy. Even the style of the cut was hideous! Melvold certainly didn't want to have dinner with the Italian. Besides the unpleasantness of the company Melvold would be the laughing stock of the dining car for sharing his meal with a circus clown.

"That fellow looks like he be in the theaters," Melvold heard the woman at the table next door mutter to her husband.

Meanwhile, oblivious to Richard's internal fashion critique, Bellini moved slowly and rhythmically up the car between the white linen islands. He seemed unusually careful in his movements as if not to upset any of his fellow diners, at least with his stance. On his face was an expression Richard could only categorize as pique. Intrigued despite himself Melvold kept his eyes on Bellini while his relaxed mood so carefully cultivated over the past half hour, evaporated rapidly. Halfway up the carriage Bellini spied Richard alone at his table. He directed a piercing look directly into Melvold's face. Then he frowned thoughtfully and nodded very slowly, almost a gesture of respect.

The action left Melvold perplexed. He could not seriously imagine that the Italian wished him a good evening. Bellini's appearance tonight carried a distinct undertone of malevolence, although if asked Melvold couldn't have articulated the reasons for such apprehension. Unfailingly polite, Melvold nodded back, almost imperceptibly so as not to encourage the Italian. He had no wish to cultivate the attentions of Marcus Bellini over an entree, and he certainly needed no interference in his romantic dinner designs.

Fortunately, Melvold was spared the indignity of having to excuse himself from Bellini's company. As Signor Bellini strolled past the table with the two brothers Richard had spotted earlier, he gave another respectful nod, this time to the two young men. He murmured softly to them, receiving a nod in reply. He hesitated for a moment, as if to sit, but then he took a table alone near the window three settings away from Melvold, back towards the Englishman. Silently he then sat, staring into the darkness rushing by outside the train.

Bellini's reappearance did serve to reinvigorate Melvold's earlier train of thought. He gazed fixedly at the Italian's back as he cogitated on the mystery of the Italian. The thoughts were still churning through his head when they were interrupted by a muted stirring amongst the diners.

He looked up to find Anne entering the car. A string of pearls at her neck blazed back at the candlelight, brighter than the burning flames and her long white dress shone as it fell away from her shoulders. She was easily the most glamorous presence in the saloon, a blazing sun among a field of soft silver stars. Slowly she sashayed up the narrow aisle. She was mesmerizingly feminine and several half-held sighs could be heard as she stopped at Richard's table where she winked at him impishly. Richard turned his head slightly to smile at her, and then he gave a curt nod to the bar. The waiter came running with the Sancerre like a page boy overawed by the presence of his Majesty.

Richard rose to kiss Anne lightly on the cheek.

"I took the liberty of ordering a bottle my dear. I hope you don't mind," he said as he strode around the table to seat her.

"Not at all," she replied, sitting and placing her right hand on the table.

She wore a rose shaped gold band on her ring finger set with sparkling diamonds.

"My grandmother's," she said, catching Melvold's glance. "A family heirloom."

"Exquisite," he murmured in reply.

"It's been a wonderful day, and I'd just love a glass of wine to cap my mood. I so much enjoy Europe by train. One simply does not find the time to sit and relax like this with the new automobiles, or the express service."

"There's a very good business case for the new large express services. More passengers per car, more cars per train, more fares per journey," said Richard, with the authority of one who has made many a successful business case for a new railway.

As he spoke the waiter arrived, satisfaction at serving such an elegant couple written plainly on his face.

"Monsieur, la Sancerre?"

He expertly removed the cork from the slender bottle and poured a thimbleful into Melvold's crystal glass.

"Excuse me," he said to Anne, as he sipped. *"Merci, c'est bon."*

He gestured to the glasses and returned to the thread of conversation as the waiter poured the wine.

"I was about to say that I do agree, it's much more pleasant travelling the old-fashioned way. We were so much more civilized before the Great War."

The waiter coughed politely.

"Ah, yes, dinner," said Richard.

He smiled at Anne and nodded towards the waiter.

"He's been waiting to take our order for quite a while."

For a long silent moment Richard and Anne turned their attention to the menu cards laid in front of them.

Richard nodded at the waiter. "For me please, the *huîtres* to start, and follow that with the *truite al Roquefort*, and for the lady...?"

Anne looked at him, eyes wide.

"Oh Richard, I'm sorry. I'm a little lost with this menu. What were those things you just ordered?"

"Oysters to start, and sea trout with Roquefort cheese sauce."

"Oh," her face fell into a moue. "Oysters aren't for me, but the trout sounds nice."

"If you will permit, *madame*," the waiter interjected obsequiously. "The *foie gras* was made fresh this evening, and our train's chef chose all the finest makings in Lyon. It would marry your Sancerre admirably."

He pronounced the last sentence with the swinging sibilance only able to be given voice by a southern Frenchman.

"Yes! Thank you, that would be lovely; and the trout to follow please."

"Merci. Pour Madame la foie gras, pour monsieur les huîtres et deux truites. Bien. Bon appetite!"

Richard smiled. A little formal French was always part of the first-class Wagon Lits experience, and formality completed the waiter bowed and removed himself from their table.

"Well, I'm quite excited about this dinner," opined Richard. "I've heard the chef on this route is quite remarkable. Apparently the London Ritz has tried to poach him twice, but he's always said no. Must like the challenge of cooking first class *à la carte* on a train."

"What did you do today?" asked Anne.

"Not a lot really. I came up here for my lunch, spent some time with a novel, and watched the fields of France roll by until nightfall."

Any further conversation was silenced as the oysters and *foie gras* were placed on their table. It was rapidly followed by two enticing plates of fresh trout smothered in piping hot white sauce.

"Oh my," breathed Anne as she took a bite of her fish.

"Yes," agreed Melvold. "That's quite one of the best things I've eaten since I got back from the East Indies.

As they finished their trout, both dawdling with the devotion of someone who has eaten so well that they never want the meal to end, Anne's eyes opened wide. "Oh Richard, I must tell you!"

She began in the flighty manner of a lady who has just remembered a well-held secret. Richard was expecting some salacity, and was therefore very surprised as Anne began, "that man, Signor Pellegrini."

"Bellini."

"Bellini. I think he might have been in your carriage."

"What?"

"I was just putting my pearls on and leaving my berth, when I happened to glance up and see him at the door to your quarters. He was facing the door, and his hand appeared to be moving towards the door handle, but then he saw me, and turned away. He walked quickly in the other direction and didn't look back at me."

Richard frowned.

"That seems a bit odd all right, but how do you know he was up to something? He could have just stumbled against the door as the train swayed."

"True, but there's something about him that just doesn't sit aright with me. Oh, and Richard, I heard one of the train conductors speak to him in Italian, and he was very rude in return. He replied in German, which I don't think the conductor understood, and then in English, which he did understand."

"Sorry, what's the problem?"

"Well, it's just that if I were abroad, in India say, and a personage of some official rank happened to ask me a question in English, I wouldn't then reply in Hindi, or Arabic, even if I spoke such uncivilized tongues! I'd be thrilled that he spoke my language and make every effort to converse back in my mother tongue."

"Oh, I see. You're wondering why he didn't just speak Italian back."

"Exactly!" exclaimed Anne. "I didn't think anything of it until just now, when I saw him sniffing around your room, but now I think about it more and more, and his whole persona strikes me as passing odd."

"It does strike me as a little strange, now that you say so," Richard replied.

He looked at his watch and stood. His intuition was positively screaming at him, and he saw Bellini turn from his table to regard him closely.

"Excuse me," he said. "I might just duck back to my cabin and make sure that everything's all right. I'll be back in just a moment."

He picked up his travel wallet and Montgomerie's package and strode purposefully out of the dining car.

Anne nodded, sipped her wine, and turned to watch Melvold leave. Bellini and the two young men, who had barely touched their first glass of beer, turned to watch him as well.

• -• •• --• -- •-

Schmidt smiled, watching Melvold as he left the dining car. Clearly grasped in his right hand was a brown wrapped paper package. The question of the whereabouts of the dossier was answered, and it seemed that Richard Melvold was more intelligent than Schmidt had credited. The stakes in the complex game Melvold and the Germans now played had been raised. In the crowded room Schmidt sensed the Abwehr were not alone. MI6 was here too, Schmidt was sure now, and Schmidt also had to admit that perhaps Richard Melvold was more cunning than what the Abwehr gave him credit for.

Still, the Briton might be on his guard now, but Agent Schmidt was confident the Abwehr could find a way to spirit off what Richard Melvold carried, if only they could get him alone. Consequently, MI6 would have to be excised from Melvold's presence. Schmidt's two young colleagues were already on the case.

• -• •• --• -- •-

The air was cold in the corridor outside cabin number five, and the lights had been dimmed so as to not overwhelm satiated diners. Alone and unobserved Richard Melvold bent quickly to check his doorknob. It was clean. All the talc he'd set as a failsafe was missing, and suddenly he didn't feel half so silly about his actions earlier.

Of course it didn't necessarily prove anything. Someone could have simply stumbled against it in the rocking motion of the train, much as he'd suggested to Anne. But in light of what Anne had told him the absent white fine dust was sinisterly accusatory.

Inside the cabin everything appeared just as he had left it. His suitcase was sealed, lying on an undisturbed bed and his toiletries hung neatly by the small washbasin. After a perfunctory glance he made to leave. Anne was still waiting and the dessert menu was yet to be explored. He turned towards his door and then turned back towards his room. On a momentary whim he decided he really should check his suitcase properly. He moved the zipper, hesitated, and shrugged.

"What the hell!" he muttered.

There was something he'd been meaning to check in his guidebook anyway. He had a vague notion of showing Anne around the *Île de la Cité*, and a quick swot up would help him sell his proposal. It would only take half a minute. He opened the suitcase and reached down through the untidily folded shirts and trousers for his guidebook, but his hands only found soft cloth. Struggling to find the hard cover he rummaged a little more and then frustratedly lifted his clothes completely from the top of the suitcase. He drew in a sharp breath, for below him the suitcase was empty. His guidebook was gone.

Melvold sat on the edge of the bed with wine buzzing round his head and blood roaring in his ears. The talc was missing because someone had been in his room. His book was gone because someone was looking Montgomerie's package. Charles Montgomerie had been murdered for what Melvold now carried. Richard made the conceptual leap instinctively. He picked the real package from where he'd dropped it on the bed, and slowly with increasing determination tore the brown butcher paper. A book slid out, just as he had originally suspected.

He hefted it up and scrutinized it closely. It was heavy and bound with a hard cover.

The cover title read, *"A History of Royalty in Bohemia,"* which puzzled Melvold.

Why would Montgomerie, who had come from Italy, have a book about Poland and Czechoslovakia as a present for a colleague? More pertinently why would anyone be willing to kill for it? One could probably buy such a book from any of half a dozen bookstores in Piccadilly. It certainly didn't look to be worth the price of someone's life.

Richard began to absently leaf though the thick paper pages. He'd only turned through the first chapter when he found his answers. The middle of the book had been excised with a penknife to create a small rectangular cavity. Hidden within rested a small loose leaf bound folder, with a beige cover.

He pulled it out, held it in his hand. It was light and felt official. It carried the faint aroma of formaldehyde as if it had just been removed from a dusty archive. Melvold turned it over and found words printed on the cover in unimaginative bureaucratic stencil.

THE WARSAW ENIGMA FILE

FINDINGS OF THE BIURO SYZFROW (CYPHER BUREAU) INTO THE WORKINGS OF THE GERMAN ENCODER KNOWN AS "ENIGMA"

COPY 3 of 5

MOST SECRET: EYES ALPHA

Melvold sat still for many minutes looking steadily at the small folio. He didn't know what he'd become mixed up in but it by far promised to be more interesting, and more dangerous he suspected, than anything he'd seen in India. There was probably very little opportunity for profit either. In opening the package seeking answers he'd only found more questions.

Slowly he browsed the dossier which was filled with strange terms. Melvold didn't know what an 'encoding rotor' was, nor an 'alphabet tyre' but he immediately realized that his earlier fantasies about being involved in some sort of spy drama suddenly had taken a sharp turn towards reality.

There was a knock on his door, shockingly loud in the huddled silence of his berth. Melvold jumped, startled. His heart raced and he instinctively reached inside his jacket for the revolver he had habitually carried while on business in the Raj.

"Bastard!" he exhaled, as he remembered that it was safely locked in a wall safe in Hammersmith.

"Hello? Richard?" came Anne's voice, muffled by the thick door. "Are you alright?"

Richard quickly put the dossier down behind his suitcase where it could not be seen from the corridor and opened the door. Anne was standing in the corridor, a concerned look on her face.

"The waiter was asking about dessert, and you hadn't come back," she said. "I was worried about you".

Melvold groped for an explanation.

"Is everything all right?" Anne asked again. "Has Bellini been in your berth?"

Richard hesitated fractionally.

"Everything is fine in here, but I've actually just developed a bit of nausea" he lied, trying to look sick. "Maybe the oysters weren't so fresh. I was just looking for some aspirin." He grinned tiredly. "Sorry."

"That's all right," said Anne. "I just wanted to make sure you were alright. I'll have the waiter bring you up some cold juice from the dining car, and you should turn in for the night".

Richard nodded dumbly.

"Thank you," he said tiredly as Anne kissed him on the cheek and shut the door quietly.

In the space of half an hour his evening had moved from happy flirtation to deadly risk. Now there was a little too much on his mind for the evening, and he was happy enough to be left alone. Certainly, Melvold had no desire to involve an innocent like Anne in such intrigues, especially as he still had no idea what was happening. There was much he really had yet to make sense of. For long minutes after Anne's departure he stood staring blankly at the Enigma Dossier, wondering what the hell he'd gotten mixed up in.

• -• •• --• -- •-

The midnight air over the English moors surrounding Bletchley Manor was cold and quiet. Denning had travelled to Bletchley to update C on the progress of their operation to retrieve the Polish data.

"Is there any word?" C asked Denning, as he stood looking out the window of his office at the dark silhouettes of fir trees.

"Montgomerie is dead."

"Yes. I saw the report."

C's voice belied his frustration.

"He had to leave Chamonix before he could make the contact with our agent. We weren't able to make the rendezvous in time. Obviously, the Germans caught up with him in Annecy," Denning explained.

"Yes, ruthless buggers, aren't they?" asked C rhetorically. "Damn," he cursed. "Murdering a British operative in France. There used to be rules about that sort of thing. The Germans are getting bold". He took another large sip of his whisky. "I don't need to tell you how important that data is to us. Those overly clever bloody Poles were at least six months ahead of us."

"Their circuit diagram would be particularly useful for our chaps over in hut one," Denning agreed.

There was mutual silence in the room, while both men considered the lost information. The only sound was snap and pop of green birch logs being ripped apart by the fire.

"It might not all be bad news," Denning said slowly. "Our man did get to Chamonix, and suddenly it seems that the Germans are quite interested in one of our nationals. Boy named Richard Melvold."

"That's not a British name." It was a question more than a statement.

"Grandfather was Dutch apparently," explained Denning. "I've done a little checking on him – spent the last few years out in India with the railways. Nothing out of the ordinary, but our agent says the Germans are all over him.

I wonder if Montgomerie managed to co-opt him somehow and then ran up towards Switzerland himself as a bit of diversion."

C raised an eyebrow.

"It makes sense," Denning continued insistently. "If the Krauts had gotten what they were looking for when they took Montgomerie they'd be halfway back to the Reich by now. I can only infer that their continued presence in France means they're still hunting for the Biuro's folio. The clock's running low, but I think the game's yet to play out."

C nodded slowly, caught by the logic.

"Who do we have down there?"

"It's Schaeffer, incognito and well covered, but ready to act should the occasion call for it."

"Tell Schaeffer to stay out of sight for the minute," C said, after a moment's consideration. "From what you're telling me it's one of our people against several of the Abwehr. Those aren't the odds I'd take at Doncaster. Charles is already one death too many."

"Schaeffer's playing things very safe. We've already made contact with Melvold but haven't identified ourselves."

"Good. Let's keep it that way. We should do everything we can to help this chap make it safely home, but if we identify ourselves to him, we just mark both Melvold and our own runner as new targets for the Germans."

"It's one hell of a bluff."

"Well," said C, "I'm more of a bridge man than poker, crass little American game that is. Subtlety is our most potent strategy now. We're holding the six of spades and trying to convince the Hun we've got the ace, while we hold on tightly to our last trump."

It was Denning's turn to look skeptical.

"All we can do is hope Jerry buys it."

C swore again.

"Damn! I hate these hastily laid on jobs."

VIII

Breakfast with Bellini

Cold air swirled wildly in Tirpitzufer Strasse and sleet hammered against pitted window panes. Wilhelm Canaris was working late again, alone by the pallid light of a small lamp set squarely on his desk. In between the rapping of the storm on the old glass panes Canaris could hear the brass bells of the great Berliner Dom chiming midnight. It was cold in his office. The old brass pipes installed before the turn of the twentieth century never seemed to handle the new oil heating system well, and he clutched his old Imperial Navy sea jacket around him. His grey brows were drawn, his face serious, and the wrinkles thrown up by his grimace made him appear more infernal than ever. A thinly veiled air of malevolence simmered in the chilly air of the room.

"What do you mean 'there's no word' from Schmidt?" he asked his aide in a poisonous voice.

"It's been three nights since our team caught up to that damned spy Montgomerie," Canaris continued, timbre rising. "The last we heard Schmidt was pursuing a British subject, Richard Melvold, an amateur who Schmidt thinks Montgomerie made a dead drop on."

The captain could only stand at attention, trying to keep his face from falling.

Canaris slammed his hand on the desk. "Three experienced agents up against a British amateur! They should have been done by lunchtime! It's nearly midnight and there's still no word. Schmidt is simply not given to such lapses."

Storm clouds had been brewing over Berlin all afternoon, and there was a deep rumble of thunder. It was muted by the heavy glazed windows, but it added to the air of menace in the room.

"Get onto Schweinstager in Paris," Canaris instructed his aide. "Wake him up, tell him to expect a cable from me. I think Schmidt needs some new instructions."

The trembling captain left with a distinct air of relief. Behind him the dark air in the office thickened noticeably as Canaris silently considered the ongoing problem of the lost Warsaw data. The cold seeped through the worn oiled leather of his old sea coat and he sighed. When he was young, the jacket had seemed impervious to any environment. It had kept Canaris safe from raking spray, cold sea winds, or rain heavy enough to drive a man through the teak deck of a destroyer, yet now the mere frigid air of a poorly heated office was enough to defy it. When he'd first donned the coat he'd been a sailor, charged with setting the course of a ship and the decisions had been easy. Now he was a spy charged with setting the course of a country and the horizon was dark and clouded. It was not the practice of the Abwehr to kill in the cities of Western Europe and yet that rule had already been broken once this operation. Of course, Canaris did not count the murder of the Syzfrow mathematicians. The cities of Poland and the bastard half breed Baltic states were another matter when it came to the business of intelligence gathering. Nevertheless, the decision had to be made, and Wilhelm Canaris made it with his usual brand of cold, rational logic.

For both the Fatherland and Canaris himself the prize in this case was so important that some risks had to be taken, and the rules broken. Subconsciously he had already decided that no price was too great to preserve Enigma's sanctity. He picked up his pen. His new instructions to Schmidt were blunt. Canaris was emotionless as he wrote the new orders. Schmidt would receive them from the Abwehr contact in Paris, and there could be no doubt of their nature or their urgency. Melvold was to be eliminated and the dossier recovered as expeditiously as possible. Canaris made it quite clear that he didn't care how public the execution was. The only restriction Canaris placed on Schmidt was that the actions of the Abwehr must remain plausibly deniable for the Reich. Otherwise as far as Canaris was concerned, Richard Melvold, Charles Montgomerie, and the rest of the British Isles could all go to hell.

• -• •• --• -- •-

Insidiously a loud rattling pierced Melvold's dreams. It rose and fell in a crescendo-decrescendo, all the while growing ever louder. Richard woke with a violent start, adrenaline pumping through his veins, thinking someone was trying to force his door! A moment later as he completed the transition from the semi stupor of half sleep to more wakeful cognition his racing heart stilled.

The jimmying noise was just caused by a loose fitting, rattling as the train rocked and swayed over the tracks. Melvold groaned to himself. He was having a bad night. In the darkness of Richard's berth, it seemed that every small movement, the creak of the door hinges, the clack of the wheels on the rail joints, was a herald of new intrusion or danger. This was the third time tonight he'd woken in such fashion. The earlier violation of his cabin was playing on his mind.

In frustration he climbed out of bed and looked at his old watch in the light of the small lamp fixed to the wall above his bed. The gleaming hands pronounced it just after three in the morning.

Sighing, Melvold rang the bell for the night porter, and pulled out Montgomerie's mysterious folio. He might as well do what he'd been putting off until tomorrow and read the damned thing. He'd have no peace until he did. There was a discreet knock on the door. It was the night porter, prompt as always.

"A double whisky please, no ice." Melvold was too tired to bother speaking French. He locked his door behind the porter and jimmied gently to ensure it was secure. When travelling the wilder reaches of India Melvold had habitually taken the precaution of carrying a firearm, but he never dreamed he'd need one in France. Although he was a good shot with a rifle and and a duck in view, he'd always found the idea of armed travel distasteful. He could stomach the internal discord while away on business, but this was a holiday. But tonight separated from an unknown murderer by a single sheet door he again felt the lack of a recourse to arms.

The door handle rattled softly. Melvold tensed.

"Monsieur?" came the voice of the porter. *"Votre boisson?"*

"Pardon," replied Melvold softly through the door.

Assured it was indeed simply the porter he unlocked the door and gratefully took took the drink.

"*Merci.*"

When the porter had departed and the door had been again secured, Melvold sat up in his bed and picked up the small folio. He settled on his bed with the whisky on the small table beside it. Awake he found the myriad small noises of the train more soothing than disturbing. He re-read the small type on the beige cover silently, but it still made no sense to him. He really had no idea what the devil this was all about.

Richard sipped the whisky slowly hoping it might help him examine the problem more fully and if not, at least it might help him sleep. He skimmed lightly through the folio looking for context, words to elucidate purpose and meaning. Complex phrases jumped out at him, "mechanical rotor" and "rotating ciphers", but without any background knowledge of the subject he could not fix the contents of the book into a workable frame of reference. He frowned and sighed and then felt an almost irrational urge to laugh, the situation was so ridiculous.

He was seemingly in possession of one of only five copies of a great secret, with no idea at all of its meaning. The only thing that stopped his laughter was a growing sense of grave portent.

From what he could put together, Montgomerie, who was dead, must have known about the folio when he'd given his "present" to Richard in Chamonix. Tonight, Melvold's own cabin had definitely been searched while he'd been at dinner. No doubt Melvold was mixed up in something dangerous. And ever since he'd met Montgomerie, Melvold had been dogged by the presence of Marcus Bellini, a blonde-haired blue-eyed Italian man, with a German passport who seemed remarkably well informed about Richard Melvold and his particulars.

Bellini's story and presence on the train were explicable, if barely, but the coincidences were becoming too strong to ignore. It was time for Melvold to investigate, and in doing so get Bellini to back off. Maybe the gendarmerie should be involved when the train arrived in Paris. From Melvold's perspective Bellini could do whatever he wanted in Italy, but there were rules in France.

Richard downed his whisky and turned off the light, resolved to confront Bellini in the morning.

• -• •• --• -- •-

Melvold woke unintentionally late due to a combination of alcohol and poor sleep. He sat up slowly, and through his window he saw an army of old red brick buildings squatting under a slate grey sky. The blue *Wagon-Lit* engine was drawing the long train through the southern outskirts of Paris.

On the floor where he'd left it last night the Warsaw dossier sat mutely and mysteriously. Richard Melvold was no wiser this morning than yesterday as to the significance of its contents. A quick glance at his watch, and he was up.

It was indeed late. Hurriedly he dressed, donning simple grey trousers, and a dark blue dress shirt. He slipped his feet into his loafers and threw on a day coat. The folio was rolled up and placed in the inside pocket. Ready to face the world even forgoing a tie, he left his berth for the breakfast car intending to find out the truth behind Marcus Bellini.

The dining car was set for breakfast and had a markedly more relaxed air than the candles and starched cloths of the previous evening. Several people lingered in a desultory manner over the remains of their repast, and the aromas of freshly toasted bread and scrambled egg made Richard's mouth water. Up at a table near the bar Richard spied Bellini. He was sitting alone. The place opposite him was still set, cutlery unused.

Gripped by a moment of decision, Melvold walked deliberately up the car, Bellini's eyes on him the whole way. He pulled out the chair opposite the Italian and appeared to hesitate slightly.

"May I join you for breakfast Signor?"

"Of course."

Bellini indicated his assent with a wave of his hand, and a lazy smile. As he sat Melvold examined Bellini more closely. The Italian was not so fresh this morning himself – there were shadows under his eyes, and small crows' feet wrinkles at their corners. Still, the gaze he turned on Melvold was calculating, examining Melvold in minute detail. In turn Richard stared back, trying to discern the answers he wanted from Bellini's cold blue eyes. Silently they looked across the table, appraising each other, seeking an advantage like two chess masters moving pieces across a hypothetical board.

"Did you enjoy a restful sleep, Mr Melvold?" Bellini asked with a sardonic smile, breaking the contest of silent wills.

"Tolerable, thank you," replied Richard.

"You had no, shall we say, company? Expected or otherwise?"

"That's none of your damn business."

Melvold struggled to keep the edge out of his voice.

"Excuse me, please. It simply seemed to me that you seemed to be, ah, engaging most pleasantly with the pretty lady at dinner last night."

"And you with the two young men, brothers I suspect. Friends of yours?"

"Colleagues of a sort, you might say. We had a most entertaining discussion over a digestif after you left the dining cart."

Bellini smiled maliciously.

"They tell me they always take great pains to lock their door when they dine all the way up here in the restaurant car. Those of us who travel frequently often see things go missing in all sorts of unlikely places."

Melvold picked up his knife and toyed with it as he eyeballed Bellini. He spoke in a low voice.

"I know what you're up to, and I'm watching you very closely."

"Me? I have no idea what you are talking about. I merely travel Europe on the diplomatic business of my country."

A polite cough at Richard's elbow interrupted their mutually antagonistic rapport. It was the waiter. Richard picked up a menu disdainfully from the table, glanced at it briefly, and put it back down.

"The eggs benedict with smoked salmon please, and don't be too light with the Hollandaise. Also, a large coffee, black, with a jug of milk on the side."

Again, Richard spoke English, and he realized that he hadn't even bothered taking the time to frame his thoughts in French. He acknowledged his own fatigue, and how intent he was on unlocking the mystery of Marcus Bellini. Normally when abroad Richard Melvold was the soul of politeness.

Bellini noticed the change of language too.

"I would swear I heard you speak fluent French in Chamonix, mister Melvold."

"I didn't realize that you had been listening to my conversations in Chamonix, Bellini."

Bellini smiled a crooked smile at Richard.

"I forgot Signor Melvold if you told me the other day what it is you do as a job?"

"I'm a man of diverse means," replied Richard, deliberately abstruse.

"Yes, but what is it that you do?" Bellini leaned forward intently over the table, watching Richard.

"I suppose you would call me a banker."

"For your government, yes? I had you labelled as a public servant, an attaché perhaps in a diplomatic service."

He paused and smiled maliciously. "Like me."

"No. I work in private enterprise."

Richard had no intentions of discussing the details of his business with Bellini.

"Ah, so you are not a supporter of the British government then? Or perhaps you simply contract to them, or other parties, when it suits you?"

Another twisted grin. Richard was being baited and knew it but couldn't help the sharp retort that came from his lips. It was the fatigue, he was sure.

"I wouldn't say that at all," he spat. "I think British institutions are probably the most modern and impressive in the world. You've only to look at the scope of the Empire, and the ease with which it runs to see that. Look at how productive the British government has been for the Indies, or Canada, and compare it to the way the Belgians abused the Congo at the turn of the century.

"But yes, if you're asking me what I think about Chamberlain and his cohorts, I wouldn't admit to being their biggest admirer, chiefly because I think that they're a little soft on some of the troublemakers on the continent. The Germans, I think, are looking to carve out a modern version of the Empire for themselves. I'm sure they've their eyes on Palestine, and quite frankly Signor, your 'premier' and his regime are not much better in my opinion."

Further conversation was interrupted by the arrival of Richard's eggs, and he stabbed one angrily with his fork. He was so intent on his breakfast that he didn't notice Bellini regarding him again across the table through narrowed eyes. Melvold's voyage of discovery into the great mystery of Marcus Bellini was not going well, but he thought that maybe some food would help him correct his course. So intent was he on eating and avoiding further conflict with Bellini that for a moment he did not notice the gradual slowing of the train as it haltingly came to a stop. A startled glance out the window revealed that the train had finished its long journey and had come to rest at platform six in the Gare Du Lyon.

Bellini made to rise, and looking up and realizing that he was to lose his chance to interrogate Bellini further, Melvold re-entered the fray.

"Look here Signor. I'm very sorry if I sounded angry or offended you. It's been a long trip, and I didn't sleep particularly well. We've still a time to wait before we can disembark. The second class have to clear the way first you know. Won't you join me for a coffee?"

"A very good idea," admitted Bellini.

He beckoned the waiter over with an imperious wave.

"Coffee, black and strong."

Melvold poured copious volumes of milk into his mug. He smiled.

"I can never agree with the way the French make their milky coffee. I much prefer to do it myself".

"I agree. There is no coffee quite like that we do at home in Rome."

"Yes, there are many things the Italians do better than the French. I for one would argue that the Flavian Amphitheater, and you will note that I use its proper name, in Rome is much more impressive than either the Louvre or the Eiffel Tower in Paris. I would argue that the Staatsoper on Unter Den Linden is more interesting again. Have you ever been to Berlin Signor?"

Was it just Melvold's imagination, or was there a fraction of hesitation in Bellini's reply?

"Yes signor, I have. You will recall on the train from Chamonix I told you I was involved in Il Duce's diplomatic corps. I have been to Berlin several times, but I have not stopped to sample many of the sights, so I cannot talk of them with any great feeling."

"Who are you Bellini?" Melvold asked in a low tone. "I'm pretty certain you can't speak Italian at all. You call your capital Rome, not Roma, and your passport is German. In fact, if you're from Italy, I'll own up to being Scottish."

There was a moment of silence while Bellini stared Melvold in the face, blue eyes piercing under his shock of blonde hair.

"Are you really so blind Melvold?" he asked wonderingly. "Can't you see the great game that's being played out around you? Can't you hear the tension, feel the whispers?"

"I'm rather sure there is indeed some funny business occurring aboard this train," replied Melvold. "I know you're mixed up in it."

"Very well," replied Bellini. He sounded unexpectedly weary. "There is indeed a way to make things go very easily for you-"

Suddenly there was a commotion at the front of the dining car, strained voices talking hurriedly in hushed French. Melvold looked up over Bellini's shoulder to see two men in the uniform of the Paris Gendarmerie talking animatedly with the waiter. He saw the waiter's arm point in the direction of where he sat with Bellini, and the two Gendarmes hurried over busily.

Alerted perhaps by Melvold's own glance, Bellini looked up just as one of the two large officers placed a white gloved hand on his shoulder. White gloves, thought Melvold to himself. Who makes their policemen wear white gloves? They were essential for a spot of miming, but hardly practical when it came to enforcing the law.

"Monsieur Bellini, oui?"

Bellini nodded vaguely.

"Yes, what?"

"*Excusez moi, je va parler en Anglais.* You are Monsieur Bellini, yes?"

Again, Bellini nodded.

"We would like you to come with us please monsieur."

"What?" Marcus Bellini appealed more volubly to Richard. "What is this? Why are you persecuting me? I am an Italian citizen travelling to Paris on business. You French, you are always molesting foreigners for no reason!"

"*Monsieur,*" continued the gendarme patiently, "we would like to ask you some questions concerning the death of a man named Charles Montgomerie. He died in Annecy two days ago."

Neither the gendarmes nor Bellini was watching Richard, so they didn't see his eyebrows shoot up in surprise.

"Well Bellini," Melvold drawled. "Seems I might have some answers in a moment."

"Who?" exclaimed Bellini, ignoring Melvold and clearly discomfited by the police attention. "I have never heard of this man, I will tell you this now."

A third gendarme, bearing gold brocade on the dark blue fabric at his left shoulder entered the car, and strode up the central corridor to the developing scene. He paused impressively, drew himself up, and regarded Bellini.

There was a dull thud as a passport dropped from his hand onto the table in front of the Italian. The crowned lion and unicorn of the United Kingdom were clearly visible.

"*Monsieur*, I am Inspector Heureusment. I overheard your conversation as I entered the car. If you have indeed never heard of *monsieur* Montgomerie, you will I am sure be happy to accompany us to our prefecture and explain to us why the passport of a dead man is hidden amongst your personal effects."

Bellini's jaw worked, but no sound came out. His shoulders slumped as he deflated, and then he stood.

"Very well, Inspector. I will come with you, and cable to the embassy of my government. I am sure that the truth of this matter will soon be apparent to you."

He turned to Melvold.

"You should be very careful in your choice of friends, mister Melvold. Many people are watching you. Remember that events move apace, and you do not understand them."

The inspector placed an arm across his chest, to stop him leaving. He looked at Melvold.

"And you *monsieur*, are you an associate of this man?" he asked.

"*Non monsieur l'inspecteur*. I am just having breakfast with him."

He smiled in what he imagined was a disarming fashion.

"I am a British citizen, travelling through Paris on my way home to London".

"Is this true?" Heureusment asked Bellini.

"Oh yes," Bellini replied with irony. "Mister Melvold is a banker, and that is it. He is nothing to do with me at all."

"Nevertheless *monsieur*, I will ask one of my officers to stay here and check your details, and record where you are staying. It is strictly procedure of course."

"Of course, Inspector. It will not be any trouble at all."

With an ironic smirk upon his face Bellini looked around the dining car as he was led out by the police. At the entrance he passed a very surprised looking Anne Hamilton. She glanced back towards the police, then hurried over to Richard.

She smiled charmingly at the gendarme as she sat in the seat just vacated by Marcus Bellini.

"Goodness Richard, first bad oysters, and now the police. I do wonder what sort of trouble you are getting yourself into."

● -● ●● --● -- ●-

Schmidt smiled ruefully at the unfolding drama. The presence of the gendarmes would make things more difficult, but it had been inevitable that they should become involved. The Abwehr team would have to lie very low for the next few hours. Melvold would almost certainly be on his guard now, between the spectacular intervention of the Parisian Police and the theft of his worthless guidebook. There was no point flushing their quarry yet. Schmidt intended to make contact with Berlin this morning and see if there was any new information available to the team. Until then, the Abwehr would continue their subterfuge.

They knew Melvold's hotel. He would be very exposed there. The Abwehr could reach him easily. The Gendarmerie would not be nearly as formidable a problem as British intelligence, and Schmidt had no fear of them. This business with the Gendarmes might delay their efforts momentarily, but then the Abwehr machine would spring into motion and finally they would dispense with the troublesome British fool.

THE LAST NIGHT

Northwest of Paris

IX

At the Golden Flower Hotel

Bellini went quietly. After his initial protests he had taken only a moment to turn and smirk back over his shoulder at Richard Melvold. Anne stood aside from the door as Marcus Bellini was escorted out to the platform and then walked silently up to where Richard sat. She rested her hand on his shoulder and squeezed gently. Pensively she looked back towards the door whence Bellini had vanished.

"We should sit for a little," she said. "It's still a little busy outside. And look," she waved her hand gently. "You've let your coffee go cold. I'll ask the waiter to bring us a fresh pot. My choice."

"Yes," Richard nodded. "It is most certainly time for a strong coffee. Damned police interrupted me just as I was about to start this one. It's cold now."

Anne strode to the bar counter to organize the refreshments, and Melvold thought furiously. He'd come to breakfast seeking answers, and it seemed now that answers he had. In the silent, empty dining car his mind turned restlessly. His instinct had been correct. Bellini was a murderer: foppish, Italian, and deadly cold; an interesting though macabre dichotomy.

The Enigma File must have been valuable indeed to Marcus Bellini. The Italian must have deduced that it was in Melvold's possession. It was the most obvious explanation for his search of Richard's cabin last night.

Melvold wondered if Bellini knew that he'd flushed his quarry prematurely. His annoyance had transmuted to determination not to be taken advantage of even though he had no idea what he carried. It could be schematics for a new engine or a strangely worded fiscal report for all Melvold knew. Whatever it was the dossier could go straight to the British Embassy when he got to Paris. He was pleased to have progressed his intuition to a decisive course of action. "King and Country" of course was always the rule for Richard Melvold, even if his time in the British Raj had left him a little jaded.

"What just happened?" Anne asked, her words breaking the veneer of quiet girding the dining car. "I missed the start of that little episode."

"It was the police," Richard said. "They've just arrested that chap Bellini."

"I beg your pardon?"

"Yes. I came to find him at breakfast. I was worried what you told me about him being in my suite, and I wanted to sound him out."

"Did you make any headway?"

"Oh, we were getting on famously. I'd just decided that I would take an intense dislike to him, he's a smart-mouth little jackanapes you see, when the Gendarmes burst in on our breakfast and arrested him. It seems he was mixed up in the murder of Charles Montgomerie. Remember, we read about it yesterday morning?"

"Goodness me, that's terrible!" Anne exclaimed.

"Quite," Richard agreed. "The French are quite tough on foreign criminals, and I hear they take a very dim view of matters like this. I hope Bellini gets a very thorough comeuppance."

Surprised by his vehemence, Anne nodded, her eyes wide. "Quite."

"In fact," she continued, "the whole thing sounds quite horrid."

Both fell into a reflective silence, and there was little more to say as together they sat alone in the deserted dining car. The gravity of the moment seemed to magnify the sense of intimacy they shared. Around them last night's burble had been replaced by only the occasional clink of cutlery being washed behind the kitchen door. Steadfast at the station even the rhythm of the train, subconscious and barely noticeable, was glaringly absent. In the idyll of the dining car Richard laid his hand gently on Anne's.

"I do have to say Anne," he said softly, "I am rather pleased with the turn of events this morning."

A moment later the waiter, cummerbund undone, delivered a small brass pot of thick Turkish coffee to their table. Richard grasped the worn round wooden handle and poured smoothly for first Anne and then himself as a gentleman should. Anne was dressed for travel today, fawn coat over a sober grey pleated skirt, accompanied by a minimum of makeup. She looked a picture, maybe a Constable, *'An English Country Lady Dressed for Travel'* Richard thought.

"You look lovely this morning Anne. I'm sorry I ruined dinner last night." He frowned, "and now our chance at breakfast has been disrupted too. We'll have to do this properly in London..."

Melvold assumed that she was probably commuting on from Paris for the Channel ferry to London, and his frown deepened with the conclusion of the thought. Her departure would be far less welcome than Bellini's.

"It's alright Richard," she said, reading his expression. She hesitated slightly, "I've been so enjoying your company that I decided to delay my trip back to London, so I cabled ahead to the *Hotel Fleur D'Or* from Lyon to book myself a room. You mentioned that you were staying there in Chamonix, remember?"

"I have to be honest," he admitted. "I can't. I'm not sure if you noticed, but I was indulging happily in the barkeep's supply of fine spirits."

Nevertheless, he intended to take advantage of his ongoing good fortune and capitalize on Anne's ongoing company. In his experience ships, trains, opportunity and women waited for no one.

"The gents I used to keep company with in India would have been proud of me that night," he continued slightly ashamedly. "'Never let a free ale go unimbibed' was the unofficial motto of our local regiment staff officers. Remind me to tell you a story or two of the company doctor one day, an absolute reprobate by the name of Husser."

"He sounds like an interesting man," she said.

"Yes, he is," Melvold shook his head ruefully. "I do miss his company occasionally.

"That said, I shall miss mister Bellini a lot less," he continued. "Your own departure however would have been somewhat less welcome."

"Yes, I'm delighted that we'll have some more time to refine our acquaintance."

She put her hand out on the table and took Melvold's in hers.

"Perhaps we'll have another chance at dinner tonight," and she squeezed.

"Of course," Melvold replied smoothly. "Allow me the pleasure of chaperoning you to your accommodation. You'll like the Golden Flower," he continued with a smile. "It's got *fin-de-siècle* European charm in spades, the sort that you simply cannot find in London anymore. I always make an effort to stay there when I'm in old Paris."

Together they finished their coffee and decanted the train for the platform by the first-class carriage. A porter dressed in black livery with his burnished copper buttons bright beneath his round kepi hat stood proudly at attention. At the other platforms trains of various shapes and sizes brooded, ready to begin a journey, some perhaps recovering from travels finished. Intermittently a locomotive would let out a large belch of steam from its boiler, filling the station dome with a sinister hissing while soft grey inverted cones searched blindly for the sky.

Pallid light filtered down through the overhead transparent panes, leeching the interior of all but the blue-grey spectrum. Against this insipid set, sober suited Frenchmen escorted fair women crowned by white bonnets to their carriages. Most overpowering was the scent of slow burning coal that lay heavy on the morning air. As she alighted Anne's hair caught the light and blazed golden against the monochrome diorama. As she stepped onto the tiled platform Richard reflected on her allure.

"This way my dear," he said jauntily as he took Anne's arm in his and began strolling towards the exit.

The blue suited porters followed behind like faithful hounds. As a train enthusiast, an interest of many years predating his work in British India, Richard was well acquainted with his present surrounds. He leaned in to whisper softly to Anne.

"They built this in 1900," he said quietly, gesturing with a gloved hand towards the glass ceiling. "It was the world exposition and some madcap French architect put that glass roof up there to impress the planet."

He raised an eyebrow.

"At the time it was hailed as a triumph, but I think it's ridiculous. Stations deserve the gravity of dark bricks and gas lamplight, like King's Cross or St Pancras. Much homelier, comforting for the traveller."

"It is quite continental, isn't it?" Anne asked whimsically.

"One decent storm and it looks like the whole lot might fall in."

"Well then," she said. "Let's hope we've no thunder or lightning today."

As they strolled off the platform the shape of a distant church spire was barely discernable through the great gusts of steam billowing intermittently across the tracks. At the concourse a group of young men made merry outside the station's cafe, perhaps waiting for their train home after a long night at the follies. Melvold thought such a scene reminiscent of one of Claude Monet's paintings - an impression of the Gare St Lazare. He'd never liked that one.

Outside on the street the air was wet, cold and biting. It carried the promise of impending downpour. Overhead the sky was heavily pregnant with dark grey clouds, and Melvold thought it would almost certainly rain. Slowly they wandered over to where one of the old city taxi cars waited. *Taxis à la Marne*, Richard remembered, in deference to a role played in that great tragic battle almost twenty years past. Bags were loaded, porters were tipped, and overhead the great clock surmounting the station began to chime musically.

"L'hotel Fleur D'or sil vous plaît. Sixième arrondissement."

Richard checked his watch. It was nine in the morning. As the old engine of the taxi sprung into life and it bounced over the old cobblestones of the twelfth arrondissement's lane ways, soft heavy rain drops began to fall on the worn leather cab cover.

• -• •• --• -- •-

The *Hotel Fleur D'Or* was one of the oldest hotels in Paris. Reclining majestically over the small square formed by the *Rue du Bac*, and the Boulevards *Saint-Germain* and *Raspail* on the Left Bank it was one of the more expensive places to stay in Paris. Richard liked it, both for its luxury, and its character.

To the casual observer the hotel's stately façade gave no hint as to its chequered history. It was built as a townhouse in the early nineteenth century for one of the many noblemen who travelled to Paris on the business of the court. Converted several times it had served as a banking establishment and also as one of the city's coffee houses when it had seen a greater breadth and volume of business than in its days as a bank.

Abandoned to ruin after an unforeseen bankruptcy, it had stood empty for several years before being renovated in the style of the Victorian era by one of London's eminent hoteliers as part of the continental expansion of his business. Since then, it had grown steadily in reputation and built up a loyal following of discerning travellers.

As a doorman in impeccable purple livery opened the great wooden doors, Richard and Anne could see why. The lobby where they found themselves was roofed by soaring arches cradling mutely gleaming crystal chandeliers in their recesses. Potted palms gave the large space an intimate, oriental feel, and scattered among them were deep laid leather couches where patrons could sit and watch the world while elegant waiters in white shirts and black waistcoats circulated to solicit coffee orders.

The concierge desk was dark stone marbled by a rich purple vein, and in the corner near the oak bar rested a polished grand piano. The walls were resplendent with gold framed paintings.

As an establishment, Richard loved it. Just as the somewhat rustic charm of the *Gustav* had seemed to him appropriate for the wooded mountain trails of Chamonix, so too did the Fleur's old-world charm suit the centre of the City of Lights.

"I love this place," he whispered surreptitiously to Anne as the surveyed the lobby. "The Gustav might have been appropriate for an alpine resort town, but the center of the City of Lights deserves this sort of old-world charm.

"Those paintings," he pointed, "they're all originals from the Parisian post impressionist masters. On Friday evenings they serve champagne here in the lobby, and there's an old American expat who plays Harlem nocturnes on that Steinway."

"It's lovely Richard," agreed Anne breathily. "Where do we register?"

"Over here," and he took her hand and made for the marble reception counter.

"Bonjour monsieur, bonjour mademoiselle!"

The smiling young woman at the desk was most welcoming.

"Bonjour, j'ai deux réservations sil vous plaît. Monsieur Melvold et Mademoiselle Hamilton," began Melvold.

He was rewarded with an admiring smile from Anne.

"Oui Monsieur, j'ai votre papiers."

"Bien. C'est possible parler en Anglais?"

"But of course monsieur," nodded the concierge in a musical lilt, switching tongue with the ease of the long practiced. "I have two suites reserved in the names you have given me. Suite ten for *mademoiselle*, and suite sixteen for *monsieur*." She turned first to Anne. "*Mademoiselle*, if you would be good enough to fill in this card?"

While Anne addressed the hotel registry Richard turned to enjoy the lobby's atmosphere. Despite his enchanting morning with Anne, he yet retained a little of last night's edginess, or perhaps he was simply fatigued. Maybe his uneasiness stemmed from this morning's episode on the train with Bellini.

Aimlessly his eyes rambled over the lobby, eyeing statues resting on half moon tables, lingering on impressionist paintings. The extensive collection of art in the lobby of the hotel was yet another reason he liked to stay here. Over several visits, he'd been trying to decide the value of a painting hanging in the corner above the grand piano, a genuine Cezanne. He turned his sight towards it and froze.

Sitting to the right of the piano was one of the young men whom Bellini had conversed with last night at dinner, he would have sworn it. Richard's memory for faces had never been good, but the mop of pale hair and the features of the face were certainly familiar. He'd had a partner last night.

Melvold frowned, and looked harder, searching for the second brother only to be distracted when Anne touched his arm.

"Richard, where do I put my surname? Is that *nom de famille?*" She pronounced the French awkwardly.

He nodded, and when he turned back to examination, the blonde man was gone.

"You must like that painting," she said with an impish grin, putting a hand on his shoulder. "You've been gazing over there for at least five minutes."

"Actually, I thought I just saw somebody I knew," replied Richard, "but…it looks like I was mistaken. I'm actually a little tired. I must have just imagined it."

"You've had a tough twenty-four hours," Anne said kindly, and then shrugged. "You should take some rest".

There was silence for a moment until the young lady at the concierge desk interrupted them.

"Excuse me, monsieur Melvold. I have a letter for you. It arrived yesterday evening marked *Poste Restante*," she said.

"I beg your pardon?" enquired Richard. "I'm not expecting mail."

"Look, here, it is definitely for you," she said as she pulled a small brown envelope from below the counter.

"Are you expecting mail Richard?" asked Anne.

"Not at all, but look, it's clearly for me." He held it up and read, "Mister Richard Melvold, care of *Hotel Fleur D'Or, Boulevard Saint Germain*, sixth *arrondissement*, Paris,".

He shrugged.

"Probably my mother. She used to write me thrice a month in Cawnpore. I'll read it later. Right now, I'm in need of a shower, and maybe some lunch. Would you care to join me?"

He stopped, realizing the faux pas.

"For lunch I mean, not the shower."

Smiling at Anne he tucked the letter inside his coat pocket.

"Thank you but no Richard. I've some small things I need to attend to this morning. In fact, I need to place a call to London, so I might be here at the concierge for some time. Perhaps I could meet you for a drink a little later on in the hotel bar. We could sit under that painting you seem so fond of."

"That sounds lovely. I'll see you then."

He kissed her on the cheek and strode towards the elevator.

• -• •• --• -- •-

In the shower, Richard finally began to relax. The cascading jets of hot water loosened his muscles, and a quick blast from the cold tap on cleared his mind. It was one of his traditional hangover cures, and though he was not feeling poorly this morning it still served to energise him. The immediate priority of his day, Melvold felt, was food, and a strong cup of coffee.

After that, he might attempt a call to London himself and find some contact details for Montgomerie's investment bank employers. Failing that, he'd visit the British Embassy. Then, it would be off to dinner and cocktails with Anne and a night out in town. The thrill of a secret job well done would add some extra spice. He was excited. He knew Paris quite well, and he was sure he could show Anne a good time. With Bellini safely under arrest there was no reason he could not indulge himself.

Ablutions finished, Melvold donned his grey linen travel suit. One must always dress well on the left bank. He looked around his room. It was immaculate, sumptuous. The dossier, almost out of habit went into his coat pocket and Melvold stopped for a moment. Why was he bothering? Bellini had been arrested and Richard's belongings were secure in the hotel room. The *Fleur D'Or* was a hotel of quality, and the dossier would be safe in his room. Still, it was obviously important, and something entrusted to him and so he was bound to keep it close. Melvold shrugged. What the hell? After a moment's searching, he found his mother's letter and put it in his pocket too. Maybe he'd read it over coffee and a croissant before he called at the embassy. With Bellini neutralized he could take his time.

As he exited the lobby, he felt the romance of Paris settle upon him. Suddenly the world seemed a happier place. There was no sign of the two young men. They couldn't be significant, Melvold was increasingly sure. Last night at dinner Bellini had probably been looking for someone new to bore with his diatribes, poor sods. They were probably off with their family now, sharing hugs and stories of crazed Italian dinner companions. Of Anne there was no sign. She probably needed a little longer in the shower than he did. He smiled wryly as he stepped out of the hotel, and turned right, walking up the square formed at the confluence of the *Boulevard Saint-Germaine*, *Rue du Bac* and the *Boulevard Raspail*.

For the moment the rain had stopped, leaving small puddles of muddy water scattered over the cobblestones. In polite society they called Paris the "City of Lights" but as he stepped around another puddle and the small mound of excrement left there by a dog on its morning walk Richard reflected that a less complimentary moniker would also fit. On the verge of the square he stopped to admire the Parisian scene. In the centre of the square a bronze cavalryman lorded over an effervescent fountain. On the peripheries cafes with striped umbrellas lined the footpaths, and the square thronged with Parisians, outside in the temporary reprieve from the rain. After so long away from the continent, so many scorching days and humid nights in the Orient, coming back here to Paris evoked old memories. He was struck by visions of boyhood trips during the Michelmas break, vacations with his friends from college, memories of the first time he'd kissed Isabelle. He stood there still amongst the heartbeat of the city. Captivated so, he didn't hear the roar of the engine or the screams of the rapidly scattering pedestrians. The attempt on his life was unheralded, and really Richard Melvold had no right to survive.

Far too late from the corner of his eye he saw the Parisians disperse like a startled flock of pigeons, but before Melvold could register anything else he was pushed brusquely between his shoulder blades. Caught off balance he sprawled to the cobblestones and rolled out onto the road. He flung out his arms, grazing the palm of his right hand and tearing the fabric in the knees of his trousers. As he fell, he turned his head right, trying to see his unknown assailant, only to be met by a splash of muddy water from the puddle he'd stepped around a minute earlier. One of the old blue taxis roared behind him, bouncing as it mounted the footpath where he'd been standing seconds before.

Above the din of the crowd, a policeman's whistle shattered the square's Parisian aplomb. It was shrilling wildly, and suddenly hands grasped Melvold as a visibly distressed gendarme pulled him to his feet dazed and bleeding from the temple. A torrent of voluble French poured from the policeman and Melvold could only mutter a very quick *"merci"* as he scanned the crowd for his assailant.

"Bastard!" he swore under his breath.

Shakily he stood and over the heads of the bystanders he saw a blond-haired figure running across the street, away from where Melvold stood. Richard only had a moment to look, and the man was facing the other way, but the shape of the shoulders, the shock of blonde hair and the method of gait instinctively identified the retreating figure as Marcus Bellini. Across the street Bellini pushed his way through the crowd and vanished. Melvold made to give chase, but suddenly the crowd closed in.

"Monsieur?" enquired the policeman urgently. *"Ça va?*

Across the street Bellini pushed his way through the crowd. Any chance of pursuit vanished rapidly.

"No, no, no, *non!*" he said to the solicitous gendarme. "The car missed me! I do not need an ambulance called. I'm fine damn it!"

"Mais, monsieur –"

"That man," raged Melvold pointing at the crowd where Bellini had been, "was arrested by your colleagues this morning for murder. What the hell are you doing man, get after him!"

The gendarme stared at him blankly. Obviously, English was not his forte.

As the adrenaline burst faded, Richard's body was racked by cold shivers. His wet muddy shirt clung to his body and the cold leached into his muscles. Bellini had tried to kill him, Melvold knew. His intuition screamed it to him. How he'd managed to fall onto the street and miss the taxi was beyond him.

He was furious with himself. His nostalgia for Paris had seduced him into a false sense of security, and he'd almost died as a consequence. What the hell was he doing walking around the streets of Paris like a wide-eyed tourist? Montgomerie lay dead, and now so nearly too was Richard Melvold.

As several more Gendarmes came running Melvold took advantage of the distraction and stepped into the crowd. Whoever was stalking him was serious. He was in danger and the streets of Paris were no place for him to be. He had to get back to the hotel. He had to rid himself of the dossier, deliver it to the authorities. Only then would he be safe.

● -● ●● --● -- ●-

Watching Melvold vanish back in the direction of his hotel from a cafe across the street Schmidt cursed. Things were moving quickly but the telegram from Canaris had been explicit. Schweinstager, the Paris station chief, had been very firm.

Without adequate time for preparations it had been a hastily laid on attempt on Melvold. The car had been driven inexpertly by one of Schmidt's colleagues. A more experienced driver would have been able to change course and certainly would have been able to catch Melvold even on the street. Unfortunately, the English would now be doubly alerted. Subtle as ever though, the Abwehr had a backup plan.

Schmidt had seen in the eyes of the young concierge the jealousy with which she regarded the wealthy customers of the *Fleur D'Or,* the longing with which she looked at the dresses of the ladies, and the jewels around their necks. A duplicate key to Melvold's room had been cheap to obtain. With Melvold injured and hospitalized or dead, (and now Schmidt didn't care), it would be a simple matter to lift the dossier from his room.

Unfortunately, their damnable bad luck had held, and Melvold had survived. Now, he would have to be flushed into the open, stalked like a game bird, and coaxed to fly straight into the sights of the hunter. Schmidt sighed, paid the bill, and walked up the street to find a telephone box and make a call. The Abwehr would need to be even more devious than Schmidt had planned. The situation called for extreme measures.

X

Hunted

When he reached the *Fleur D'Or* Melvold burst into the hotel foyer with a presence of a drowning man breaking the surface and gasping for fresh air. It had taken him more than half an hour to extricate himself from the rugby scrum that had developed in the *Place Vendôme*. Uninjured except for a head graze, he'd had to thrice refuse to offer of an ambulance from the overly solicitous gendarme. His overwhelming desire had been for the safety of the hotel and reaching the lobby was both a physical and mental relief.

The lobby itself was little changed from earlier. Music floated in the background. There were a few patrons, all dressed respectably in their business suits or day dresses who looked up disapprovingly from their various *tête-à-têtes* to frown at Melvold's torn and sodden grey linens. Being damned by raised eyebrows and hushed voices was the least among Melvold's concerns. As he stood in the doorway breathing heavily a concerned bellboy, recognizing Melvold from his earlier check in, approached him.

"Is everything all right *monsieur*?"

"Yes, thank you" he replied, after a moment's hesitation. "I slipped over on the wet cobblestones that's all. I think I'm all in one piece."

"Do you need anyone, a doctor perhaps?"

Melvold held his temper.

"No, that's all right. I'm just going to go upstairs and change. Thank you."

Melvold could see the questions striving to burst from the bellboy's lips but he simply smiled and nodded his head slightly.

"Very well *monsieur. Au Revoir.*"

The boy's quite remarkable restraint in not exercising his curiosity was great testament to the refinement of the *Hôtel Fleur D'Or*.

Fully conscious of his incongruity in the elegant lobby Melvold threw his jacket over his shoulder, nodded at the concierge and made for the elevator, all the while ignoring the many stares directed at his back. It was a very sodden attempt at panache.

At the fifth floor he stepped out and walked slowly down the corridor. He fiddled with the old iron guarding room sixteen and looked wistfully down the corridor to number ten, Anne's suite. He was still looking sideways as he stepped forward into the doorway. When he turned to look into his room, he stopped halfway through the portal, shocked. The room was a picture of devastation.

His suitcase was cut open and ruined, his clothes were strewn randomly about the floor. This time the vandal hadn't even bothered to fiddle with the brass buckles on the old leather straps. Irrelevantly, Melvold thought to himself that his suitcase was almost an antique and deserved more respect. Clearly whomever had ransacked his room had been in a hurry.

The rest of his suite had been equally defiled. On top of the small bedside bureau rested Melvold's travel wallet, empty and desolate. His passport, cash and traveler's bank notes were all gone. The envelope holding Montgomerie's card had been torn open, and the card itself was lying on the floor. Around the card lay the drawers of the bureau where they had been pulled out and their meagre contents scattered on the floor. When he picked up his black patent leather dress shoes from the floor, he found that they too were empty. Even the spare notes he habitually rolled up in the toe of the right shoe as a form of security had been taken.

This was not the casual rifling his luggage had undergone on the night train from Lyon. This time the search had been truly thorough. Even his bedspread had been pulled down, with the top half of his mattress lying slightly askew as if the mattress had been moved to check underneath. With every item he discovered searched or missing Melvold was formulating the opinion that although this looked to have been a quick, messy robbery it was very professional. Bellini was loose again.

He must have been back to the hotel while Melvold was detained in the square. Twenty minutes would have been enough head start. Luckily Richard had kept the dossier in his jacket this morning, although if that car hadn't missed, he'd be lying dead in the road and it wouldn't matter a jot.

Melvold wandered into his bathroom for his tincture of merbromin to dress his grazed knees only to find it even more of a mess than the sleeping area. Smashed glass littered the floor, and there was a distinct smell of cologne in the air.

"Bugger, that was expensive," he muttered to himself.

Besides the remnants of his cologne bottle on the floor was his toiletry bag. His small wooden handled shaving brush and his tin of shaving paste, lid missing, were scattered with the rest of his ruined toiletries on the tiles.

Anger simmering inside Richard returned to the living area. The game had changed again, catching him unawares and he'd only just escaped serious injury at the hands of Marcus Bellini this morning. Melvold still held the Warsaw File, but now he was without passport and money and all the while his enemies were becoming more ruthless.

He sat on his bed with his head in his hands with thoughts racing feverishly through his brain. He simply didn't understand. Richard was fairly sure that Bellini had been in his room on the train from Lyon to Paris. This morning, only pure serendipity had saved his life. At the centre of everything was a mysterious dossier from Warsaw, given to him by a dead man. Whatever was going on was high stakes, that much Melvold could determine. Now he found himself hunted.

Did Bellini act alone? Who was behind him, and why was the dossier so important to them? Most importantly, what the hell was he supposed to do with the damned thing? There were so many questions that Melvold had no answer for.

Slowly he scanned the wreckage of his room and the detritus on the floor. Woodenly he picked up his jacket from where it had fallen in the doorway and dropped it on the bed. His gaze rolled around the room and settled back where the crinkled envelope of his mother's letter peeked out from the inside pocket of his jacket. Not really caring, he picked up the letter. Might as well read it, scrunch it up and then throw it on the floor with the rest of his belongings Melvold thought bitterly.

As he made to tear open the envelope, he hesitated slightly. It carried an express French postmark, with a Chamonix stamp. It had probably travelled to Paris on the faster mail train from Lyon after Chamonix. It would have arrived in Paris the previous evening and been delivered this morning to the Hotel.

Perhaps his initial assumption that it was a letter from his mother in London was incorrect. She had always expressed disapproval of France and never travelled even to Paris. She'd certainly never go to Chamonix. Richard's uncle had died here in the great war, and she'd never overcome her subsequent prejudice.

Melvold's eyebrows rose as he continued to regard the envelope. Even a simple letter was cloaked in mystery, a minor one to be certain, and fortunately for once the answer was easily available. Without further hesitation Melvold tore open the envelope and pulled out a thin sheet of writing paper. The paper was headed with the crest of the *Hôtel Gustav* in

Chamonix, and the words were delineated boldly in black ink. It was dated three days previously.

Melvold,

I hope this letter finds you well and safe in Paris. Forgive my presumption, but if you are indeed reading this, there are now certain facts you need to know. I am sorry to have involved you in important matters against your will and without your knowledge, but unfortunately as of tonight, stranded here in Chamonix, I have no choice.

I confess to having lied to you. My real name is Charles Montgomerie, but I have nothing to do with the banking industry. I work for His Majesty's government in a somewhat discrete capacity, and it is in this role that I am in Chamonix. I am tasked with carrying documents important to the security of our nation. I have carried these all the way from Poland, only to be checked in Chamonix by an early snowfall.

Needless to say, there are those in the service of foreign governments, notably the Third Reich who would be glad if the information I carried never made it to Britain. They have dogged my steps since I left Warsaw. They are here in Chamonix, I know, and they are closing in on me. I am alone, my rendezvous has not arrived. I am fast running out of viable options. Suffice to say that losing my charge to the Germans is not something to be considered.

Thus, I have conscripted you. You are a citizen of his Majesty's government, and as such I know you will do your duty. What you carry must reach British soil, whether it be the embassy in Paris, or the address I have given you in London. I intentionally did not reveal to you the true nature of the task I have set you – the enemies of our country are always watching, and I think ignorance in your case, and the facade of innocence which accompany it are possibly your best defence. If you have reached Paris though, it is time you knew what is happening.

Tomorrow morning I leave for Annecy, and I will not see you before I go. I will attempt to lead those who chase me north, away from you. Hopefully the time you have gained by this will allow you to safely and easily reach Britain. God willing, I will see you again in London, and we can share that pint you promised me at your club in Hammersmith.

Lastly, a word of caution. Trust no one. Those who seek me are resourceful, and most ruthless. They will not reveal themselves to you voluntarily, nor will they consider any request for quarter. Even the most innocuous person may be an enemy. I am hopeful that my employer will send you some help, but by far your best hope is to always be on your guard.

Good luck.

Charles Montgomerie.

Amongst the remains of his possessions in the centre of his ruined room Richard Melvold sat quietly, mind churning like the waves of Cornwall before a winter storm. His first thought was that he should have trusted his instincts, that he was wrong to take Montgomerie's package but then instinctively his mind rebelled. Such a thought was deeply unpatriotic, anathema to the core of his being.

He was enough of a realist to know that he was in deep trouble, and the fact of that choice was now completely irrelevant. The question was what to do about his situation.

Richard had faced difficult business decisions before. Once he'd had a rifle pointed at him in a stock deal gone sour, and on at least two occasions he'd nearly gone broke, but this was much more serious. This trouble was personal, not amenable to silver pounds and letters of credit. He'd been happier before he'd had explanation for the events of the last two days

"Jesus," he swore. "The bloody Nazis are after me."

Silently shaking his head, he got up. Here he was running moneyless and without passport chased by the spies of the Third Reich, spectres in the shadows of France. There was a slinking air of unreality about the whole episode, as if Melvold was caught in a fever dream, a nightmare that there was no waking up from. He shook his head again. This was no dream.

His paranoia had turned into real danger, and now he needed some real help. There was no way he'd get back to Britain with no money and no passport. He screwed his eyes up and thought hard for five minutes. Surrender was not an option. It was time to run and he had no choice. Just as Montgomerie, isolated in Chamonix had had to take a chance with Melvold so too would Melvold himself have to seek aid.

He stood. While his clothes were strewn recklessly about the room, none of them were ruined. Moving slowly around the room Melvold picked over his scattered belongings. Eventually he found a black high necked woollen pullover and a change of trousers that weren't too creased and pulled them on. He rescued Montgomerie's card from the floor and tucked it securely in the inner breast pocket of his grey jacket.

He spent five minutes in the bathroom rescuing the remains of his cologne and freshening up, and he stepped out into the hall. He strode down to suite ten and knocked on the door. There was no answer. Melvold's heart leapt into his mouth. His intuition was screaming again, a wave slowly building, threatening to break and drown him in anger. Anne was completely innocent of the entire affair, but he knew the Nazis would judge her guilty by her transient association with him. Bellini had commented on it previously, he recalled. He would struggle to accept her being harmed simply because of her proximity to him.

He knocked again without success and tried the door handle. It was locked. He jimmied it forcefully, without success. He was just about to give up and head downstairs to demand the concierge open the door, when he heard Anne's voice behind him.

"Whatever is the matter Richard?"

She sounded a little surprised to see him outside her door.

He wheeled, to see Anne dressed in outdoor guise, standing in the corridor with a bag in her hand. It was the kind one might find in any of a hundred boutique stores around the *Galleries LaFayette*. He sighed relievedly. She'd been shopping. Wordlessly, Richard took her hand and lead her back up the corridor. He opened the door to his room and heard her sharp intake of breath as she surveyed the wanton disarray. She turned to him again.

"Richard! What is going on?"

Her tone was quite forceful.

"You look quite wild around the eyes."

"Perhaps it's better if we talk in your room," Melvold suggested softly.

"Oh Richard, I'm not sure that's quite proper."

"Please Anne, it's important," he said steadily.

She held his eyes for a moment, nodded and fished in her handbag for the key. As she opened the door, he held out his arm in a gentlemanly manner, ushering her in from the corridor. He closed the door behind him and locked it, much to Anne's surprise.

"Richard, what is going on?" she asked.

He sat down on the edge of the bed, planted his hands by his hips for support and looked up at her.

"Something very strange has been going on for the last few days," he began. "Not between us, but while we've been together there have been some other events in the background."

"Bellini?" she asked. "I've been thinking about him. He must just be a thief, or a confidence man. It doesn't matter now anyway, he's under arrest, locked safely away somewhere horrible, I'm sure."

"That's the problem, you see," retorted Melvold. "He's not. I just saw him in the city."

"He was arrested!"

"Anne, it was him, I know it," Melvold replied evenly.

"Very well, but I don't see how that explains your room."

"I think he's got some friends, two brothers."

"Yes, I remember them from dinner on the train last night. I also think I told you, I thought I'd seen him trying to break into your berth."

"Someone had been in my berth Anne. My suitcase had been searched."

"But why, Richard? What is it about you that criminals would want to keep harassing you? I understand about petty crime, it's quick, it's opportunistic, but this sounds much more serious."

"I think it is," he replied.

He reached into his outside pocket and withdrew the Enigma folio which he handed to Anne.

"They were looking for this," he said softly.

"What is it?" she asked, a frown creasing her pretty features.

"I don't know," he answered truthfully. "Remember Charles Montgomerie? The man from Chamonix?"

She nodded.

"He gave me this three nights ago, hidden inside what looked like a gift package. Asked me to take it to someone in London. Didn't tell me what it was all about, wanted to keep me in the dark I expect. I didn't realize what I was carrying until after I found some things missing from my cabin on the train."

"So," Anne began slowly, still frowning, "whoever went through your bags on the overnight from Lille, who is presumably the same person who's turned out your room, was looking for this document that Montgomerie unknowingly foisted off on you in Chamonix."

"That's the way I've been reading it, yes."

"And you think it was this Italian man, Bellini, who was responsible?"

"Yes. He's clearly not Italian. He can't speak the language, and he owns a German passport. He was arrested this morning for murder, but now he's free. I'm fairly certain that he just tried to kill me in the small square down the road."

"What?" she exclaimed.

"Pushed me in front of a car, vanished into the crowd. But I saw him as he left. While I was stuck there being mothered by the local police his two accomplices must have been back here, ransacking my belongings."

"Richard, this is quite serious," Anne said slowly.

"But you see, the problem for Bellini and his friends is that they haven't got what they wanted. Since I first discovered that someone had been through my bags on the train, I've kept the document Montgomerie gave me on my person. It wasn't in my room this morning, it was in the pocket of my jacket."

His resolve was firming up, clearly audible in the timbre of his voice.

"These bastards have taken my money and my passport, but they haven't got what they need. Call me stubborn, but I simply can't bring myself to let them win. The trouble is I'm running out of resources, and options."

There was another silence as the cold grey light reflected off the clouds outside through the large bay window in Anne's room. Then, slowly, Anne responded to the unspoken plea in Melvold's words. She kissed him gently on the lips and spoke.

“Then I’d better help you I suppose. After all, we’re in this together now. I think the best thing to do is try to get to the British consulate. It’s down on *Rue Du Faubourg St-Honore*, near the *Jardin Des Tuileries* just before the *Élysée Palace*. Last time I was in Paris I had to call in on some business.

“It’s not too far at all from where we are. They don’t allow normal vehicles that far up the *Rue Faubourg*, but if we took a taxi towards the garden, we could walk across and be at the embassy in no time at all.”

“Anne, I don’t know if I can allow you to do that,” Melvold said gallantly. “I came here to ask you for help, a loan of some money to get me back to Britain. These people have killed before, and if you come with me you will be putting yourself in danger.”

He hesitated.

“Look, I’ve been in a few close scrapes before, seen my share of danger in India. You, however, are a lady, and innocent. I don’t want you to get hurt Anne.”

“It’s all right Richard,” she reassured him. “I’ve travelled quite a lot, and although you don’t know it, I’ve had to look out for myself before. We’ll be fine. We’ll get the mess sorted out and be safe in the Embassy for lunchtime.

“Here,” she continued, handing him a linen satchel. “Put the document in here. You’re going to look very silly walking around Paris with no possessions and a book sticking out of your pocket.”

Mutely, Melvold nodded. He could recognize sense when he heard it.

• -• •• --• -- •-

Fifteen minutes later as Melvold and Anne left the foyer of the *Fleur D’Or*, Schmidt evinced a tight-lipped smile. Luck had not run the Abwehr’s way this day, but the pendulum of fate always swung, and in the end usually came to hang dead centre. Melvold was a surprisingly canny quarry for an amateur, obviously hardened by his time abroad, but sooner or later Schmidt and the other agents would run him to ground.

He was running for the embassy now, Schmidt knew. It was the sensible, and therefore entirely predictable, next move. Paris today was cold and wet, and not many people would be outside. Down by the Seine, the *Jardin des Tuileries* was foggy and almost deserted. Schmidt's colleagues were already positioned there, waiting eagerly for their chance to finally claim that which they had chased all the way from Warsaw. Melvold was walking into a trap. No one would see him die in the cold mist by the banks of the Seine.

XI

The Winter Garden

Outside the winter closed in over Paris. Festive and gay in summer, as the days shortened and grew dark the French Capital took on a Dickensian melancholy, a mood that seemed appropriate for such a jaded place as the Garden.

In the mid sixteenth century, Catherine De Medici, bereaved queen of Henry the Second, had ordered the construction of a new grand palace on the site of the disused Paris tile kilns. By all historical accounts the palace and its grounds had been grandiose by the standards of the day. Named *Tuileries* from the French for "brickworks", the palace had seen much of the glory of France. At its zenith the palace had served the sun king, Louis the Fourteenth, as a temporary home while as he awaited the completion of his own grand palace at Versailles.

Its fortunes had fallen in tandem with those of the French royal family. For Louis the Sixteenth, the *Palais Tuileries* had been first an imperfect refuge during the storm of the Revolution and then a prison after his arrest by the Paris mob. Napoleon had taken the palace as his chief residence, restoring it to the heights of glory but then in the nineteenth century the Paris communists had burnt it down in defiant gesture of anti-imperialist sentiment.

Finally, the burned-out shell of the jaded palace had been demolished, and now all that remained of the once great building was sixty acres of parkland. The *Jardin des Tuilieries*, last gift of a lonely Florentine queen to the city of Paris. In summer, snapdragons snapped and petunias popped under apple trees crowned with blossom. In winter, the garden was cold, and spectacularly desolate. A chill mist billowed across empty flowerbeds interrupted by leafless trees. Hunchbacked forms gnarled by decades of aggressive pruning brooded silently and beneath the skeletal trunks were park benches, empty, desolate, and burdened by bitter frost. Black-fingered branches rose gracelessly towards the sky, arches fanning out in silent protest against the biting cold. Bare dirt spattered with shrivelled leaves carpeted the ground.

The winter of 1938 was cold and already there had been too many bitter frosts for the grass and trees to survive. The garden was a cemetery of the botanic, a tundra where the ghosts of Parisians past stalked amongst swirling, sorry memories.

As Richard Melvold looked in through the tall iron fence that guarded the garden he shivered. Together with Anne he had alighted from the taxi on the southern border of the park. The day was becoming colder by the hour, and the morning fog was thickening. The swirling mist was so dense that he could barely see twenty yards. Trees, benches and dirt simply faded into infinite grey.

The cold bit into his face, penetrating through to his bones and thence seeping into his courage and resolve. The British consulate had seemed such a good idea in the warmth of Anne Hamilton's room. Now, he was having serious second thoughts.

Holding Anne's hand, Melvold turned to regard the rest of the street. Opposite the entrance to the garden was a typical Parisian cafe, wicker chairs unfilled on the pavement, menu board standing optimistic in the cold air. His gaze drifted across the glass face of the café, watching his and Anne's reflections play across the panes.

There were people inside, blurred faces poorly visible through the dirty panes. He saw young lovers sharing coffee, a family having lunch, and suddenly there it was: a shock of blonde hair over ice blue eyes gazing steadily back out at him. Bellini, Melvold was sure. Or was he? A second later, he wasn't so certain. The face had turned away as quickly as Richard had seen it, and fine detail was obscured by the glass.

Melvold shivered, not because of the chill in the air. He turned back to Anne as she finished paying the taxi driver and watched as the cab sped off with a loud bang, leaving them alone in the street with only the mist billowing through the gardens for company.

Anne noticed the worried look on his face.

"Are you alright Richard?" she asked.

He nodded and gestured with his chin towards the garden gate.

"We should get cracking. It's cold out here."

Anne took his hand and squeezed, and they walked towards the garden in silence. Together they passed beneath the old iron gates without speech, subconsciously intimidated by the skeletal majesty of the wintry garden. For long moments they walked briskly, at least ten minutes, and then Richard brought them to a halt. He hadn't remembered the garden being so wide on a north-south line.

"I think we might have been turned around here in the mist," he remarked.

"No, I think we're all right," Anne murmured. "Just a little further, I'm sure."

Melvold shrugged and then nodded.

"We should get this over with."

Together they walked on, and as they continued the cold grew yet stronger. Suddenly a gust of wind opened the fog. Their path ahead stretched for a long span between the trees and flowerbeds, and Richard stopped, pulling Anne up short with him.

Sitting on a park bench ahead in the distance were two young men of equal height. They had no books, no instruments. They were merely sitting in the park, waiting. Richard suspected they were waiting for him.

"Richard, –" Anne began, but he motioned her to silence.

Her voice must have carried in the cold air, because the two young men turned. They stood, and even a hundred yards away Richard could see they were indeed the two brothers from the Lyon train. One of them pointed to Richard and gave a cry.

Richard tightened his grip on Anne's hand.

"Run!" he barked.

Melvold didn't wait. Still holding Anne's hand he spun and sprinted, pulling her along and ignoring her protests. As they careened blindly through the mist, Richard fired off a silent prayer that he and Anne were moving back towards the Southern gates. Around them the grey closed in again, shattered shockingly by the thunderous report of a pistol in the distance behind them. A second later the bark of the elm nearest Richard flew from the tree with a wet clack. He risked a glance over his shoulder, but there were only the shadows of the trees to be seen in the fog.

"They must be firing blind" he panted. "It's too foggy in here for sharp shooting."

He pulled her hand urgently.

"Come on, we need to get out of this garden! There's a maze of back streets here in the old district down by the river. If we can get into the buildings we can lose them in the fog."

He began running again, this time with purpose. There was another report from the pistol farther in the distance, this time with no impact. Melvold's heart leapt.

"That was softer," he panted to Anne. "They're firing blind, in the wrong direction. They may have lost sight of us."

By the old gate where they'd entered the park Richard lunged left and pulled Anne with him, racing down behind the Louvre. The district was completely blanketed by fog now and the street behind them was silent. After another block Richard stopped to take his bearings.

He and Anne were in an alley behind the *Palais du Louvre*. He felt cold sweat on his forehead. Beside him Anne was taking great gasping breaths, hands on her hips. Together they continued at a more sedate pace for another block until looming in front of them an old Art Deco Paris Metropolitan sign announced an entrance to *Pyramides* Station. Struck by an idea, Richard stopped dead.

"Come on," he said to Anne, dragging her down the station steps.

"Where are you taking us Richard?"

"Who knows? But if we get on a tube carriage and run for a few stations, we'll be far away from here and out of reach of those two murderers. There's no way they'll ever be able to find us if we get off at a random stop," he explained, as he rushed up to the empty ticket counter. "There's a train every three minutes, and we can't run forever. This will put us in the clear."

"But Richard, the embassy-"

He cut her off.

"They were waiting for us Anne. The British Embassy isn't an option. We need to lose them, get out of Paris and get home while they sniff around here."

Anne looked hard at him and nodded curtly.

The platform below the station was mercifully empty as the train screeched in. Alone Richard Melvold and Anne Hamilton stepped up to the carriage. Silently, the doors closed behind them, and with the brassy protest of rusty wheels the Paris Metropolitan Railway pulled them to safety.

• -• •• --• -- •-

A stream of curses ran running steadily through Schmidt's mind. Foiled again! Damned breeze, vagaries of mist, revealing the ambush a moment too soon! Melvold had succeeded for the third time in evading the Abwehr, and now he had vanished into the maze of the Metropolitan while Schmidt's team was left combing the deserted paths of the *Jardin des Tuileries*. Something would have to be done. Paris was simply too big, and the job was too hard here. Melvold would have to be lured out into the open, to somewhere he could easily be disposed of. He was lucky, but that would not save him.

• -• •• --• -- •-

Richard and Anne alighted safely five stops south of *Pyramides* station. The earlier surge of adrenaline had worn off, and by now Melvold was most shaken. He stood on the platform and looked at Anne.

"What the bloody hell are we going to do now?" he asked bitterly.

The constant stress of the last twenty-four hours was beginning to weigh more heavily on him.

"We've got no money, no passports, and I don't even have a fresh change of clothes. Those bastards tracked Montgomerie all the way from Poland. It won't take them very long to find us in Paris if we don't get out of here."

"Richard, take a few deep breaths, calm down, and let me think for a moment," Anne admonished.

Her pretty face went quickly through a range of contortions.

"Firstly, we're safe for the moment. Getting on that train was a good idea, but we shouldn't linger here on the platform. That's not the done thing in Paris, and anything we do that marks us as out of the ordinary will make it easier to find us."

She took Richard's hand firmly in her own. It was rather warm, he noticed as she led him towards the stairs to the surface.

"Incidentally, where have we ended up?" she asked as they climbed the stairs.

"We're at *Saint-Germain-des-Prés* station. It's only a few blocks from our hotel, but I don't think we should go back there. That's sure to be the first place the Germans look for us. They'll be watching closely."

Anne steered Richard into one of the ubiquitous Paris sidewalk cafes, and they sat in one of the corners, away from easy viewing in the street. She ordered herself a coffee, and Richard a beer. He glanced surprisedly as her as the waiter brought the drinks over.

"I thought you could use a stiff drink," she explained, "and I couldn't remember the French for whisky."

"Jolly good," he mumbled by way of reply as he sipped.

The beer was a welcome distraction from the problems at hand.

"Now, we need to think about this objectively for a moment," Anne began, as Richard sipped his beer.

It was ice cold and quite malty. In other circumstances, he would have quite enjoyed it, and in fact would probably have looked forward to having several more.

"Whoever it is chasing you has obviously marked you as a target, which means if you try to run, they'll be waiting and they'll catch you. Our best option I think is to assume as low a profile as possible, blend in with the common French, and try to slip by these people unnoticed. They will be looking for a fugitive running hard, not a couple travelling slowly and innocently."

"Anne, that's very sweet of you, but you don't have to be a part of this. I got myself into this trouble, and I couldn't possibly put you in danger. You should head away, not travel with me.

"And besides, we still don't have any money, or any passports," Richard protested.

"That's the beauty of our situation Richard. You've been made a mark, but I'm still an unknown. No one will be looking for me. While you stay here, in fact, you should have another beer," they both smiled at this, "I'll slip back to the hotel, pick up my purse and my passport, and some other small essentials that every lady needs. I'll leave my bags in my room, so no one notices I'm leaving, and then I'll come back and meet you here. We'll scoot across to the *Gare du Nord* and get on a train for Lille. We'll travel together, as husband and wife."

She smiled again.

Richard was quite impressed by the clarity of Anne's thought.

"Jolly good idea actually," he said.

"If we travel together, we'll be much more inconspicuous. We should have no trouble reaching Lille. From there it's just a short journey to the coast, and we can hop over the channel to Britain. Once we're in England, we'll be safe, and the issue of your stolen passport can be cleared up at leisure."

"You're right," Richard pronounced, his optimism returning. "I'd much rather explain myself to His Majesty's customs than be exposed out here while I replace my papers."

"We can do this Richard," Anne said very seriously.

"I'll wait here, but you just make sure you take care of yourself."

He smiled into his glass as Anne stood up and walked quickly out the door.

• -• •• --• -- •-

In a rare happenstance for early winter, it was sunny in Buckinghamshire. Anaemic yellow sunlight devoid of warmth filtered in the first-floor windows of Bletchley Manor, bleaching the tableau of C's office. C himself sat at his large oak desk, faced by Alan Denning in a high-backed paisley armchair. The remains of a rather good platter of tuna sandwiches sat mutely on a sideboard, next to an uncorked bottle of Beaujolais red.

"Any news from Paris?" C asked.

"We've just had a cable – it looks like the Germans have made another attempt on this chap Melvold. Tried to shoot him in the *Jardin des Tuileries*. The middle of bloody Paris of all places!"

"They're getting desperate then."

"I agree."

Denning's face was solemn in the insipid sunshine.

"Looks like he lost them. Slipped off into the Parisian back streets, then vanished into the subway. Not too shabby for an amateur."

"Is there anything we can do?" C asked.

"Last we heard, Melvold had given the Abwehr the slip. Cable just in now in fact. He probably won't shake them for long though."

C grunted. "Does he have what we need?"

"We confirmed it yesterday, on the train from Lyon."

"Does he *still* have it?"

"It's not in his room. The Abwehr searched it earlier, and we've been in since. If you want more proof, the Krauts are still trying to kill the poor bugger. There's only one conclusion to draw."

Denning said it with the air of a doctor pronouncing a diagnosis.

"It might be time to ask our asset in Paris to begin taking a more active role," he continued.

C raised his bushy eyebrows.

"I still find it unbelievable you've managed to get one of our people in on this so quickly."

Denning smiled.

"Of course. Schaeffer picked him up in Chamonix. We've been watching Melvold for almost his entire trip. You should know that I always have an ace in the hole."

"I didn't know you were a poker man."

"I'm not really. Learned the phrase off some of our colleagues in America while I was the MI-6 liaison in Langley. It seems appropriate for this sort of predicament thought. Sounds dashing."

"Does he know about us?"

"No. He's done terribly well without our help. At the moment he's our stalking horse. Schaeffer's using him to draw the Germans out, helping him keep running. Interfered with their search of Melvold's room on the train, stayed in close contact in Paris. Actually prevented him being run over this morning. We're keeping it all as quiet as possible. We can interdict the Germans if we need to, when we need to. Schaeffer can move on a moment's notice."

C noticed Denning's grin was decidedly crooked now. He grunted again, this time in concession.

"You always win at bloody bridge too."

Denning nodded happily.

"Anyway, Schaeffer is in Paris, on Melvold. I'll cable some instructions and see if we can get our boy home."

The smile vanished, and he became deadly serious.

"This boy Melvold has eluded the Nazis for more than forty-eight hours with none of the training or resources we give to our men. He's done good work for us, and I want him home alive."

"Not to mention the Enigma data."

"That would be nice too," agreed Denning. "Schaeffer's good at hiding in plain sight, and Melvold's still running. He's not bad at the game either, and I don't think he even truly knows he's playing. We'll have him home, C."

"That's why I employ you, Alan. You know what's important. When this young chap gets back to London, you should invite him up here for a whisky and a chat. Never know, the fellow might be partial to a hand of cards or two."

XII

North by Northwest

An hour later Richard surreptitiously checked his watch for the third time. Anne had been gone longer than he'd expected. He hoped she was safe and that everything was alright, but even if there had been a problem he doubted he'd be able to do anything.

Returning to the *Fleur D'Or* himself certainly was not an option. He was a marked man and the Nazis chasing him were proving ever more ruthless. At this stage he wouldn't put it past the Germans to stage a shoot out in the hotel lobby. So, having no other options, he waited.

The cafe itself was becoming busier by the minute as lunchtime approached. Every time the door opened Richard cast a suspicious eye over each patron. Melvold sat like a coiled spring, the tension wound tightly within him ready to rage free at the first sign of trouble. Fortunately, neither Marcus Bellini nor his two accomplices were to be seen.

After another ten minutes Richard began to relax. The clientele streaming in the doors were just workers coming in for an early lunch. To appear inconspicuous and blend in with the company Richard ordered another beer and a bread roll filled to bursting with chicken and salad. After all, it was lunch time, and he was hungry.

He'd just finished his roll and was working slowly on the second glass of beer, when the cafe's door opened again. Anne strolled in casually carrying her black handbag, and Richard exhaled very slowly between tightly stretched lips, relieved. She appeared relaxed, but when Richard glanced at her face there was determination in her eyes and barely concealed strain at the corners of her lips. Something was wrong and insidiously Melvold's heart rate began to rise.

"Richard!" she exclaimed without a hint of tension in her voice.

Nonchalantly she strolled over to kiss him on both cheeks. It was a perfectly natural gesture seen thousands of times daily in the cafes of the French capital.

As she leant forwards her hair brushed Richard's left ear and she whispered softly, "we may have a problem."

Melvold nodded to show he understood.

"How lovely to see you dear," he said.

He smiled at the caf\e in general, continuing the elaborate charade between himself and Anne Hamilton.

"We are late!" Anne exclaimed loudly, for general consumption. "Come, let us settle your bill and depart."

Richard thought she was overplaying things a little, she was speaking English after all. But the idea behind her role playing was correct, and certainly there were many English residents in Paris. Speaking bastardized French probably would have been far more incongruous, he realized.

Outside the cafe on the street Anne took his hand and began walking briskly back towards the metro station that they had arrived at after their escape from the Garden.

The midday meal was a time almost sacred in its importance to the average Frenchman, and even in the cold there were a great many people out. There was a general bustle in the air and hidden by the noise of the street it was possible for Richard and Anne to talk softly without fear of being overheard.

"What's wrong?" Richard asked her.

"I may have underestimated our pursuers," she answered. "I think one of them saw me as I left the hotel, and I think he might have picked me up."

"Damn!" Melvold exclaimed with feeling. "We'll never be rid of these bastards! Where to now then?"

"The *Gare du Nord.* We can take the train for Lille from there. We should go there now, quickly and directly. While we are in Paris with so many people around, I doubt that they will try anything further. We are safe in the crowds, and we should take advantage of this time."

"You're right. Besides, there is always the chance they will lose us in the throng."

"You're an optimist, I see," replied Anne with a tight-lipped smile.

By now they were descending the stairs to the cavernous body of the station. The platforms were busy now and Melvold casually scanned the crowds.

"I can't see anyone we know. Can you?" he asked.

"Fortunately not," answered Anne as the metro screeched into the station.

Aboard the carriage a quiet sense of foreboding settled over the pair. All the way to the *Gare du Nord*, Richard watched the indifferent faces of the commuters on the Paris metro. Bellini and his cohorts were nowhere to be seen. Melvold knew though that they were near. He could feel it.

• -• •• --• -- •-

From the very same metro carriage, Schmidt watched Melvold intently. The man was close to breaking. Soon it would be time for the Abwehr to finish their chase. Victory, home, accolades were all at hand.

• -• •• --• -- •-

Canaris hastily tore the envelope off the latest communique from Schmidt. Finally, it had come, mid morning while he was meeting with the cabinet in the Reichskanzlei. As he read feverishly his mood darkened. Still the British eluded them! The morning's debacle in the *Jardin des Tuileries* was madness!

Schmidt was lucky to still be on the outside of the French gaol system. Firing Lugers in the middle of Paris with the Gendarmes on the alert! Canaris knew his instructions had been fairly blunt, but a gun battle in the middle of Paris?

He cursed vehemently, but as he continued reading he began to smile slightly. His thick eyebrows rose as he considered the telegram's contents. Schmidt had a new plan, outlined in brief for him. Melvold was leaving Paris, running for home. In the cold northern forests of France away from the heart of that decadent city, he would be alone and exposed, easily disposed of. There would be no help no witnesses, no incidents. Even MI-6 could not reach him there.

At the bottom of the telegram was a request for help. Schmidt needed a route of egress from Northern France. He nodded to himself. A boat could be arranged. The smile had widened. It was demonic now. Borders could be opened, transport could be made available. The treasured dossier would be in Berlin within days. He knew his faith in Schmidt had not been misplaced. The race had been long, the game had been great, the moves had been subtle. Victory would be very sweet. Wilhelm Canaris picked up a telephone and began to make the necessary arrangements.

• -• •• --• -- •-

On the platform at the *Gare du Nord* throngs of people pushed and shoved. Early afternoon was a peak time for travel, and Richard worried that Bellini and his cohorts could be mere feet away, hidden by the crowd. He clutched his borrowed linen satchel tightly.

As the one thirty to Lille pulled up to the platform children's voices could be heard in happy exclamation of the fact to their parents. Melvold read the works plate of the engine as it passed him. It was an older train again, and it would be slow he judged. There were five carriages, each long and lacking closing doors to fully insulate the inside from the cold air whispering up their steps. Richard looked around again. Still there was no sign of any pursuit. Anne saw him canvassing the crowd.

"Richard, stop. You look like a man with something to hide. They are here, never fear, and they are watching us."

She smacked him gently on the hand, like he was a small child who needed calming.

"I'm wishing I'd brought my revolver to France," he muttered discontentedly.

"What, so you could cut someone down here, on platform three?" Anne asked sarcastically. "You'd spend your life in a French gaol."

"Right," he agreed curtly.

Reluctantly Melvold stopped his search and looked at the tickets in his hand. They were seated in carriage five, near the back of the train. As the engine stopped, Anne gathered herself, and walked to the front of the train.

"Anne, we're actually seated in the rear carriage" he pointed out.

"I know," she replied tersely. "Come on, quickly!"

He shrugged and followed her into the first carriage. They were almost last to get on, and as they stepped into the carriage, the conductor's whistle blew. With a great blowing of steam and a high-pitched whistle, the train began to shunt slowly forwards. Inside the carriage Anne took the lead, and began walking briskly down the central aisle, heading for the door between the first two carriages.

"What are we doing? Scouting the entire train?" he asked.

“Come on,” she replied again. “We need to hurry.”

Richard shook his head. She obviously intended to walk the entire inside length of the train on the way to their berth. He’d never understand women. Why they hadn’t just got on at their own carriage was beyond him.

As they stepped between the carriages he noticed that the train was still moving quite slowly. It was an old engine indeed, he thought. Through the windows of the second carriage, he could still see the platform and the station drifting slowly by.

“This bucket of rust will take hours to round the first bend!” he protested.

“I know,” replied Anne quietly.

The carriage was full. At first glance Richard could again see no one suspicious. There was a young couple with their children, there sat several businessmen with their top buttons undone. Halfway down the carriage, one passenger was largely obscured by a broadsheet newspaper held in front of him. Anne was still striding briskly down the centre aisle with Richard closely in tow when with a jolt, the engine picked up speed.

Richard stumbled sideways at the unexpected movement, and the arc of his outstretched arm knocked the obscured passenger’s newspaper down. It took him a second to get his balance, and he was picking himself up preparing to apologize, when he froze still bent double. He was staring at a face topped by a mound of blonde hair. Beneath the locks ice blue eyes regarded him coolly. Marcus Bellini smirked and nodded politely to Melvold.

For Richard the atmosphere in the carriage had frozen like salt water spontaneously crystallizing in the cold. His heart stood still and he expected to see the shape of a revolver in Bellini’s hand at any minute. His right fist clenched instinctively, ready to smash Bellini’s chin before he could draw a concealed weapon.

Suddenly Anne was leaning forward breaking the silence. “Excuse us *monsieur*,” she said blithely, giving no sign she had recognized, or indeed even seen Marcus Bellini. “My husband can be quite clumsy.

“Come Richard, the train is leaving, and we must find our seats.”

Coolly she took Richard’s hand and resumed their passage down the corridor. Every muscle in Richard’s back was tense, expecting the cruel, hot bite of a bullet at any moment, but he and Anne reached the door at the far end of the carriage, and stepped out into the clear cold air between the second and third carriages. As the door closed behind them, Richard spoke.

“Anne, that was Bellini-”

She cut him off with another curt wave.

“Come on!” She spoke louder this time. “Quickly now!”

The last of the station’s platform was sliding by to their left. Quickly Anne led him into the third carriage, but instead of heading towards the central aisle and the seating area, she took him by the hand to the door that led back out to the platform. She stuck her head out to confirm that there was still platform beneath them and turned to Richard. She spoke rapidly.

“The train’s not moving very fast at all. We have to jump, now!”

And with that she stepped down from the last stair onto the platform, in the direction of the train travel to minimize any disruption to her momentum. Richard gave an exasperated grunt. It was quite a jump, but if Anne could make it so could he. Besides the idea of being stuck on a train with Marcus Bellini and his co-murderers really didn’t appeal.

He looked forwards and saw the end of the platform approaching a bare five meters in front of him, and with a deep breath stepped down. It was that or remain on the train. He stumbled badly; he hadn’t taken the precaution of stepping in the direction of travel as Anne had. He’d been too worried about falling off the end of the platform.

Fortunately, after three or four unsteady steps, he stopped without falling and thus avoided ruining his second set of clothes for the day. As he righted himself the rest of the train slid by as the engine accelerated further. He caught a glimpse of the amazed conductor looking through the back window at them gesticulating animatedly. Then the train was sliding away around the corner to the north of the station.

He turned to Anne. The rest of the platform was completely empty. She was smiling at him. He embraced her, and kissed her fully on the lips, twirling her around. Finally, realizing that for all their solitude that he was still in a very public place, he put her down. She was laughing.

"That was absolutely amazing!" he exclaimed. "I thought we were in very serious trouble for a moment there. Although I do wonder now how we're going to get to Lille."

Anne's clear blue grey eyes looked straight into his. "Oh Richard," she began in an exasperated tone. "We were never going to Lille."

"We weren't?"

"No. I told you we were being followed. The whole point of getting on that train was to do what we just did so we could shake our pursuit. Finding Bellini and confirming he was on the train was just a bonus."

She smiled.

"That train goes all the way to *Sarcelles* before it stops again."

"*Sarcelles?* I don't know it."

"It's a small village about fifteen miles north of Paris. In that old banger it will take Bellini at least an hour to arrive and that's before he makes his way back to us. In short, we've suddenly plenty of time to make Calais."

"Calais?" Melvold was truly confused now. "Usually when I'm this confused it's in the context of several whiskies and John Husser's company. I haven't got my mind around your plan at all, I'm sorry my dear."

"Yes Calais. The other reason I chose the *Gare du Nord* was that the main coach station for Northwestern France is just across the street. We can take the afternoon service to Calais. There's a late mail boat that departs for Dover. If we make that, we can be in England by midnight. Misdirection and subtlety are our methods of choice to counter our pursuers' speed and power."

Richard's eyes narrowed. With the adrenaline flowing through his arteries, and the frigid air in his lungs, his mind was racing, and his thoughts were crystallizing. He looked back into Anne's eyes, searching for some answers.

"You seem to be awfully proficient at this misdirection and cloak and dagger business."

"Is that a question, or a statement Richard?"

"I'm definitely fishing, Anne."

Anne hesitated.

"Well, I may not have been entirely honest with you when I told you I was just a student. I also do some work for the government, in a less official capacity."

"Do you mean-"

"No, Richard, just a hint, that's all," and she winked at him. "We need to get off this platform. We've probably gained an hour or two, but we do need to get moving. Misdirection aside, time is still a big factor. They'll know we have to be heading for the channel somewhere."

He nodded, and taking her hand in his this time, he led her off the platform.

"Let's find a bus," he said. "It's time to go home to London."

XIII
To Calais

"Anne, that was quite brilliant," remarked Melvold ten minutes later as they stepped onto the cobbled path beneath the sandstone main arch of the *Gare du Nord*. "I've always tried not to be an ungracious victor but," he smiled evilly, "I do quite relish the thought of Bellini stewing all the way to *Sarcelles*".

Anne raised her eyebrows at him just for a minute, encapsulating mischief and devious triumph with a mere twitch of her forehead.

"If we had time for a Pernod, I'd toast a long trip and a slow locomotive."

"Quite," agreed Richard. "I hope that old banger shakes him to bits. Hopefully this coach you've set your sights on is reliable."

"It will be Richard. We've bought ourselves time and space. Marcus Bellini will never catch us now," she said firmly, determination providing a steely spine to the assertion. "Come on then!"

She lifted the hem of her dress as she stepped onto the glistening grey stones of the street.

"The afternoon service leaves at a quarter after two, and if we're not on that we won't make the launch at midnight."

Melvold checked his watch. "It's only ten to the hour. We've plenty of time."

Grey sun glistened on the wet cobbles as they crossed the street,

"Do you know," he continued as they entered the dilapidated brick warehouse that had been converted into a station for coaches, "I've never taken a coach before. Looked into them in India for one of our shorter passenger lines but never could see the benefit."

"I think you'll find it less exciting than the glamour and romance of the 'iron horses'," replied Anne.

"What, no middle-aged man in tails and a top hat above wooden doors, gilded wheels and six white steeds?" he joked.

"More like ordinary folk, who travel for need rather than pleasure."

The inside of the warehouse was dimly lit. Pale light streamed in through high set windows, catching pale motes of dust circling morosely above the thin crowd. Beneath banners tersely proclaiming destinations, men downcast and gloomy in their sober woolen work clothes quietly transacted for tickets.

Behind the ticket stalls stood buses of all shapes and sizes. There were open topped Volvos which Melvold thought would be brutally cold in the late French winter evening. Next to them stood sleek silver Renaults that looked like something from the future. Anne took his hand and pulled him briskly towards the far end of the row of ticket vendors. Behind the short line at the ticket booth stood their bus to Calais. It was painted deep vermillion, barely visible in the evening light which glinted off windows held by mahogany frames. A chrome grill held two large headlights at the front of a smooth rounded engine house.

"That's an English bus!" he whispered to Anne. "I rode something similar last time I was on the Brighton strand. I can't remember the make, but I'm sure they build them up in Birmingham."

"Yes, it's the executive service, run largely for travellers from the Isles," she replied. "They chose a familiar vehicle so those overwhelmed by continental culture would have at least one familiar element after they got off the Dover Ferry. I understand it's quite popular."

"Fair enough," he shrugged.

"More to the point it's quite fast," she stated. "And speed is our ally now, if we're to reach safety before we see Bellini again."

During their brief conversation they had reached the front of the ticket queue. Anne turned from Richard to the vendor.

"Deux billets s'il vous plaît."

"Pour Calais?"

"Oui."

"Hold on Anne," Melvold objected. "You told me over dinner you didn't speak French."

She looked back at him and smiled. "I lied," she admitted. "But you were having so much fun showing off your linguistic skills that I didn't want to interrupt."

Minutes afterward Melvold found himself boarding the bus with Anne. She picked a seat towards the rear and pulled the brocade curtain.

"It's rather dark!" protested Melvold.

"Yes, and now no one who might still be looking for you will chance a glimpse through the window," replied Anne.

"Bellini couldn't possibly be here!"

"Richard," Anne laid her hand on his and looked at him earnestly.

This closely within the confines of the bus he could smell her, the light rose waft of perfume floating above the scent of her golden hair. She looked him directly in the eyes, her pupils grey, almost translucent in the evening light.

"It would be a mistake to assume that Bellini acts alone. The Germans are most efficient".

For long moments she held his gaze, and slowly he nodded.

"You're right. You're absolutely right".

He nodded again.

"It would be a mistake to lose the game now in the final tricks. Besides," he continued. "It's quite nice to be alone with you in the dark."

This last was accompanied by a mischievous smile and a lift of his brow to take any coercion out of the comment.

"Richard!" Anne exclaimed in a high-pitched whisper. "Do behave!" and she slapped him playfully on the right shoulder.

He leaned in closely, so that his lips were by her ear.

"Thank you, Anne, for everything," he whispered.

He felt her head turn ever so slightly, so that her cheek lightly brushed his. He sensed rather than felt her head pull back in preparation to turn towards him, but just before she could make the critical movement backwards, in the rush before the kiss, the engines of the bus roared into life and broke the moment of rapture.

Anne pulled her head back completely, looked him in the eyes, smiled, and then straightened up and began fiddling to fasten her restraining belt.

"Bugger," whispered Melvold under his breath as he did the same.

• -• •• --• -- •-

Schmidt's eyes were closed, head resting back. It had been a beautiful move on the train for Melvold to shake the pursuit, reminiscent of Montgomerie's daring effort outside Krakow, but even now the hunt was drawing to a close. Never one to show emotion, Schmidt's nerves and expectations were hidden well below an icily calm demeanor. Nothing could be done for hours now, but at last Melvold was theirs.

Taking a rare moment to relax now, while all the pieces in the complex game of chess moved in their final turns, Schmidt reflected on the chase. It had been a marathon, an epic endeavour, and not even Agent Schmidt with ice water for blood was unmoved by the scope of the task that the Abwehr had laboured to complete.

They had infiltrated and destroyed the Biuro Syzfrow and in return been undone by a lone, clever, desperate British agent. The plans had left Warsaw in the hands of the enemy and Schmidt had chased Montgomerie across the Reich.

They had missed him by a hair's breadth in Vienna, and Montgomerie had opened up some distance. Persistence had paid off and Schmidt had called Charles Montgomerie to account in Annecy. Enter Richard Melvold, who unexpectedly stood between the Abwehr and victory.

The book said Melvold was a buffoon. He was an adventurer, on occasion a dilettante, skilled in finance but naive to the ways of the darker dealings of nations. He'd been lucky, but there had to be more than that. Melvold remained a mystery to Schmidt. It was impossible for an amateur to evade agents the calibre of Schimdt's colleagues. There was another factor here at play, something the Abwehr could not see. The thought momentarily disturbed Schmidt, but then it was dismissed with cold disdain.

Melvold was cornered, run to ground. His castle had fallen, and the king was exposed. The further one entered into a game, the more pieces one eliminated, the more predictable the moves became. Schmidt saw tonight the impending completion of a long and arduous assignment. Melvold was now so desperate that he was predictable. Lille or Calais, the options for a return to England were binary. The train was the only way to reach Lille, and if Melvold wasn't on it he must be running for Calais. Schmidt squinted in the poor light, trying to divine the time on the watch dial. It was 3.15 in the afternoon. Melvold would be in Calais in a few short hours, and the brothers were already in place.

To be sure the Abwehr's old adversary MI-6 were still to be considered. They had been marginalized, prevented from entering the delicate dance of the great game Schmidt played, and now before the sun rose on another day

Schmidt would be triumphant. They had struggled to send Melvold any assistance. They'd certainly sent Montgomerie none. The game was at an end. Unconsciously Schmidt smiled.

• -• •• --• -- •-

Melvold awoke with a start. For a moment he was quite disoriented. There was a deep growling hum as the engine of the bus chugged onwards and outside the sun was setting, filling the bus with a burnt orange light.

"What...?" he muttered.

"Easy Richard," said Anne softly, laying a hand gently on his leg. "It's all fine. We're on our way to Calais, remember?"

"Of course," he muttered. "Excuse me, must have nodded off. It's a bit hypnotic, this bus caper, isn't it?"

Outside the French countryside raced away, leafless trees and tightly shuttered cottages in silhouette against clouds rimmed gold from below.

"Where are we?" he asked.

"We just passed Amiens," replied Anne. "The bus stopped briefly so that people could stretch their legs, but you were sound asleep. I didn't want to wake you."

"Too much beer at lunchtime," observed Richard. "It always put me to sleep in India too. I always thought it was the heat, but I suspect it's actually the alcohol. What time is it?"

"It's almost turned five. We were just outside Paris when you nodded off. One minute I looked and you were watching *Montmartre* roll by, and the next time I looked you were out. You must have needed the sleep!"

"It's been quite a long few days," he replied. "How far are we from Calais?"

"Less than a hundred miles. We should be there just before eight."

"And what time does the mail launch leave?"

"Usually a little after nine."

Richard narrowed his eyes as he looked at Anne. Lord she was pretty! But somewhere deeper in his mind, intuitively, inductively, he was starting to believe that she was more than she seemed.

"Anne, you seem to know an awfully large amount of the comings and goings of unusual means of transport," he ventured.

She looked at him and raised an eyebrow.

"It's just that I've never met an English lady who knows that there's a late-night mail launch from Calais, let alone what time it leaves," Melvold continued, mentally grasping at the edges of an idea which kept slipping through his consciousness.

"You told me you did some unofficial work for the government," he said. "I thought you probably meant some diplomacy, some analysis of data, something that you probably wouldn't mention in polite society," he continued. "Not the sort of thing one can talk about at dinner."

He smiled. Anne turned her head, looking out the window at empty fields burnt by the setting sun's gold light.

"But it's more than that I think," he stated, a tone of certainty entering his voice.

Peripherally observed fragments, events of no individual significance, disparate actions and words all met together in his mind.

"You've been watching me since we met in Chamonix. You're not a diplomat, or an analyst," he stated, drawing a hand up to her chin, turning her head so that she faced him directly.

"You're a spy."

She kissed him, suddenly without warning. Not the kiss of an actor, but the kiss of a lover, full, passionate, hot and breathy.

"Richard," she breathed. "You're-"

"It doesn't matter Anne," he responded, cutting her off. "We'll talk about it back in London, together." And he kissed her back as the bus rolled on into deepening evening.

● -● ●● --● -- ●-

C had judged it time for a whisky. He was sitting in a high-backed chair, feet up by a crackling fire. The Warsaw affair was coming to a close, and the outcome was far from certain. A thousand thoughts about the chase ran through his mind, simultaneously everything and nothing.

A knock broke his reverie, and he looked up as Denning entered his office with a solemn face.

C sipped his Talisker and asked a multitude of questions with a single word.

"Melvold?"

There was a note of hope in his voice.

"He's broken from cover," answered Denning. "Telegram in this afternoon via the bank. It's going to be Calais."

"Does he have our package? Not much bloody point playing if there's no money on the table," C snorted.

"Yes, we've confirmed it," nodded Denning. "If this boy makes it to our launch and delivers us Montgomerie's charge, unknowing, chased halfway across France by the best agents the Nazis could field, it will be quite the miracle."

"If he delivers Alan," said C, "we need to invite him up here for a chat. We are going to need some good people in the coming years, if what we see in Europe comes to pass."

He sipped his whisky again.

"Agreed," replied Denning. "I've looked into his past a little more. He's a sharp one, this Melvold. Knows his way around some of the seedier areas of the world. There are a couple of wonderful stories that our man in India has dug up. If he lives, remind me to tell you about the way he dispersed a group of bandits intent on holding up one of his trains."

"I see. Are we ready for him?"

"Yes, we are. Schaeffer's in place," said Denning confidently, nodding.

• -• •• --• -- •-

Night had fallen earlier in Berlin, and once more the Mephistophelian features of Wilhelm Canaris were frowning and smiling at the same time. Alone, in the secrecy of the director's office, he read Schmidt's last telegram and smiled.

The Führer had been furious with Reinhard Heydrich when he discovered that the leaked enigma secrets had been within the grasp of his Sicherheitsdienst for a week and yet had slipped silently through the German security net. It had been a serious blow to the prestige of both agency and man. Serve that strutting peacock right, thought Canaris savagely. If what Canaris read was true, victory was finally in Schmidt's grasp.

Such a bold and complex operation would surely propel the Abwehr into the dominant position in the eternal politics of Germany's intelligence services, and in doing so, would assure the ascendancy of Admiral Wilhelm Canaris for months to come. Everything would be settled, tonight.

XIV

Schmidt

It was well after dark when the coach finally entered the *Rue Royal* on the island of *Calais-Nord.* The evening had settled heavily on the city and the bus slid by high angled gables in the gloom. Melvold let out a sigh, a slow exhalation of tension.

"We made it," he whispered, squeezing Anne's hand.

"Yes," she replied.

"It's about bloody time too," he said. "It's been a rough two days, and I'm starting to feel rather strung out."

Anne squeezed his own hand back. "We're almost there, Richard," she murmured.

The shadowed face of the *Musée de Belle Arts* slid by, grim and forbidding, and then the bus slowed as it entered the south margin of the *Place d'Armes* on the northern aspect of the city. The plaza was lit poorly by the light of several gas lamps. They stood upon workmanlike iron poles and cast a desultory yellow glow that could not stretch out to overcome the darker reaches of the square.

"Plenty of places out there for villains to hide," speculated Melvold restlessly as the bus came to a halt. He received another squeeze in reply.

Outside tendrils of mist circulated restlessly and as he stepped off the coach Melvold inhaled the damp heavy air. Bitter salt, wet and heavy, settled on his tongue. It was an unpleasant feeling, more so because it was mixed with the miasma of rotting fish and vapour from the squalid water of the harbour. He grimaced as he looked around the square, searching for any sign of Bellini or his two blonde henchmen.

Anne stepped off the bus behind him and noticed his expression as he turned in his survey.

"Richard, what is it? You don't look happy at all."

"I'm not," he answered as he finished his slow sweep of the square. "Charming place, architecture, aroma, atmosphere. None of it does much to lighten my mood. It's been years since I came to Calais, and I don't think it's improved much."

"I know it's the closest port to England, white cliffs and all that guff," he continued, "but I simply can't make myself come to France this way. I much prefer *Le Havre*, from the line out of Bournemouth. It's a longer trip but much nicer."

"You might be alone in your preference there you know. Most of England comes to France this way," Anne pointed out. "Even those who do so discretely."

And she slapped his thigh and began to stride away from the bus.

"Yes, I know," Melvold sighed as he followed. "Look, once upon a time, in the sixteenth century, this city was one of the jewels in the crown of greater England. It was a commercial hub, the gateway to the continent, where millions of tonnes of highly valuable cargo - lace, silk, tin, wool, lead - passed every year.

"Now it's known for its fishing, and with that comes that ever so slight odour you can smell on this evening's breeze. It's also a hive of activity for the hardline French socialists. They call themselves the *cartel des gauche*. Calais might be a port of call for English tourists, and even a home away from home for spies, but it's not exactly my natural environment as a venture capitalist, my dear."

He continued as they reached the middle of the square. "Now, take all that unpleasantness, and add the strong possibility that a murderous German posing as an Italian buffoon is somewhere out there in the cold dark fog, contemplating putting a bullet in me, and I'm sure that you might understand why I'm not ecstatic about being in Calais tonight."

There was a momentary pause, and Anne reached out to touch Richard's cheek gently.

"Richard," she said calmly, "everything will be fine".

Melvold took a deep breath to fortify himself. "You're right," he said. "Time to do our duty for King and Country." He looked at his wristwatch. "Near enough to eight o'clock," he pronounced. "Where does this mail boat you speak so fondly of leave from?"

"That way." Anne stretched out a hand to point across the square. "We cross this square and follow the road down to the main harbour. It's not far, five minutes perhaps. There's a launch that makes a run at nine, so we've time to make the dock before she weighs anchor. Usually, a few shillings each will earn one a berth in the galley for the crossing."

Melvold rubbed his head with his right hand.

"I still don't have a passport," he said crossly.

"Yes Richard, but by then we'll be back on English shores. If you're detained for a few hours by British customs I don't think you need to worry about whoever's chasing you abducting you from their offices, do you?"

"Good point."

"We should shake a leg then, shouldn't we?"

Melvold nodded.

The *Place d'Armes* was largely deserted as Anne and Richard walked across. Several cafes had space marked on the main area for food service, but tonight they were all shut. Cold winter weather and a failing economy provided little incentive to open at such an hour.

Anne and Richard stole across the edge of the square in the shadows. Above them the *Tour du Guet*, a relic of medieval times stood silent sentry in the gloom. They stole down a backstreet, walking down a flight of cobblestone stairs made slippery by the cold night air.

They slipped past a derelict apartment block with paint peeling on its walls, and then they were out onto a a long wide cobbled promenade by the town's main canal. Here the gas lamps had not been lit, and the only light was cast from alleys in which the apartments were still inhabited.

Without his overcoat, dressed only in his black sweater, Melvold shivered.

"It's cold down here by the ocean," he said.

"And the fog is closing in quite rapidly," replied Anne quietly.

• -• •• --• -- •-

"It's amazing how slowly time passes, isn't it, when one is waiting for news?" asked Denning.

He and C were still in the office, and the bottle of Talisker was at least a good third emptier.

"Bloody mind numbing, if you ask me," replied C. "This is the part of the job I hate most."

The two men lapsed into silence for a moment. The fire filled the room with its own conversation, a combination of short crackling exultations and muted pops as an underscore.

"Never really trusted Schaeffer," remarked C, finishing his glass. "Damned man always seemed a bit flamboyant for my taste. Still, he gets the job done, I must admit."

"He'll be ready," Denning reassured C. "We'll have Melvold and the prize safely back to London before dawn."

• -• •• --• -- •-

Walking down the stairs and away from the poorly lit square Melvold found that Calais had changed again. Cobblestones and closed cafes were replaced by empty mooring spaces, some filled with the detritus of a busy but impoverished shipping industry, others empty. Rust dripping across wood like congealing blood coated the docks, and the miasma of rotting catch grew stronger. In the distance dim lights glowed, smeared across the evening fog, and seawards a sparse forest of rake thin black masts rose above the grey mist. A chill wind blew cold air off the water to sweep the dockside and aside from the cry of an orphan gull the river concourse was completely deserted.

• -• •• --• -- •-

Alone in his office, Wilhelm Canaris had another glass of Schnapps. It was almost time. He might even attend the opera tomorrow night, indulge a lifelong love once the operation was complete. He walked to his sideboard, and poured another glass, and then dropped the needle of his gramophone down onto the disc below. It was Mendelssohn, something happy.

• -• •• --• -- •-

Melvold found the desolation of the Calais docks strangely heartening. Stopping at the base of the stairs he looked out over the boardwalk. Stepping off as he pointed Richard's voice rose determinedly.

"That's it Anne. We're almost there!"

He strode off confidently towards the forest of masts.

"It's a mailboat, and a ride back to England for us."

Grasping her arm, he pressed forward.

As they moved towards the harbour proper the air became even thicker, dampening all sound.

"Goodness, it's thick here," Melvold remarked. "And completely desolate. I imagine all the locals are inside by the fire, drinking Armangnac, or something equally horrible."

He felt a strange need to make conversation, as if the rhythm of words would somehow counteract the encroaching darkness. Beside him, suddenly, Anne stopped. She grasped Melvold and brought him up short.

"Richard, look!" she exclaimed urgently.

He had been striding out just ahead of Anne towards an empty riverside bench by the entry to the docks. He turned back to her and then looked hard again at the bench. He froze. In his haste to embark on his ride home, he'd missed the two symmetrical upright silhouettes sitting ramrod straight in the gloom. He half turned, so as to speak quietly to Anne, pushing her behind him.

"Anne," he whispered urgently. "Those chaps look like the two brothers from the train, the ones who were with Bellini. We are in awful peril."

"Richard -"

He cut her off.

"Anne, there's no time. We are both in mortal danger."

He took the Enigma file and Montgomerie's card from his pocket and thrust them into her hands.

"I don't think they've seen you yet, and they may not realize who you are. I'm going to run off into the alley to our left, draw them off. If they chase me, you might be able to slip past and make the mail launch."

He turned back, intently watching as the two shapes began moving, seeking any clue as to their intent, any sign of a weapon being drawn.

"Richard..." she said firmer this time, behind him.

There was a hint of steel in her voice that Melvold hadn't heard before. He hadn't yet turned to face her because he was still watching the approaching duo. As they walked towards him, he saw the taller man on the left reach into his pocket. It was difficult to be sure in the gloom, but the shape in his right hand looked awfully like a revolver.

"Anne -" he began firmly, motioning her away.

"Anna."

She pronounced the name softly, in a voice that cut through the mist and made Melvold's blood run cold. He turned slowly to face her. Gone was the smiling gentle face of an English lady. Hard blue eyes gazed back at him, unwavering, unblinking. In her left hand Anne Hamilton held the card and the folio that he had thrust at her a moment before. Extending from her right hand was the deadly cylindrical barrel of a Luger machine pistol, pointed directly at Richard Melvold's chest.

"Anna," she reiterated. "My name is Anna Schmidt."

She smiled sardonically.

"I am sorry to disappoint you mister Melvold, but Anne Hamilton is a lady who does not exist."

"To think," Schmidt continued, "that I had chased that bastard Montgomerie all over Europe for this," she waved the Enigma dossier, "and now you simply hand it to me in sight of the British coastline!"

She laughed bitterly.

"It has been quite a chase, Richard Melvold. Tell me, how long have you worked for British Intelligence?"

"I....I don't...." stammered Richard as he raised his hands. "I don't know what you're talking about."

He was manhandled from behind, one of the two brothers frisking him roughly to ensure he had no weapon.

"Come now, you may be honest with me," continued Schmidt. "Do you think my superiors in Berlin will believe that it took three of their finest agents four days to catch an amateur running across France?"

She raised the gun to level it at Richard's eye line, as her two accomplices frisked him. Richard simply shook his head.

"I don't know what to say Anne," he said.

"Anna. Please sir, have the manners to use my name correctly now that we have truly formally introduced ourselves."

"Anna then," he responded. I'd never met Montgomerie before Chamonix, and I have nothing to do with the British government."

"Rubbish!" she barked. "You made a switch in Chamonix, professionally. You set a trap for me on the train that I was not expecting. You cheated us in Paris, where you were supposed to die, and then you lead me down to the metro to shake off any pursuit from my colleagues. You would have me believe these are the actions of someone who is not from MI-6?"

"Yes," he answered truthfully. "I guess I'm just a jolly good sport when it comes to these cloak and dagger shenanigans. Must have read too many of the pulp penny dreadfuls as a younger man."

It was a flippant answer, but as he said it Melvold raised his head to look her directly in the eye. If he must die, then as a good British man he would not do it on his knees.

There was a prolonged silence, while Schmidt contemplated Melvold's face. Both her accomplices had moved forward to stand with her, and Melvold could see that they were indeed the brothers he had noticed on the train to

Paris. Each of them also carried a Luger, each of them pointed it at Melvold. No stranger to firearms or danger, Richard knew that with three firearms covering him he had no chance of disappearing into the fog.

Schmidt slowly lowered her pistol, looked Melvold up and down and smiled. It was not the ladylike English beam of Anne Hamilton. It was colder, crueller, a smile that expressed triumph over the world rather than affection for the beings in it.

Slowly she paged through the Enigma dossier. She spoke softly to her underlings in German, unintelligible to Richard. Schmidt finished flipping through her document and turned to Montgomerie's card. She opened it, and her smile widened. She looked up at Melvold.

"Wonderful people, you British," she said disparagingly. "The audacity of subtlety. Montgomerie was one of the best agents I've ever come across. We will talk about his exit from the Reich for years to come. And now, even out of time and options, he has the audacity to disguise a secret worth destroying nations for as a birthday present."

She waved the Engima dossier at Melvold. "It's a pity to take this off you. Montgomerie tried hard."

"You played me very well Anna," said Melvold evenly. "All the while I was concentrating on your colleague, Bellini, you were worming your way into my confidence. I thought I was trying to get into your affections, but really you were worming your way into mine."

Anne Hamilton, Anna Schmidt, Melvold corrected himself, laughed.

"Bellini is a complete fool," she said scornfully. "I will leave you to the further pleasure of his company, if he ever resurfaces."

Melvold remained silent.

"You should know, Richard Melvold," Schmidt continued, "that Charles Montgomerie pulled an amazing switch on us," she motioned with her Luger to her two colleagues, "on a train outside of Krakow. I very much enjoyed the chance with you to pull the same trick on Mister Bellini this afternoon in Paris. That particular caper will loom long and large in the history of the German intelligence services."

"Glad you enjoyed yourself madame," muttered Melvold.

Schmidt stepped closer to Richard. She moved up to stand in front of him, and again she was provocative, alluring. He could smell the rose scent of her perfume, see the slight scatter of freckles across her nose. Suddenly, Melvold smiled. He leaned forward and whispered in her ear.

"You know Anne, it's been entertaining," he murmured *sotto voce*.

He turned his head and brought his lips to hers. It was a passionate, forceful and commanding kiss and Anne's lips lingered on his, hot and breathy. Behind her he heard the sounds of her colleagues raising their revolvers and he put his hand around her waist, pushing forwards so that he presented no profile as a target.

Surprisingly, Anne kissed him back, crushing her mouth against his. She dallied for another moment, then bit his bottom lip and pulled away breathing deeply. Suddenly she slapped him, a loud crack over the deserted boards of the river walk.

"Richard, I should kill you where you stand. You have seen me in my true identity, and this exposure will render me vulnerable in the future," she said. "Secret agents, even more so than women, must have some secrets".

"But," she continued with a deep breath, "killing you here would make life extremely tiresome. We," she gestured at her colleagues with her Luger, "are still a very long way from the Reich, and a gunshot might bring an overly curious Gendarme. A murder investigation would make our journey home much more dangerous."

She smiled wolfishly and did not pull away from Melvold's embrace. She pulled the card from her left hand, and pressed herself more firmly up against Melvold's chest, teasing his cheek with the hard edge of the cardboard.

"So instead," she said, "we are going to leave you here alive. As a little memory of me," said cruelly, with a downwards twist of the mouth, "I will even leave you with this card."

She kissed him again, forcefully, passionately and then stepped back flushed with the triumph of victory. Then she laughed.

"Take it to British Intelligence. Tell them it is a gift from Anna Schmidt."

Anna Schmidt smiled even more broadly and again waved her pistol at her henchmen. Tripartite, guns focused on Melvold's chest, they backed slowly away and vanished into the fog leaving Richard alone on the dock.

XV

Schaeffer

Melvold shivered in the cold evening air. His mind refused to accept the events of the past quarter hour: Anne Hamilton, Anna Schmidt, a German pointing a revolver at his chest.

Although he hadn't known Montgomerie personally or understood what he'd been tasked to carry, Melvold still felt a profound sense of disappointment. Another man had died for what he'd carried. He himself had been betrayed. In all his years in the colonies, he'd never fallen victim to such a convoluted lie. The damned woman made the worst confidence trickster in the Cawnpore bazaar look like a sainted bloody priest!

Slowly he walked forward past the park bench where moments before Schmidt's accomplices had waited to interdict him. He put his hand on the fraying wood and slowly sank to the worn seat. He took a deep breath and didn't know what to do next. The Baum and Mercier chimed softly once, announcing the half hour.

"Doesn't bloody matter now, does it?" Melvold asked no one in particular. "Stuff the mailboat. Might as well find a good hotel and take the real ferry in the morning."

Absently he considered this thought, alone in the mist. The card that Schmidt had left him as a parting insult was still in his left hand, and he tapped it idly against his thigh. Still debating the choice of a ride home to London tonight and the morning ferry, he opened the envelope and read:

DEAR C

Hope you enjoy this!

MONTY

For a moment, Melvold stopped thinking about the hotel, and forgot his bitterness about Anne's betrayal. Without the distraction of the Enigma Dossier, he looked properly at the card for the first time.

"Deuced odd," he muttered as he turned the card over again in his hands.

It was quite large for such a small inscription. It was plain and white, with something incomprehensible written in large, gilded letters on the front.

"Must be Polish for happy birthday," he surmised.

A thought, something important, flirted with the edges of his mind. It was ungraspable, the gestalt of an astute man teasing his own consciousness. Melvold knew it was important, if only he could quantify its content. He stilled, contemplative in the dark, all thoughts of the mail launch driven from his brain. It was there, the card made no sense, and....

Shockingly loud footsteps cut the stillness of the night, patent leather tapping out a staccato beat on the cobbles of the riverside. It took Melvold a moment to register the sound, and as he started he looked up squarely into the muzzle of another gun.

His first thought as his heart leapt was that the Germans had returned to retract their earlier clemency, but then as his eyes focused he saw this was not so. This barrel was long and silver, with a snub mark set above the barrel to allow more accurate sighting. Schmidt's weapon had been thin and grey, concealable, the weapon of a spy or assassin. This was the sidearm of a soldier. It was an Enfield, Melvold realized, the standard issue for the British army. Hands resting between his knees Melvold looked up above the gun barrel into the unsmiling face of Marcus Bellini.

There was a pause as each contemplated the other and then Melvold spoke.

"What do you want, you German bastard? Your friend has already made off with the prize. She went that way," he gestured with his chin towards the fog ridden alley leading away from the harbor, "after saying some rather uncomplimentary things about you. Why don't you sod off and join her? Find a schnapps, and celebrate in one of those seedy living rooms you people call a pub."

Provoking Bellini might not have been smart, but Melvold was irritated and tired. His concentration and calculation had led him to this point tonight. Why not try reckless abandon?

"Get up."

Bellini spoke flatly, with no evidence of the caricatured Italian accent that he had used on the train from Lyon. He waved the gun in front of Melvold's face in a direction that pointed vaguely further down the pier.

Melvold stood slowly, not taking his eyes off Bellini's face.

"Walk," Bellini waved the gun again in the direction of the ghostly forest of masts rising from the harbour. "Bring your birthday card."

He smiled evilly.

Melvold pocketed the card as instructed and began to walk towards the docks, Bellini at his back.

"I'm getting rather tired of having guns pointed at me Bellini," he said. "I've already had someone I liked very much do the dirty on me tonight. Having a German disguised as an Italian pointing an Enfield at me is not doing wonders for my disposition. Too many double crosses will do that to a man you know."

"You recognize the gun then?"

"I've several close friends in the military," Melvold said, with a bitter laugh.

"Interesting. Do you still keep in contact then?"

"I don't think that's any of your damn business."

"You should calm down Mister Melvold. It's been a trying day for everyone."

"Excuse me Bellini," he replied. "I don't often mean to be rude, but in your case, I'm prepared to make an exception." Richard took a deep breath. "Perhaps I'll calm down if you tell me what you want," he continued. "Why aren't you off with Schmidt and your other colleagues, running back to your Nazi masters for a pat on the head like good little bloodhounds? The Enigma File is gone. Why bother pointing a gun at me now?"

"Let me simply suggest that I don't like to leave loose ends lying around."

Richard turned to look at Bellini, who raised his eyebrows and gestured for him to keep walking.

Bellini herded Melvold up the concourse in silence for a few more minutes until they came to a yacht moored against the stone wharf. It was an ocean-going vessel, sixty feet long and dull grey. It bore no naval ensign, nor name upon the transom. Insofar as much as it was possible for a boat to look secretive, this one did. Two burly crewmen were standing on the deck, one coiling rope and the other staring at the two men on the dock. Both were silent and neither seemed bothered by the spectacle of Bellini menacing Melvold.

Melvold stopped, and turned to Bellini, who grinned evilly.

"Climb aboard," he murmured maliciously with another gesture of the Enfield.

Melvold stepped up the gangplank. Bellini motioned towards the cabin and nodded at the crewmen. Richard stepped under the canopy over the helm, and down three stairs to the door. Concentrating on any chance he might have to win free of Bellini's captivity, he missed hearing Bellini speaking to the crew.

"Open it, please," he heard over his shoulder as he felt a prod in the small of his back.

He reached out and turned the handle. The door was unlocked. Melvold walked into a surprisingly plush cabin, at odds with the subdued exterior of the vessel. Warm wood paneled walls framed a large leather settee beneath two framed paintings of racing yachts beating windward at full sail. A mahogany dining set was bolted to the floor in the middle of the cabin and beyond on the sideboard was a crystal decanter filled with amber liquid, resting amongst matching lead oxide cut glasses. Bellini entered the room behind Melvold and pushed the pistol harder into his back.

"Please sit down. The settee is most comfortable."

As Bellini spoke there was a strangled mechanical gargle followed by a throbbing dull hum as the motor of the yacht kicked over and sprang to life. Subconsciously Melvold sensed the gentle rhythmic sway of the deck that announced the boat was underway for destination unknown to him.

• -• •• --• -- •-

Spray kicked up, wetting Anna Schmidt's face. She and the two brothers were aboard a fast motor launch, racing out to join a Hamburg flagged merchant ship in the English Channel. Canaris was organized as ever, she thought. She would soon be back in Berlin, basking in the glory of a complex and successful mission.

Richard Melvold had been very resourceful, for an amateur. He'd also been quite devilishly charming at times, and at others nothing more than an awkward schoolboy. German men were rarely so reticent about expressing their interest in her, a situation she usually discouraged. There had been none of that from Melvold. She reflected that despite her ability to impersonate the English she did not understand them.

It surprised her as she stood on the back of the launch watching the lights of Calais recede that she was thinking of Richard Melvold with a touch of fondness. Truth be told her heart had raced as they kissed. Perhaps that was why she had let him live. She smiled in the dark.

That had been a first for Anna Schmidt, normally so ruthless and so cold. The Englishman had seen her, knew her true identity, and would be sure to pass the information on to her enemies in the British Intelligence service. Sparing Melvold had not been smart, had not been professional.

As the boat moved further into the channel she gripped the Enigma Dossier tighter, and reflected that sometimes, she did not understand herself.

• -• •• --• -- •-

"Going to ply me with a few drinks before you shoot me and drop my body in the channel?" Melvold asked as he sat. "I hope the whisky is good."

He spread his hands expansively and shrugged. Despite his words he held himself tightly, like a coiled spring. If it became apparent that Bellini meant to attack him Richard Melvold intended to die fighting.

"Single malt. The Isle of Skye's finest" smirked Bellini. "Ice?"

"Just a drop of water please."

And then something so unbelievable happened that it took Melvold a moment longer to register than it should have.

Bellini turned to the sideboard, presumably to mix the drinks, but as he did so he put the Enfield down on the table in front of Richard. It was such a basic mistake that disbelief almost prevented Melvold from moving. The glasses clinked together as Bellini poured, and the Richard sprang into action. Bellini must have heard but could not turn in time with hands full of glass tumbler. Melvold grasped the gun and extended his arm towards Bellini.

"You fool," rasped Melvold, panting. "Turn around."

Bellini turned calmly.

"Your whisky," he said, laying the glass on the table and pushing it towards Melvold. Then, as if Melvold was not pointing a gun at him, Bellini sat and sipped from his own tumbler. Speechless, Melvold watched him. He simply couldn't believe the Italian's nerve. Surely no one could be that calm.

After another minute that to Melvold seemed more like an hour, Bellini spoke.

"It's not loaded old boy," he said, as he took another sip of his whisky.

Melvold stared at him disbelievingly. He looked again at the gun, then aimed wide of Bellini and pulled the trigger.

There was a metallic click, but nothing else happened. Frustrated, Melvold pulled the trigger again, and shook the Enfield in frustration.

"Couldn't risk anyone getting hurt you see," continued Bellini placidly. "Of course, I did have some bullets in there earlier when the Krauts were holding you up. Might have needed to shoot if it looked like they were going to do anything a bit rash, but once they'd snuck off, I unloaded the chamber."

Bellini reached into his right coat pocket and dropped three small silver cylinders on the mahogany table with a metallic rattle. He looked at Melvold expectantly.

Then, amazingly, Bellini's pattern of speech registered in Melvold's mind.

"That's a bloody London accent!" he exclaimed. His eyes narrowed, and he looked across the table. "Who are you Bellini?" he asked. "No lies this time. The Enfield might not be loaded, but I can still club you mightily with it, and I have to tell you that I'm quite worked up at the moment."

Bellini stood to face Melvold.

"Actually, the name's Schaeffer, Harry Schaeffer," he said, holding out his right hand for Melvold to shake. This he did, dazedly.

"Please sit down Richard," continued Bellini cum Schaeffer. "You've had a very long four days. Won't have you a drink? I assure you, you are entirely safe"

Melvold fell into rather than sat in the chair opposite Schaeffer. Overcome, he finished the contents of his glass with a single swig.

"That's better old chap," encouraged Schaeffer as he stood. "Let me fix you another one."

Facing the sideboard, he turned his head to continue speaking. "You must be famished too. Once we're safely out into the channel, I'll have Wooldridge jump into the galley and fix you something to eat. We're not stocked for a long voyage, but I'm sure we can manage a sandwich or two."

"In fact," continued Schaeffer as the pitch of the boat suddenly increased markedly, "I imagine we're just clear of the harbor seawall now. Excuse me for a moment please."

He stood and exited to the deck. Alone in the cabin Melvold looked around him for any clue as to what was really going on. A brief search of the sideboard revealed two British passports, sitting on a pile of others, all of varying nationalities. He opened a Dutch passport, to be confronted by a photo of Schaeffer-Bellini, but this time the name was different again. A French document bore the same photo but a third different name. Beneath this was the German passport that Melvold had seen on the train from Chamonix. All the foreign passports Melvold checked bore photos of the same man, but no two names were the same. He opened the first British passport.

"Harry Edward Schaeffer," he read. "Born in Brixton, London."

He drummed his fingers idly on the sideboard as he digested the name. He opened the second British passport and froze. At that moment he heard the cabin door open again, and silently cursed that he hadn't had the forethought to reload the revolver. He turned accusingly to face Schaeffer, face dark with anger again.

"This is mine," he spluttered furiously at Schaeffer, waving the passport.

"Yes," said Schaeffer mildly. "I was going to give it back to you, but I see you've already found it.

"You ransacked my room in Paris!"

"Actually, old boy, I didn't," countered Schaeffer urbanely. "That was the Krauts. They wanted to drive you towards Anne Hamilton, who was of course Anna Schmidt, a German agent. Without your passport you were never going anywhere except towards her door. Quite a clever scheme really, draw you away from Paris, recover their quarry, dispose of you as they saw fit and not anyone the wiser."

"Yes," growled Melvold. I'm aware of how that played out."

"Well, you see," continued Schaeffer, "I reasoned that the Nazis wouldn't risk carrying your passport with them. Appallingly incriminating if they get searched. After I'd decided that, it was a simple matter to search the garbage at the *Fleur d'Or* and retrieve your passport."

Melvold raised his eyebrows.

"Thank you," he said grudgingly.

There was a knock at the cabin door, and Schaeffer opened it slightly, to retrieve a plate of fresh sandwiches. He shut the door again firmly and placed the sandwiches on the centre of the table.

"Ploughman's," he said. "Help yourself please."

Richard simply looked at him.

"Help yourself," repeated Schaeffer, "and I'll explain to you what's occurred the last four nights."

• -• •• --• -- •-

Alone again in his office, working by lamplight, Wilhelm Canaris read the radio message from the *SS Stiermark*, presently making way in the English Channel. Schmidt had been successful, and Canaris clenched his fist in triumph. Enigma's secret was safe. The U boats of the Kriegsmarine would sail, and the Royal Navy would be powerless to stop them. Germany's ascendancy was at hand.

XVI

Melvold

Melvold had to admit the sandwich was delicious, and for a few moments he was taken away by the tang of the pickled gherkin and the sharp bite of the Stilton cheese. He'd already finished one and was reaching for a second before his mind returned to the issue at hand.

"Sorry Schaeffer," he mumbled around his mouthful. "I find stress always works up quite an appetite. Used to be the same after an all-nighter in the colonies. The harder the work, the hungrier the man. Friend of mine, chap called Husser, used to have a theory, something about hormones and the kidney or such rot."

He looked up to see Schaeffer smiling at him.

"You seem to have recovered your equanimity very quickly."

"Yes, I always find my mood improves when I'm not famished."

Melvold spread his hands expansively and leaned back in his chair. "It's patently obvious to me that if you meant me any ill will, it would have befallen me by now. We've been sailing half an hour, and you could have shot me just after we cast off the docks back in Calais."

"In fact," Melvold continued, "I have a suspicion that this time you've told me the truth about your name, and where you come from."

"That's rather a leap of faith isn't it?"

"Yes, it is," admitted Melvold. "But it's a strong hunch, and I made a lot of money in India playing them. I've learned to trust myself."

He paused and focused his gaze on his ersatz adversary.

"What I would like is to know why? Why the charade? Why pass yourself off as the worst Italian caricature since Chaplin played Rome?"

"I admit, it wasn't my greatest impersonation. The trouble is the whole damned operation got laid on so hastily that I didn't have any time to organize better cover. The only papers I had on me when I was ordered after you were my own – obviously out – a German passport, and a horrible mockup of some Italian gear.

"I couldn't get back to Paris station to change my documents and make Chamonix in any sort of good time. So, I had to go with what I had. The real hell of it is that I don't even speak Italian.

"That passport was only in my valise because I used it to slip into north Africa last month. No one there would know Italian from Greek, so it was fine. In Europe, of course, the story is a bit different. Talk about ham fisted acting!"

"It was pretty terrible," agreed Melvold. "So, now that I have a name, why don't you tell me who you are. I've already met a German girl posing as an Englishwoman. I might as well find out the truth of Marcus Bellini too."

"Quite," agreed Schaeffer. He hesitated. "Where to begin?"

Melvold waited patiently.

"As you might surmise," Schaeffer continued, "I am, in common terms, a spy."

"Yes, I'd gathered," replied Richard drily. "That's hardly news."

"More accurately, I work for Branch 6 of British Military Intelligence. As you might now correctly infer, so did Charles Montgomerie. In loose terms I suppose you would refer to us as the foreign service. I am Anna Schmidt's counterpart. We had her fingered as the main opposition quite early on in the piece, but what we didn't know was who you were old son."

"Me?" asked Melvold, surprised. "I'm just a chap from back from the colonies, looking for some sophistication on the continent."

He spread his arms again, gesturing blankly at the air in the cabin.

"No hidden agendas here."

"Yes," Schaeffer agreed. "We know that now. The office has done some checking up on you, see? But at first, you could have been anyone for all we knew; Anna Schmidt's accomplice, an independent contractor, an American disguised as a Brit, absolutely anyone! And what Montgomerie was carrying was so important that we couldn't risk losing it.

"He knew," continued Schaeffer, "that he had been run to ground in Chamonix. I hadn't been on the scene long enough to make contact with him, or deal with the Germans, so he knew he had to take a chance."

"So, he hit on the idea of giving his package to me?"

"Precisely! Exactly! Montgomerie knew the Krauts had caught him. He dumped the prize on you and ran off as a decoy to the mountains. Figured you," Schaeffer stabbed Melvold in the chest with his middle finger, "were too ordinary to attract any notice.

"And when he fixed on you in desperation, knowing he was caught, I thought that I would need to sound you out, see who you were and who you worked for. Montgomerie had taken a huge risk, and so we needed to see how it would all play out.

"Waltzing up to you and announcing that I was a British spy is simply not the way the game is played. So, I had to improvise."

"The ridiculous questions on the train from Chamonix?"

"I was going to come clean in Lyon, but then when the Germans re-appeared I thought it might be better to hang by in the shadows a little longer. Thought it might make your life easier if I acted as a stalking horse. Interfere with their plans, draw their attention away and all that, give you a clear run to Paris. On the other hand, announcing myself to you would just have put two of us in the Lion's den. Much safer with me on the outside, protecting you."

"I'm still a bit cross about you going through my things on the way to Paris," remarked Melvold, irritably. "Not exactly gentlemanly and all that."

"I did save your life in Paris though," countered Schaeffer.

"What?"

"Saw that car mount the pavement," explained Schaeffer as he sipped his whisky. "Did the only thing I could think of, pushed you out into the street away from its path."

Melvold stared at him, stunned.

"I thought you tried to kill me," he stuttered.

"No, old chap. Saved you. Sorry to ruin such a nice suit."

Schaeffer shrugged.

"But if you were on my side, why break into my sleeper carriage?"

"I didn't touch your effects old boy," parried Schaeffer.

"I caught a thief, red handed. Set a trap for him that he fell into nicely, while I kept Montgomerie's package in my pocket. Then, Anne mentioned she'd seen you in my cabin over dinner."

Melvold stopped, seeing the inherent contradiction in his reasoning which brought him up short. "But then, she would, wouldn't she?" he smiled wryly. "The nerve of the woman."

Then he grinned at Schaeffer rakishly.

"I do have to tell you Schaeffer," he said, "she kisses with quite a lot of enthusiasm".

Schaeffer stared at him for a moment and then burst out laughing.

"Quite!" he stuttered. "Glad you enjoyed your evening old son."

Melvold waved an arm dismissively.

"I've interrupted you," he apologized. "Please continue."

Schaeffer took up where he had left off.

"Returning to the train, I actually interrupted her searching, probably why she sprung your trap. Bit unusual that. Our experience of the Germans is that they're very careful. Once she realized what she'd done, she took the opportunity to prejudice you against me. She's clever, that one. Obviously didn't take her very long to work out what my game was. Lucky she just didn't stab me in my sleep on the way to Paris. I kept my door double barred that night I can tell you."

"Turns out she was rather vicious, doesn't it?" agreed Melvold.

"Absolutely. Schmidt and her two companions are both very nasty pieces of business. I thought in the dining car that she might have her cronies come up with some mischief towards you, so I made sure to keep a close eye on them. Lovely dinner service and all, but very hard to enjoy while one is carrying an Enfield in one's tuxedo."

"Quite," agreed Melvold.

"She had her minions plant Montgomerie's passport on me and sidelined me with the gendarmerie. Very clever on her part, took me quite a bit of time to talk my way free. French police are sticklers for procedure you know. I had to phone his Majesty's consul to get out of the knick."

Melvold sipped his whisky and finished the glass. He held it up for a third, and Schaeffer stood.

"Then," continued Schaeffer, "those filthy buggers tried to run you over while I was off the scene. It was pure serendipity that I'd managed to get out of the police station in time to knock you free."

He placed another full glass by Melvold's left hand.

"And I do have to tell you that the switch she pulled with you on your way out of Paris was absolutely beautiful to watch, if a little inconvenient," Schaeffer continued, shaking his head. "Right out of the academy, that one.

Montgomerie would have been proud of it. He used to teach it. Probably pulled the same switch on them on his way out of Poland."

"He did," replied Melvold.

Schaeffer raised his eyebrows.

"She told me," Richard clarified.

"Marvellous," sighed Schaeffer.

There was a brief pause in the conversation.

"I still don't understand, Schaeffer." Melvold's voice was puzzled. "You seem awfully upbeat about this whole affair."

"Please don't think for a moment that I am Melvold. Montgomerie was an old and valued friend. I've known him for a very long time. It was all I could do not to shoot that Nazi harpy and her two friends down in cold blood on the docks."

"Why didn't you then?" countered Richard. "I like to think that if such evil had befallen me, my friends would not be so lax in extracting vengeance."

"Because that's not the way we play the game old boy," said Schaeffer, his voice a mix of steel and sadness. "We all know the risks. We all signed up to play. Think about it. If I start a shoot-out, perhaps the prize ends up in the water, ruined, and the krauts win. At that range you're also very unlikely to survive when bullets start flying. So, shooting and risking the loss of the packet that Montgomerie worked so hard to deliver safely, and risking your life unnecessarily, would have been to dishonour his memory."

A moment of hesitation struck Melvold. Schaeffer clearly hadn't realised the full extent of what had happened.

"Harry," he began hesitantly.

Schaeffer looked squarely at him.

"You know Schmidt took it? The file?"

"Yes, old boy. I do."

• -• •• --• -- •-

C looked up as the door to his office opened without a knock. Alan Denning strode in, looking very pleased with himself. C had been reading quietly by lamplight, and the fire was burning quietly in the background.

"Well?" asked C, looking up from his reading.

"Schaeffer just radioed the bank from the Channel. He's aboard the launch, and Melvold's safe with him."

C sipped his whisky in silence, pierced only by the dim buzz of the lamp on his desk, and the rhythmic crackle of the burning logs.

"Does he have what we want?" he asked quietly. "Charles Montgomerie died for this you know. Hell of a price to pay if we haven't succeeded."

Denning paused.

"Schaeffer says he does," he replied. "Apparently the Germans took off with the dossier but left the rest of the package with Melvold."

C straightened in his chair. He drained his whisky on the fly and threw the small folio he'd been reading on the desk.

"Capital," he said relievedly, rubbing his face between his hands.

He looked up at Denning, fingers crossed over his mouth. "Glad we got this boy Melvold out too. He's done a damn good job racing the Nazis across France. I suspect we might need a few more men of his resourcefulness in the coming years."

Denning nodded thoughtfully.

"I did mention that to Schaeffer," he said.

• -• •• --• -- •-

"You see old boy," explained Schaeffer. "Montgomerie was a very crafty fellow."

Melvold looked at him, puzzled.

"Let me expound a little," Schaeffer said. "I know you've been abroad lately. In fact, the office knows quite a lot about you. I'm sure you've kept up with the news on the continent. The Germans are playing up, getting rather full of themselves."

"You're right Schaeffer," rejoined Melvold. "I have been away, but even in the Colonies we heard about the travesty that was the Sudentenland. Poor Czech bastards."

"The inside word in London is that the serious members of our government, the ones who don't have lunch with Chamberlain and his friends, expect the Reich to look past the Baltic states. The Führer has signed up the Russians and the Italians.

"Despite the *entente* from the Great War we don't expect any help from the East. We've all been out for months, chasing leads on the continent, trying to find out anything we can about the Reich. The insiders at Admiralty House fear Hitler's going to try to come West."

Richard snorted derisively.

"Let him," he said, raising his glass. "The Royal Navy taught the Germans a lesson thirty years ago. Rule Britannia and all that. The waves are ours."

Schaeffer regarded him steadily.

"They're building a navy to rival ours," he said. "Three years ago, they laid down the keel of the biggest battleship the world has ever seen. Launched her three months ago. She's christened the *Bismark*. Named after their Chancellor who united the Germanic city states in a sea of blood and iron. They've a fleet of raiders, ready to starve us out, cut us off from the Empire."

He paused.

“I understand the issues,” replied Melvold, “but what the hell does this have to do with Charles Montgomerie, Anna Schmidt and a small book about something called Enigma?”

“Think about it Melvold. The RN, pitted against a more modern fleet of greater firepower.”

“Yes, quite a battle. But the Empire rules the seas. We’d decimate them as they sailed out through the Heligoland Bight.”

“What if I told you that we couldn’t read their signals?” asked Schaeffer.

“That’s not possible,” replied Melvold. “Even the best radio can be intercepted. I used to deliver sensitive telegrams by hand in Cawnpore, prevent any unwelcome ears listening in. I’m sure His Majesty’s Navy is more resourceful than me.”

“The Germans have developed an encoder that we can’t break. Imagine, their fleet of submarines loose in the Atlantic, decimating our shipping while their Panzers pound Europe. It would be a disaster for the civilized world!”

Melvold thought silently for a moment.

“Enigma,” he said.

“Exactly!” exclaimed Schaeffer. “Enigma is the codename of the device. Some of our very clever friends in Poland have been working on the problem. There’s some chaps up in the midlands who do the same, but the Poles are a bit closer than us.”

“That’s what Montgomerie was carrying,” said Melvold. “That’s what the folder was. And now the Nazis have it,” he trailed off wordlessly, and there was silence in the cabin. “Bugger!” Melvold exclaimed a moment later.

• -• •• --• -- •-

"Pour yourself another drink Denning," continued C. "And me one while you're there please. Sit down, and we'll toast the memory of Charles Montgomerie."

Denning wordlessly poured a rather generous measure of the amber spirit into a glass for himself and then refilled C with a similar amount. He sat opposite and regarded the head of MI-6 silently for a moment.

In the still of the room the fire cracked suddenly, startling both men from their reverie.

"Charles Montgomerie," intoned C solemnly.

"A good man," Denning replied, eyes downcast.

They clinked glasses and drained them in a single gulp.

Between them, on the desk rested the papers that C had been reading. Both men looked down at the title:

THE WARSAW ENIGMA FILE

FINDINGS OF THE BIURO SYZFROW (CYPHER BUREAU) INTO THE WORKINGS OF THE GERMAN ENCODER KNOWN AS "ENIGMA"

COPY 2 of 5

MOST SECRET: EYES ALPHA

They were silent for a moment, and then Denning rose to refill both glasses once more.

• -• •• --• -- •-

Harry Schaefer tutted and shook his head at Melvold's despair.

"I told you Montgomerie was clever," he said. "The Enigma File was a decoy, a bluff within a bluff. Give the Krauts something to chase, and hopefully they'd take the bait."

Melvold frowned.

"You were too clever for them," assured Schaeffer. "If you had let them take the dossier on the train to Paris, we could have all spared ourselves a lot of trouble. The chaps up at Bletchley Park have had an identical copy of that dossier for the last four months," he continued blithely. "What was yours? Number three? I can't quite remember, but I think it's number two that's sitting in a file up there now."

"Then why the farce, the chase?" asked Melvold irritably. "I'd only just met Charles Montgomerie, but I did rather warm to him. I can't believe that Admiralty House would ask him to die for nothing."

"They didn't," replied Schaeffer. "While we have all the technical data, what we can't do is put it into a working model. The Poles, on the other hand, had. What we needed was their circuit diagrams, allow us to do the same."

"But I don't have any circuit diagrams!" exclaimed Melvold. "I had the dossier, and a bogus birthday card, and that was it!"

Schaeffer cocked his head, contemplated Richard for a moment, and laughed.

"May I see the card?" he asked evenly.

Melvold rummaged in his pocket and held out the large white card. Schaeffer took it wordlessly and put it on the table. From beneath the table, he produced a match, which he struck.

"Now hold on a minute -" began Melvold.

"Relax Melvold," replied Schaeffer with another laugh. "I'm not going to burn it. Watch," he said, as he held the match close to the card, against the unmarked surface.

For a moment, nothing happened, and Melvold started to wonder if Schaeffer was slightly mad. Then he started. As the blank surface of the card warmed, lines started to appear. Within a moment the blank facing page of the card was covered in a maze of scribbles, connecting boxes and zig zags beneath mathematical notations.

"See old boy," remarked Schaeffer, raising an eyebrow. "A bluff within a bluff. I told you Charles Montgomerie was a clever fellow. This is called sympathetic ink, only appears when the surface it's written on is hot. The file was a decoy, and the card was always the prize. Smart people in Warsaw. Hell of a way to send a secret."

"They're the diagrams you were after?" asked Melvold.

"They are," confirmed Schaeffer. "Let me pour you another dram, celebrate our success and all."

Melvold remained silent, while Schaeffer stood and poured two more large measures.

"Charles Montgomerie," he said, raising his glass as he handed the other to Richard Melvold.

"Charles Montgomerie," replied Melvold, returning the gesture.

"You know Schaeffer," said Melvold a few moments later, holding his glass up to contemplate the whisky in the amber light of the cabin. "It occurs to me that you've told me rather a lot in the last half hour. I've heard about the British Intelligence Service, its top-secret project to break the German Navy, and rather a lot about you."

He sipped his glass.

"Not that I don't appreciate the information and all. Just seems to be an extensive debrief given the circumstances. It would seem a bit odd that your employers were happy to have me run around London with a head full of their secrets."

Schaeffer paused for a moment.

"Melvold," he began. "I think you probably aren't quite on top of what's going on here. You made it all the way across France chased by three Nazi spies. Anna Schmidt is one of the Reich's best, we've seen her work before. She's almost unbeatable when it comes to a game of sharpened knives."

"Luck, nothing more."

"No," demurred Schaeffer. "You showed a great deal of poise under pressure, and some courage under fire. We did some digging into your past, saw what you'd achieved in the Colonies. You're a sharp one Richard Melvold, and we're going to need people like you in the coming troubles."

Melvold stared straight across the table at Harry Schaeffer.

"Excuse me?" he asked.

"Melvold old boy," replied Schaeffer, jovially as he set his glass on the table with an air of finality. "I'm not debriefing you. I'm recruiting you."

EPILOGUE

The Moors of Bletchley

24 hours later

Beneath a slate grey sky pale sunlight streamed through the skeletal birch trees that crested the ridge above Bletchley manor. The day had been short and cold, and in the valley by the river the morning's frost still clung to the brown grass.

The black Bentley pulled up at the door of the manor, and two men alighted.

Shortly afterwards, there was a knock at the door of Sir Hugh Sinclair's study.

"Enter," called C shortly.

Alan Denning was also present, and both men rose to greet their two guests.

The first man, with a shock of blond hair still unkempt, strode across the room and handed Charles Montgomerie's card, covered in circuit diagrams to Alan Denning.

"Thank you, Schaeffer," said C. "Job well done."

He turned his eyes past Schaeffer to the second man, tall with wavy brown hair, who was regarding the office with a great deal of interest.

"Mister Melvold?" asked Sir Hugh Sinclair.

The man nodded wordlessly.

Denning extended his hand silently, and Melvold shook it.

"Sit down son," continued Sinclair. "I have a job offer for you."

END

●- -●-

Author's Note

I have never been inclined toward lengthy commentary at the end of a novel. Once the story is told, it ought to stand on its own.

I wrote *Four Nights in France* as a work of escapism — something to be read on holiday, on a train journey, or in a quiet evening's pause from the world. My hope was simply to tell an engaging story set against a moment in history that continues to fascinate me.

My sincere thanks go to my family, whose patience and careful reading helped shape this book, and to close friends who offered encouragement when I needed it most.

While certain historical figures and institutions appear within these pages, the events of this story are entirely fictional.

Most of all, I hope you enjoyed the journey. I am most definitely looking forward to Richard Melvold's return.

Luke Lawton

www.ingramcontent.com/pod-product-compliance
Lightning Source LLC
LaVergne TN
LVHW091128080826
845145LV00008B/2082